Shadow Over Southwold

By Suzette A. Hill

A Little Murder
The Venetian Venture
A Southwold Mystery
Shot in Southwold
The Cambridge Plot
Shadow Over Southwold

The Primrose Pursuit

Shadow Over Southwold

SUZETTE A. HILL

Allison & Busby Limited
11 Wardour Mews
London W1F 8AN
allisonandbusby.com

First published in Great Britain by Allison & Busby in 2021.
This paperback edition published by Allison & Busby in 2022.

A CIP catalogue record for this book is available from
the British Library.

10 9 8 7 6 5 4 3 2 1

ISBN 978-0-7490-2731-5

Typeset in 10.5/15.5 pt Sabon LT Pro by
Allison & Busby Ltd

Printed and bound by
CPI Group (UK) Ltd, Croydon, CR0 4YY

To the happy memory of Alexander Wedderspoon

PROLOGUE

'You must admit it does rather cast a shadow,' Miles Loader observed.

'What does?'

'Dewthorp's dispatch. I mean to say . . .'

'His dispatch? But he died.'

'Oh yes, he did that all right, but what I want to know is why and how. Personally, I think there is more in this than meets the eye – mine at any rate.'

Reggie Higgs put down his drink and gazed at his companion in some puzzlement. 'But surely you know?' he said, 'It's common knowledge. It happened when he was exercising Mrs Peebles' dog at Dunwich and he fell off the cliff – he was always clumsy. Rather bad luck as it had been his birthday. First of April. I know that because he told me the other day when he was browsing in my shop. He was very taken with a little figurine of Punchinello and said that as his birthday was imminent it might make an appropriate present to himself.'

'Hmm,' the other mused, 'All Fools' Day. Fate's joke in poor taste, one might say. But then, Horace Dewthorp was no fool, or at least I never got that impression. Clumsy, perhaps, but hardly one to be pottering about on the cliff's edge. Not like him at all.'

'The police say the dog had probably put up a rabbit, was rushing too near the brink and Dewthorp had pursued it, tripped on a jagged piece of chalk and went headlong over. His cap was caught in a tuft of gorse, and a dog lead and whistle found near the body. I think he had a slightly dicky heart, so I suppose it cut out when he fell. I gather the dog was found by a cyclist who recognised the name on its collar, shoved it in his basket and took it back to Southwold. Apparently, the dog was quite unperturbed – though Mrs P. was annoyed. She thought Dewthorp had lost it. The irony is the poor chap wasn't all that keen on canines and had only agreed to exercise it as a favour. She had been laid up with the pox.'

The normally phlegmatic Dr Miles Loader (DPhil, History, Oxon.) almost choked on his whisky. 'The pox!' he gasped. 'You mean to say that prim Peebles has caught the—'

'Chickenpox,' Higgs grinned. 'A visitor's small child passed it on to her. It wasn't a bad dose but enough to keep her confined for a bit and out of harm's way, or at least out of our way.'

'That's certainly a relief,' Loader mused. 'I don't fancy

Southwold being menaced by murder and syphilis!'

'Ssh,' Higgs hissed nervously, glancing round at the small back bar of The Crown Hotel. Though never loud, Loader's voice was clear and precise, and the two words had cut the air like a knife. Luckily, there was only one other drinker present and he seemingly engrossed in his newspaper. In an undertone Higgs urged his companion to control his imagination. 'Dogs chasing rabbits are one thing, but we don't want wild hares being sprung all over the place. Southwold is a homely little town, and it would be a pity to have its cheery image tainted by ugly rumour. Bad for business.' Reggie Higgs ran a small but choice antiques shop off the high street.

'Conversely,' Loader murmured slyly, 'it could be very good for business. The public take a perverse pleasure in the grim and grisly, and a local killing might have them flocking here in droves.'

His friend brightened. 'Ah, that's a possibility, I suppose; hadn't thought of it like that. Perhaps I should increase the Sèvres collection. I was thinking only the other day that it's starting to look a bit sparse. It could do with a fresh injection.' He paused, and then added, 'Since we are on the subject, perhaps we should refill glasses and toast old Horace. He may have been teetotal but he can hardly complain.'

'Not now he can't. Your turn, I fancy.'

In fact, contrary to Dr Loader's assumption, Dewthorp's mishap cast barely any shadow over the little town, or indeed the peaceful cliffs of Dunwich – and it certainly did not bring the hordes of visitors that he had jovially predicted. Naturally, the victim's passing caused an element of shock, but the proverbial nine days' wonder probably amounted to no more than three. The dead man had not been a denizen of Southwold, making only occasional visits up from Cambridge in order, as he had jocularly declared, 'to escape the cloistered racket and to breathe some decent sea air'.

Recently retired from his post as senior clerical administrator at one of the Cambridge colleges and with no immediate family to claim him, he had been free to indulge his two interests: wildflowers and Suffolk's wartime coastal defences. And while he had been perfectly affable, being teetotal he had rarely ventured into any of the local hostelries, and except for a few acquaintances such as Miles Loader and Reggie Higgs, on the whole had seemed content with his own company. Sometimes he would be seen strolling on the common or along the seafront, and occasionally settled in the Sailors' Reading Room absorbed in its newspaper archive. In his early visits he had stayed in a guest house run by Mary Peebles, but the arrangement had lapsed and he had instead rented a small flat near the pier for his periodic retreat from Cambridge's 'cloistered racket'. His death, though sad, had generally been regarded as one of life's unfortunate accidents – except perhaps by the sceptical Loader, an inveterate reader of crime novels.

CHAPTER ONE

A month later, in Cambridge itself, a drama of a more scandalous nature was being discussed.

'Naturally I cut him dead, quite dead,' Emeritus Professor Aldous Phipps announced with relish. He glanced around at his assembled colleagues in the senior common room of St Cecil's, seeking smiles and murmurs of approbation. Few were expressed.

But one voice spoke out: 'Yes, but you have to admit he is pretty tall, a good six-foot-two I should say.'

Phipps turned a glacial eye upon the speaker. 'A non sequitur if I may so, Smithers. What has height to do with my cutting of Hapworth?'

'He may not have noticed you,' John Smithers replied amiably. 'Perhaps his mind was fixed on higher things.'

This elicited not just smiles but a loud guffaw from Dr

Maycock, St Cecil's Senior Tutor. 'He has a point, Aldous, you must admit.'

Phipps glared. 'I admit no such thing. Dr Smithers is being gratuitously personal, and I can assure you that Hapworth saw me most clearly. In fact, I rather think he was about to strike up a conversation – which is why I immediately lowered my eyes and spoke to my dog.'

'Ah the compliant Popsie,' Smithers murmured, 'a charming confederate. Where is she, by the way?'

'In her basket enjoying the sleep of the just – not something you are familiar with, I imagine.'

Smithers shrugged and lit a cigarette, disdaining reply.

'Ah well, Aldous,' Maycock interjected hastily, 'I don't suppose you will be the only one cutting him. I daresay Canterbury & Co. have also withdrawn the hem of their chasubles – or soon will if the press gets its way. The newspapers are already muttering about resignation.'

'Inevitable, I should have thought,' snorted Mostyn Williams, the college bursar. 'After all, with one hand in the till and the other up a choirboy's surplice I can't see that he has much choice in the matter.'

The master, who had been mentally honing his address for the forthcoming Founder's Day, woke up and winced. Really, must Mostyn be quite so crude? Besides, nothing had been proved about the allegations and it was currently only gross rumour. He cleared his throat. 'If you don't mind my saying, Bursar, aren't you being a trifle premature? The Reverend Hapworth may not be to everyone's taste, but by all accounts he has been a sound pastor at St Bernard's and is apparently highly esteemed by the upper echelons of the Mothers' Union.'

'Oh well,' said Smithers, 'if he is approved by the Mothers' Union then he must be all right.' He turned to Professor Aldous Phipps: 'Wouldn't you say so, Aldous? Frankly if I were you, I should be jolly careful whom I cut in future. After all, it wouldn't do to have phalanxes of heated ladies bearing down on you, would it? Not your scene at all, I shouldn't think – wrathful or otherwise.' He lowered his left eyelid and stubbed out his cigarette.

This time it was the turn of ancient Phipps to keep silent, but he thought the more. He had never approved of the fellowship the college had bestowed upon John Smithers; and in his view, having spent a research year at Yale the young man had returned to Cambridge even more distasteful than before. Cocky young pup! Phipps frowned thoughtfully at his neatly pared fingernails, pondering how best to ruffle that slick confidence.

A week later John Smithers' slick confidence was indeed ruffled – not by the sly wiles of Aldous Phipps, but by the fate of the Reverend Stephen Hapworth. The cleric had been found at half-mast under Clare College Bridge: hanged and blowing in the wind. Or at least, that is how the new cub reporter of the *Cambridge Clarion* had originally put it; a version hastily modified by the editor.

Given the rumours surrounding the victim, suicide of a somewhat public nature had been the first assumption. But once it was revealed that the dead man had sustained a heavy blow to the back of the head, such view was quickly revised. The man could hardly have engineered his own end unaided: the bludgeoning surely suggested another hand at work. But it was evidently the rope, and not the blow, that had actually carried him off, the immediate cause of death being asphyxia. It had been a quick end, apparently – neck instantly broken and thus no unseemly heavings. The despatch would seem to have been executed by one conversant with the process.

Members of the public with a love of the lurid and knowledge of such matters, had discreetly checked the movements of the erstwhile public hangman, Mr Albert Pierrepoint; but were disappointed to learn he had been otherwise engaged on the Isle of Wight, mentoring one of his successors. So at least that was one possibility ruled out. Still, with luck there would be plenty of scope for others. Amongst the college common rooms and drinking holes of Cambridge, speculation thrived.

It thrived too in the discreet back bar of Southwold's Crown Hotel, where, sipping a vicious gin cocktail and wearing a smile of placid sweetness, Dr Miles Loader opined that the murdered Reverend Stephen Hapworth, his third cousin once-removed, had been a bugger of the first water and it was merely surprising that he hadn't been given the chop years ago.

His companion on that occasion, Miss Isabel Phipps, nodded in vague agreement, saying that in her view there were an awful lot of them about.

'What, buggers?' asked Miles, a trifle surprised.

'Oh, well yes, those too, I suppose. But I was really thinking of all those in need of the chop . . . Take my brother, for instance.' She sighed and contemplated her sherry.

14

'Do you mean the Cambridge one, the Classics chap? But I thought he was rather a distinguished scholar – a professor, isn't he?'

'Oh yes, a venerable emeritus. In theory he's retired, put out to grass. But that doesn't stop anything.'

'Stop what?'

'His habits. He is fussy, tiresomely nosy and obsessively neat.'

Miles smiled, eyeing the unruly hair, laddered stocking and trailing scarf; and recalling the habitual debris of her sitting room, said, 'Well, admittedly neatness is not your strong suit – charming though your house is – but I can't really see why that should bother you. I thought you hardly ever met.'

'We don't, but we are about to soon,' she replied grimly. 'He is coming to stay – in a moment of madness I invited him. Apparently, the college authorities have decided to renovate a couple of the grace-and-favour houses where he lives. One of them is adjacent to his own and he says the noise will be intolerable, the mess deplorable and it will disrupt his work and shatter his nerves. The dog too will suffer. Thus, he is coming here for the interim.'

'With the dog?'

'With the dog.'

Miles cleared his throat, and murmured tentatively, 'But you are not terribly fond of dogs, are you? And what about the hedgehog, won't it object?'

Isabel shrugged. 'Thomas will have to take his chance with the rest of us; and from what I gather the dog is small and spends most of its time asleep in its basket . . . No, the real bore is having to stock up with that searing dry sherry he likes. Takes the skin off your teeth, it does! Typical of Aldous not to be satisfied with a decent amontillado like the rest of us. I remember when we were children: not content with the usual ginger beer, he always had to lace it with some foul-tasting liquor scrounged from Daddy's drinks cabinet. Lethal stuff!' She screwed up her nose in painful memory.

To assuage the memory her companion went to the bar to order replenishments. Poor old Isabel, he thought wryly, quite a handful. Still, I suppose she'll cope; she generally does. But will the hedgehog? Even lazy dogs are known to rampage.

Returning to his seat he was slightly surprised to see his friend smiling broadly. 'Well,' she said brightly, 'at least Aldous will be able to give us the lowdown on why your cousin met such an untimely end. He is bound to have a theory, he always does.' She took a sip from her glass and nodded appreciatively. 'Now that's what I call a drinkable sherry. They do a very good one here.'

About to sip his own drink, Miles Loader paused and replaced the glass on the table. He gave a discreet cough. 'Uhm . . . well as I said, only a distant cousin: third, once removed. It hardly counts,' he added hastily.

'It's still consanguinity – or all relative, as the police might say.'

'Police?' Miles was startled. 'Oh, but I doubt if they would be interested in me. I mean to say, he and I lost touch years ago. A figure from the past, really. He was a very tenuous connection, very tenuous indeed.'

'And yet you say you didn't like him. So, you must have some knowledge or have made an assessment. And besides, the police love digging up the past, it's their favourite hobby. If they think there is some extramural connection, a friend or relative who could be helpful, they are bound to make enquiries, especially as Southwold isn't all that far from Cambridge. Anyway, if nothing else, at least dear Aldous will have an angle.' Isabel downed the dregs of her sherry and, gathering handbag and evening paper, stood up. She consulted her watch. 'Ah, just in time to order that rotgut from the off-licence.'

'When does your brother arrive?' Miles asked.

'Not till Saturday. Six days of liberty. Toodle-oo.'

Miles gave a vague wave and settled to his cocktail. But somehow it had lost both its savour and his attention.

Instead, he ruminated about the dead cousin. His thoughts went back to his time as an adolescent, canoodling and a bit more with a girl in a cornfield. The process had been going well until bloody Stephen leapt up from behind a circle of stooks, toting a butterfly net and pair of binoculars. He had said he was trying to catch a Brimstone Yellow, but the binoculars suggested other, more human interests. Days later, the bugger had approached him for money, muttering about God, the wrath of parents and the sins of the flesh. Miles had clocked him one, and mercifully the older man had taken the hint, backed off and dropped the matter.

Stephen Hapworth had later become a clergyman, and other than at an occasional family funeral Miles never saw him again, being careful to keep a wide berth. Time had passed and water flowed. And now the chap was a murder victim in Cambridge, and a rather spectacular one at that. Intriguing, most certainly, but hardly his business. Embarrassing, really. Sanctimonious sod.

As Miles Loader was brooding dispassionately upon his relative's unseemly fate in Cambridge, in London's fashionable Sloane Street – untouched by clifftop fatalities and corpses dangling under bridges – Felix Smythe, proud proprietor of Smythe's Bountiful Blooms, was telephoning his good friend Professor Cedric Dillworthy.

'I've just had such a lovely surprise in the post,' he exclaimed, 'you'll never guess what!'

'The Queen Mother wants you to supply a floral collar for one of the corgis,' Cedric suggested drily. (Her Majesty's patronage of Felix's flower boutique was a source of exquisite joy to its owner – as evidenced by the daily and meticulous polishing of its Royal Appointment plaque.)

'Oh, very funny, I'm sure,' Felix sniffed. 'No, it's from Suffolk, from that group of Aldeburgh musicians I encountered when we were up there a few years ago. You remember, the distinguished composer and his friends who kindly invited me to their soirée at Crag House. Charming.'

'But I thought they had dropped you,' Cedric said casually.

'Dropped me? Most certainly not. What on earth do you mean!' Felix's look of glee was replaced by a scowl and he very nearly stamped his foot.

'Well, you didn't receive a Christmas card this year, did you?' Cedric replied mildly.

'Card be damned. I've got better than a card, I can tell

you. What I have received is an invitation – an invitation to join them in a little celebration.'

'Celebration of what?'

Felix hesitated. He wasn't sure – he would have to check the wording. Had it been to do with that concert place in Aldeburgh, the Jubilee Hall? Maybe it was an anniversary of its founding; something like that, probably. But the essential thing was that his name was on the guest list. Clearly, he had found favour after all. They had been an engaging group, he recalled, and he had done his best to fit in and make a suitable impression (not easy with scant musical knowledge). Yes, a party in Aldeburgh was a most enticing prospect. He must cancel all other engagements . . . unless of course Clarence House should require him to discuss the next flower order. One could hardly cancel HM!

'Celebration of what?' Cedric repeated patiently.

'Come to supper tonight and I might tell you,' Felix said airily. 'Oh, and do bring that bottle of Montrachet you prised out of Angela Fawcett. I'll make some bouillabaisse and we can pretend we're on St-Jean-Cap-Ferrat again chez Mr Somerset M!'

'I did not prise it,' began Cedric indignantly, 'I merely asked if . . .'

But his words were lost, for replacing the receiver, Felix had bustled off to deal with fish and travel arrangements.

When Cedric arrived that evening at Felix's slightly over-ornate flat, it was to find his friend less exuberant than he had expected. Despite the delicious aroma wafting from the kitchen and two wincingly dry Martinis standing sentinel

19

on the mantelpiece, its occupant appeared worried.

'Hmm,' Cedric remarked quizzically, handing over the Montrachet, 'you sound a bit piano, thought you might be doing handstands by now.' He took the proffered Martini and they sat on the sofa while Felix revealed his woes.

'It's too bad,' he complained, 'I telephoned the Sandworth – you know, the hotel at Aldeburgh on the seafront and which was so good to us when we stayed there before – but they say they don't have a vacancy for the dates I want. Apparently if I check with them later, they might be able to help, but for the moment nothing's doing. I did think of the other one at the opposite end of the front, but it's closed for repairs.'

Cedric asked if he had tried The Swan or Crown at Southwold.

'Yes, but they are full up too. It's maddening!' As often when in a state of agitation Felix ran his fingers through his short spiky hair and pouted. Apart from the pout, the *en brosse* style crowning his thin features made him look not unlike an older version of Tommy Steele.

'You might be able to find a pub in the outlying district, some of them do rooms these days.'

'Spending hours on the telephone and then taking pot luck with some meagre hostelry out in the sticks is not my idea of fun,' Felix replied haughtily. 'Naturally, if I am to mingle with the musicians and to make the best of my time with them, I shall need a decent base in or close to Aldeburgh and to which I can invite members of their circle for a drink – should chance arise.'

'Ah, like the tenor, I suppose,' Cedric said slyly.

Felix gave a careless shrug. 'Anyone who is convivial, naturally.'

As it happened, Cedric felt sorry for his friend. Some people could cope with such irritants but he and Felix shared the same respect for the smooth and predictable. Having something planned and then finding those plans blighted could be most tiresome – galling even, especially if the project had been special (as it clearly was to Felix). He studied his Martini, and suddenly had an idea. 'I'll ask Miles Loader , he may be able to help. In fact, I could telephone him now if you like.'

'Who's Loader – a travel agent?'

Cedric explained that Dr Miles Loader was a historian he had encountered from time to time at publishers' parties and various academic events, and who happened to live not far from Southwold. 'He was abroad last time we were there, otherwise I would have introduced you. Quite a pleasant cove, though I haven't seen him for ages. Anyway, the point is he is bound to have various local contacts and may be able to fix you up with something suitable. You never know, it's worth a try.'

Felix agreed, and brightening somewhat, went off to the kitchen to attend to the bouillabaisse. Whether the Loader person would be any good remained to be seen, but as Cedric had said, it was worth a try. He prodded the fish and hoped.

An hour later, with a second Martini under their belts and most of the burgundy gone, matters were considerably lighter. Miles Loader had been very helpful, explaining that he had a niece on the staff of the Sandworth who might pull a string on Felix's behalf. With luck she could fix him a room in time for the party. It wasn't certain, of course. Meanwhile, as a safety net, Miles was sure he could find him a decent guest house in Southwold and from where, if all else failed, he could easily drive over to the party.

The news mellowed Felix and he cordially invited Cedric to join him in Suffolk. 'I don't mean to attend the party,' he said quickly, 'the invitation only mentions the one name and it might be infra dig to bring another, but we could spend a few days up there, do a bit of touring around and perhaps even go into Norfolk. After all, we aren't due on the Riviera with dear Willie and friends till September – ages away. A little preliminary jaunt would be a warm-up before the Big One.' He winked.

'My dear boy,' Cedric exclaimed, 'I wouldn't dream of gatecrashing the musicians' thing – one would feel terribly awkward. No, no, that's absolutely your pigeon. But certainly, a little break from London would be most refreshing and I'm sure something can be arranged. Mind you, at the moment I am a bit tied up with the paper I'm writing – that new archaeology journal wants a fresh angle on the Cappadocian hermitages – so I may have to come up later. But meanwhile, for your sake let us hope that Master Loader does his stuff.'

As it happened, Loader did his stuff rather well. Given hints of a slap-up meal at The Swan, his niece at the Sandworth assured him that in the event of a cancellation Mr Smythe would be the first to be informed. There was also a chance that a room currently being refurbished might become available, and she would see that it was reserved. Thus, things seemed promising. But wisely Loader had also enquired of Mrs Mary Peebles in Southwold, whose guest house though small, was centrally placed and generally deemed reliable. When he had told her that Mr Smythe's plans were somewhat fluid and that his stay might be cut short, he had feared she might be tricky (she sometimes was), but surprisingly there had been no objection. 'Provided he doesn't bring a mistress or hordes of offspring, he can be as fluid as he chooses,' she had said tartly. When Loader relayed this proviso to Cedric, the latter remarked that he could think of few things less likely.

So that was the programme: Felix would stay in Southwold on the off chance of de-camping to the hotel in Aldeburgh, and at some point be joined by Cedric. Other than replenishing his favourite cologne and filling up with petrol, all that remained was to give meticulous instructions to his new assistant not to address the Sloane ladies as 'duckie', and on no account permit General Withers to run up a tab. The latter may have served superbly in the Great War and knew a lobelia from a camelia, but in other ways his memory was 'playing tricks'. Especially, it seemed, in matters financial.

CHAPTER TWO

Mrs Peebles' visitor was not enjoying his stay. The house itself was comfortable enough (despite the lack of finer touches, such as real flowers instead of plastic ones). And being just east of South Green, it was an easy stroll to the sea and the high street. But apart from its central position there were other places Felix would prefer to be – principally, of course, Aldeburgh's stylish Sandworth. Yet even a far-flung establishment of the sort he had earlier disdained would have done; at least in such a place the bar chatter might have amused. The problem was his hostess. He didn't like her.

Polite, correct and efficient in supplying the necessary amenities, the lady did not seem unduly pleased to have him as her guest – despite his tactful gift of some specially selected amaretti from Fortnum's. Most women would have been delighted and twittered fulsome gratitude, even offered him one after supper. Huh! Far from it. After a cursory word of thanks, she had thrust the beribboned box into a sideboard as if it had been some cheap little chocolate bar from Woolworths, and nothing more was said – or seen. A sensitive soul, Felix had mentally bridled. Standing in the hall trying to ease his foot away from an overly attentive Yorkshire terrier, he felt a flicker of regret. He was not used to such indifference. Still, he had reasoned, not everyone could be charming and doubtless things would go all right. In this he was correct . . . up to a point. And the point was reached on a number of occasions.

Initially, however, things went smoothly enough. She had offered him tea, enquired after his journey, agreed with him about the oddity of some of the local road surfaces and declared that personally she blamed the government – her favourite scapegoat, Felix was to learn. But there were others too, including the dustmen, the window cleaner, the postman and the local doctor. 'Such a fool,' she sniffed, 'if he had had his wits about him, I would never have suffered that dreadful disease.'

Nervously Felix had enquired to what disease she was referring.

'My chickenpox of course. If he had diagnosed the thing earlier it could have been treated. As it was, I was laid up for weeks – well, two weeks, at any rate,' she said indignantly. 'In fact, I was so weak that I was unable to exercise Freddie. The poor little thing had to be taken out by Mr Dewthorp, and he came a cropper all right!'

'Really? In what way?' Felix had asked politely, slightly

bored and wanting to get to his room to unpack; it was essential that his shirts and new suit be put on hangers.

'Fell off the cliff at Dunwich and broke his neck. They say he had been running after Freddie and missed his footing. Typical. When in doubt blame the dog, it's always the way.' She gestured at the Yorkie snuffling in its basket.

'Oh dear – and, er, is the gentleman all right? In a neck brace or something?'

'Neck brace? No, he's dead. That bit of cliff is very sheer and I've always said it should be railed off. But will they listen? Of course not! If you take my advice, Mr Smythe, you'll keep well away – especially in those shoes. Slippery soles, I shouldn't wonder.' She glanced disparagingly at Felix's neat and impeccably polished footwear and changed the subject, impressing upon him that breakfast would be served at eight-thirty sharp and that if he wanted anything beyond the usual porridge and boiled egg, he would need to give advance notice and it would be added to his bill. 'Nothing faddy in this house,' she had said briskly, glancing at the dog as if for endorsement. 'Isn't that so, Freddie?' The creature stared back glumly.

After an indifferent supper, and realising that breakfast would be devoid of his usual lapsang souchong and lavishly buttered croissant, Felix slipped out to stroll around the town and telephone Cedric to give a less than rosy report of his landlady's charms. 'Not my idea of a merry widow,' he had muttered.

While sympathetic, his friend observed that perhaps, after all, he should have gambled on the Sandworth being free. Felix pointed out that in that case he would have risked missing the musicians' party.

'Ah well,' Cedric had replied jovially, 'it was ever thus, dear boy. It just goes to show that we have to pay for our pleasures.' It was not a riposte that Felix had appreciated. Nevertheless, cheered by the thought of the party, he returned to the house pondering which tie to select for the occasion and whether he should wear a waistcoat.

At breakfast the next day, slightly to his relief, it was not Mrs Peebles who served him but a young woman. She introduced herself as Elsie and said she 'did' for Mrs Peebles and that if he wanted anything extra for his breakfast, she could probably obtain it without 'the old trout' knowing. Slightly taken aback by such Christian charity, Felix hastily said he was perfectly content for the moment but would give it careful thought in the days to come. After she had gone, having toyed with a small amount of the greying porridge, Felix decided he would accept Elsie's kind offer.

Moving the bowl aside, he sat back, took out his cigarettes and glanced around for an ashtray. His quest was interrupted by a voice from the door. 'If you must smoke, Mr Smythe, there is always the garden – the back garden by the compost heap, not the front.'

Unused to loitering by compost heaps, Felix hastily replaced the cigarettes and falsely indicated that he could do without. Then in an attempt to appear helpful, he offered to adjust one of the pictures: the ubiquitous scene of stampeding elephants. 'It's just the teeniest bit crooked – and in any case, I think you might find it better displayed on the opposite wall where the light is brighter and its colours would be echoed by the . . .'

Foolish Felix, he might have known.

The suggestion was met by a stony stare, and his voice faded as she said, 'It looks perfectly straight to me. And as for moving it – well, it's always been there. It's where it belongs.' The words were uttered with curt finality, clearly marking the end of the matter. Discussion was out. Felix flashed a compliant smile. Bitch, he thought mildly.

However, that little hiccup was small compared with a discovery he made in his room half an hour later. Having decided to wear his waistcoat for the Aldeburgh party, to his dismay he found he had omitted to pack it. All other essentials were there: a sheaf of ties, the Jermyn Street eau de cologne, nail clippers, Cartier cufflinks, brilliantine to quell his spiky hair – everything except the Sod's Law of a waistcoat. It was too bad! He pursed his lips and gazed irritably at a badly embroidered doily on the bedside table.

But as he brooded it occurred to him that such a garment might be found in Southwold. Doubtless long odds, still you never knew . . . And then with a start, he did know. Yes, wasn't there a gents' outfitters in Market Place? On a corner, he seemed to recall, with a name beginning with D – Dennis or something. He had passed it a couple of times on their previous visit and remembered Cedric getting some socks there. It had looked quite a decent place, in fact just the place that might keep a small but select range of waistcoats. He would investigate immediately.

Thus brightened, Felix dashed down the stairs, narrowly missing Freddie who lurked on the bottom step, and almost tripped. The dog gave a piercing yelp, which elicited a similar sound of protest from its mistress emerging from the kitchen. She held an envelope in her hand.

'Ah, Mr Smythe, I thought you might be going out. I wonder if you would be so kind as to post this for me? I would like it to catch this morning's collection from the post office.' She thrust the letter at him, adding, 'Oh and by the way, you will be careful not to tread on Freddie when you return. The poor little fellow is quite fragile, you know.' She gave a frosty smile.

Fragile? Felix thought. According to her the little tyke had already been the cause of one death. Who knew what others it was planning! He took the letter and hastily assured her the post office would be his first port of call.

He had gone as far as the garden gate when he was hailed from within. He turned round to see Elsie waving a duster and emerging from the porch. 'Ah, glad I've caught you,' she said breathlessly, 'Mrs Peebles forgot to tell you. There's been someone on the blower, some professor bloke. He left a message while you was upstairs after breakfast.'

'Really?' asked Felix, rather startled. 'What did he say?'

The girl frowned and concentrated. 'It was something about a change of plan, something to do with an article what's been postponed so he's got more time. Anyway, he's coming sooner than he thought. Yes, that's it . . . he's arriving by train late tomorrow afternoon and staying with that Dr Loader over in Blythburgh, who's picking him up at Darsham station. He said to be sure to tell you.'

Felix was pleased – but also peeved. 'So why didn't Mrs Peebles mention this when she was talking to me only a few minutes ago?'

Elsie shrugged. 'Like I said, she forgot, or so she said. She was banging on about some letter she wanted you to post so I suppose it slipped her mind.' It would, Felix thought grimly. It would serve her right if he too forgot. But decency prevailed, and making his way to the high street he continued on down to the post office.

As he walked, enjoying the morning air and the early stirrings of dogs and people, he thought about his two previous visits to the little town. What curious dramas – unsettling to say the least. Still, all had been resolved eventually, and mercifully the parts played by himself and Cedric had escaped the press. This time, of course, the visit would be free of such surprises. Well, unless someone propositioned him at the Aldeburgh party. He grinned, and passing the Orwell house stopped to light the cigarette he had been denied at breakfast.

He reached into his pocket for his lighter and Mrs Peebles' letter fell out. He stooped to pick it up and was struck by the name of the addressee: an H.R. Dagwood Esq., somewhere in Aldeburgh . . . Dagwood? Why should that name strike a bell? He frowned. And then he remembered: oh of course, Dagwood Bumstead, witless husband of Blondie, the American cartoon character. The comic strip had been a regular item in one of the popular papers and the only enlivening feature of a dentist's waiting room. Felix recalled his effort to recreate the legendary Dagwood sandwich, a structure of gargantuan proportions; but the project had been scorned by Cedric, who had made it clear

30

that his own taste was for a lightly sautéed turbot.

By now he had reached the post office steps, and banishing images of Dagwood and his sandwich, hastily shoved the perishing letter into the pillar box. With commission discharged, he eagerly retraced his steps in search of the vital waistcoat.

He was in luck. Yes indeed, the young lady assured him, only that morning they had received a fresh batch from the suppliers. 'They look very smart – just your style, I should think, sir.' Felix recognised the tactic, he used it himself. Flattery was a useful tool in the commercial world. Still, he couldn't help feeling pleased, and taking three samples from the counter entered the fitting room.

For some people, the process of choice would be simple enough: remove jacket, don items, select best or cheapest; exit fitting room and produce chequebook. Not so with Felix. The operation was lengthy and complex. Each item had to be tried at least twice, its colour, fit and texture assessed, seams examined, label approved. And then the burning question: would it be fit for purpose? I.e. would it impress without being obvious? And what about his ties – which would it suit best? Too much of a contrast might be crude, and yet too little a mite dull. It was all a question of nice balance. Frowning at the mirror he pondered the matter and had just reached a firm decision when he heard a voice in the main area. 'Huh! That little chap's taking his time, isn't he? What's he doing, trying on the crown jewels?'

Felix was indignant. He had every right to take his time. What did the man think he was doing, buying a packet of fags? Defiantly, he remained where he was, admiring his choice before emerging to stand at the counter behind the other customer, a tall and burly man in aggressively loud tweeds who was smoking a cigar. The man looked over his shoulder, glanced briefly at Felix and turned back to the counter. 'That'll be all, dearie,' he said to the girl, 'just the shirts today. I'm in a bit of a hurry, got plenty to do,' and lowering his voice muttered, 'unlike some people, it seems.'

Needless to say, Felix heard the words only too clearly – as was no doubt intended. He stared pointedly at the other's loud check and crêpe soles, and his eyebrow arched ever so slightly. But such signs of disdain were lost on the other, for the next moment the man had grabbed his package and was striding to the door. 'Shall I put it on your usual account, Mr Dagwood?' the girl asked.

'That's it, girlie, got it in one,' was the curt response, and the next moment, with a clang of the bell, he had left the shop.

Felix returned the assistant's polite smile, while inwardly incredulous. Would you believe it? The very name on the letter he had just posted! Obviously, the man was a Suffolk local, and therefore quite possibly the intended recipient. Huh, it just showed how right his mother had always been in her insistence that truth was stranger than fiction and coincidences ten-a-penny. 'Just mark my words,' had been her favourite phrase. He gave a wry smile, prompted not so much by his mother's mantra than by the disparity between the fictional Dagwood and the distasteful reality. At least D. Bumstead had been funny.

Although piqued by the incident, Felix was delighted with his purchase; and to compensate for the sparse breakfast slipped into the café by the bookshop to guzzle a pancake and plan his day. What a nice surprise that Cedric should be appearing so soon. What had the girl said – that he was being collected by the Loader chap in the late afternoon? Perhaps he should book a table for the three of them at The Crown. He would call Cedric that evening to check. As he spooned more jam on to his pancake, an idea struck him: he could buy his friend a present, a cheerful gift of welcome. A bottle of wine? A book? The shop next door had a fine selection . . . He pondered. No, not a book, Cedric's tastes were somewhat eclectic and it would be easy to make a mistake. Wine? He had plenty at home. Perhaps something frivolous, like the giant toy panda he had seen in the draper's window. Had it been for sale or merely a means of displaying the swathe of pink silk wound round its neck? On reflection he doubted if it would suit Cedric's austere humour. No, it would have to be something beautiful and unexpected, something which would give pleasure here yet which he could continue to enjoy back in London. He wondered if that little antique shop was still trading, the one he had noticed on his last visit; some of its stuff wasn't bad. Perhaps he might find something there – it was worth a try.

Pancake demolished, Felix left the café and sauntered into the street . . . then hurtled back inside to retrieve the waistcoat. Clutching the precious parcel, he turned into the alleyway and looked for the shop. Yes, it was still there all right. He went in and began to browse. His eye roved over various knick-knacks of little account and a plethora of Edwardian fish knives and napkin rings. But there was some decent porcelain, including a couple of Sèvres soup plates (but Cedric was no cook and rarely dined at home) and a rather fetching Parisian clock. Would that appeal? Possibly. However, its fulsome price tag made him look elsewhere. Suddenly his gaze alighted on an etiolated flower vase, which looked suspiciously like a Lalique, though judging from the modest cost it was more likely to be 'in the style of'. All the same, it was very striking. As he brooded, envisaging where it might be best displayed in Cedric's neat drawing room, the shop's owner appeared from somewhere in the back.

'Ah yes, a nice bit of repro, that,' Reggie Higgs remarked. 'Most of those pieces are pretty scrappy and you can tell immediately, but this one's got an artistry all of its own. Very graceful.' Felix agreed and had already decided where it might be placed.

'Nice on its own, of course, but shove a bunch of lilies in it and Bob's your uncle!' the other said encouragingly. No further words were needed and the deal was clinched. But then it occurred to Felix that he could give the vase to Cedric with lilies already in place; a charming gesture, which Cedric was bound to appreciate. Why wait till their return to London? Would he find lilies in Southwold? Or even peonies, for that matter.

He asked the man, who shook his head. 'The grocer in High Street often has flowers, though I've never seen lilies there – daffodils or bedding plants, that sort of thing, but nothing stately.'

Felix asked if there was a nursery nearby. The man looked doubtful. 'The nearest one is over at Saxmundham, but I don't know if they do lilies – bulbs perhaps, but you want them in bloom, don't you.' His face brightened. 'I tell you what, you could try Isabel – Isabel Phipps. She's got a passion for lilies and grows them galore in her greenhouse. You never know, she might give you a few. Get on her right side and she couldn't be nicer, a friend for life; wrong side and she's rotten. Still, I suppose we're all a bit like that.' He grinned.

Felix nodded. He had already met the rotten side of one female recently, but he would take a gamble on the Isabel person. Reggie Higgs produced the address and agreed to keep the vase until required. Thus, free of the encumbrance, but being careful to take his earlier purchase, Felix set off on his quest. He hadn't far to go as the slightly ramshackle house was just off South Green. Approaching from the rear, Felix was reassured to see the top of a glass roof behind a thick hedge. With luck, this would be the woman's greenhouse.

CHAPTER THREE

Harassed by thoughts of her brother's imminent arrival and disposing of the more obvious dust in the spare bedroom, Isabel Phipps was in no mood for visitors. However, she was slightly intrigued – and disarmed – by the neat and shyly beaming stranger standing on her porch. The little chap had even executed a sort of bow. He was clutching a parcel. Was he a refined delivery man, perhaps? He looked harmless enough, and certainly a diversion from her present chores.

Felix hastily introduced himself, at the same time whipping out his business card: 'Smythe's Bountiful Blooms', its heading discreetly underset by the words By Royal Appointment (essential information, naturally), and explained his mission. 'It's my friend, you see, he is arriving tomorrow and I wanted to give him a little gift of welcome, something rather special and . . .' He described his visit to the antiques shop, the attractive vase and Reggie Higgs's advice. 'He says your lilies are truly superb.'

Isabel gave a gracious nod. Yes, she thought, they were superb and it was nice of Reggie to have said so. 'I'll show you if you like,' she offered, 'but the ground's rather rough so be careful where you tread, and watch out for the hedgehog, it can get testy.'

Lilies almost within his grasp, Felix could brave anything – even testy hedgehogs. He followed her eagerly to the large greenhouse where he was assailed by a scent so overpowering that for a few heady seconds it was as if he was back at Mr Somerset M's villa on St-Jean-Cap-Ferrat. Delicious! Rarely had Isabel's greenhouse had such an appreciative visitor (or one so knowledgeable of hothouse flowers and their arrangement) and both she and Felix spent a happy time meandering in its fragrant warmth discussing varieties and cultivation. She very much doubted whether her brother would take such an interest when he arrived.

Naturally, Felix had offered to pay for the lilies; but when the moment of choice came, she would not hear of it and insisted on giving him far more than the few he had selected. They agreed that for maximum life the petals should be tightly closed but with just two or three open to give a splash of colour. 'I'm sure your friend will be delighted,' she said.

And so he blooming should, Felix thought.

Slightly to his surprise, she insisted he stay for a cup of coffee and a sandwich. 'I don't normally bother with lunch, which means I get a bit peckish by this hour and crave a snack to tide me through till supper.' It was a nice gesture which Felix happily accepted.

She led him into a large sitting room, an attractive blend of faded elegance and homely disorder. There was a scattering of books and newspapers and in an alcove a half-finished jigsaw, three of its pieces on the floor. While she was out of the room preparing the sandwiches, he went to pick them up and was surprised to see that the design depicted not some popular rural or civic scene, but was a vibrant pastiche of abstract art; a pastiche so fiendishly obscure as to confound even the most ardent of admirers. Felix gazed down at the dazzling cacophony of form and colour and wondered if she painted. But there was no sign of an easel, which in view of what lay before him was probably just as well. What he did note, however, was that her wall pictures were straight, well hung and of some interest – unlike the Peebles variety.

They spent a congenial half-hour chatting about flowers and the Queen Mother, Felix having modestly let drop that he was one of Her Majesty's more favoured suppliers.

'And is she really as charming as her photographs suggest?' Isabel asked.

'Oh charming, charming,' he replied effusively, 'couldn't be more gracious, and then of course—'

'What about the corgis,' she broke in, 'are they charming?'

Felix hesitated. Should he tell her of the little bugger that had nipped his ankle, or the one that pawed his trousers leaving indelible marks? No, it wouldn't be fitting. He cleared his throat. 'Less so,' he said drily, and turned the subject.

Before he left, Isabel asked where he was going to put the flowers overnight. 'A bucket of water and a dark corner would be best,' she advised, 'I expect Mrs Peebles can help.' Would she? he wondered. Supposing the old trout was allergic to lilies, some people were and she was bound to be one of them. Or would say so.

Isabel must have seen his doubt, for she said, 'I tell you what, why don't you take them back to Reggie and he can put them in the vase all ready for when you want them. He's very obliging like that. Besides,' she winked, 'good for trade – you might be tempted by something else.' Felix agreed that it was quite possible, and having expressed warm thanks for her generous hospitality, pottered off back to Reggie's shop.

Its owner readily agreed the arrangement and Felix returned to his lodging feeling quite perky. It had been a most productive day. Cedric would arrive shortly, there was the gaiety of the Aldeburgh soirée in store, and with luck he would soon be free of his tiresome hostess. Since the dreary breakfast, things were surely looking up.

In this he was sorely misled.

His purchase unwrapped and once more paraded, Felix considered the evening ahead. The prospect of another supper in the Peebles establishment did not greatly appeal and he had just decided that he would see if they had a spare table at The Crown, when there was a brisk rap on the door. It was his hostess, looking moderately affable.

'Ah, Mr Smythe,' she said, 'you and I have a date tonight, we are to dine together.' It was an announcement that caught Felix unawares, and she must have taken his startled look of dismay for mere surprise. She gave what approximated to a smile, and added, 'You see, it's my bridge evening but my usual partner has a cold and the other girl is useless, so I shall stay in for an early night. I've laid the table for two and we shall have some excellent local cod and a little of that nice Blue Nun – just the thing to go with fish, I always say. Oh, and I expect you could manage some cherry tart for dessert, it's my speciality.'

Without waiting for a response, she shut the door and he heard the sound of her footsteps crossing the landing to her own room – presumably, he thought glumly, to don her glad rags. He turned his mind to the proposed menu. Cod wasn't his favourite fish, but if it was local and freshly caught it might be pleasant enough. He also had a penchant for cherries. The wine was not to his liking, but well chilled it could do – better than plain water, anyway. Oh well, he sighed, nothing lasted; he would put a brave face on things and be his suave and charming self. After all, she might produce the amaretti.

No such luck: the amaretti did not appear. The tart was dry, the wine warm and the fish, which could indeed have been excellent, was smothered in a commercial salad cream so vinegary that it almost seared his throat.

His mother had once called him her 'little Trojan' – why, he couldn't imagine, zest for warfare not being in his nature. But that evening, gamely tussling with Mary Peebles across the table, he certainly felt like a Trojan. Initially things had gone quite well. He had made complimentary comments about the tiresome Freddie, which had clearly pleased her, admired the view from the dining room window and agreed with her that the government hadn't a clue what it was doing. (Actually, he rather admired Mr Macmillan but it might have been unsafe to say so.) He then enquired as to what her interests were, to which she replied bridge, golf and the fallen.

He was slightly puzzled by the last. 'Er, the fallen what? Oh, I see . . . you mean our gallant war dead.' He wondered if she belonged to the British Legion and was an inveterate poppy seller.

'Fallen in the wars? Certainly not. Nothing belligerent like that! I refer to the world in general, of course, those fallen morally by the wayside and in need of firm but charitable guidance. There's a little group of us who meet once a month over at Orford and offer up our prayers – nothing formal, you understand, but sincerely meant.' She leant towards him: 'Tell me, Mr Smythe, are you a believer?'

Felix was wrong-footed. 'Uhm, well, yes and no . . . I mean to say—'

'No, I thought not. Or at least, one of the many lukewarm ditherers. Most people are like that, well-meaning but ultimately ineffectual – spiritually, that is. Still, I am sure you are a most talented florist.' She gave a patronising smile while Felix seethed. Mean well? No, he bloody didn't mean well, he didn't mean well at all. She could fall under a bus the next day for all he cared! However, his association with Cedric and with the more demanding of his clients had taught restraint, so he merely smiled and drew her attention to the rays of the dying sun catching the tops of the trees and the tip of the lighthouse.

'Yes, very pretty,' she remarked indifferently, and helped herself liberally to the putrid salad cream.

Felix stared listlessly at his plate with its half-hearted potatoes and ruined cod. He took a sip of the warm wine and winced. But then he had an inspiration. Embroidery, that was it! His napkin bore the same spidery traces as the tablemat in his room . . . and, as he now recalled, there was something similar on the hall sideboard, its purpose obscure. Adopting a tone of rapt enquiry, he said, 'I see you ply the bodkin; such a soothing hobby I always find.'

For a moment she looked puzzled (as well she might) but then grasping his meaning said, 'Oh yes, quite the little needlewoman I am, learnt it at my mother's knee.'

But not well enough, he thought acidly. Perhaps the knee got in the way.

'Actually, I do a little myself,' he murmured modestly. 'Nothing remarkable, and it takes a long time, of course. But so far I've managed six dining-room chair covers and – if you'll excuse the boast – a rather fetching fire screen with baroque flowers and an intricate pattern of—'

She had put down her knife and fork and was staring at him intently. Interest? Not exactly. 'Well,' she said, 'I have never heard of a man doing that sort of thing, certainly nobody I've ever known.' She paused, and then added, 'And I suppose you cook as well – one does hear of certain gentlemen doing that, I mean apart from those peculiar French chefs.'

Not half as peculiar as your effing cod, Felix raged. He tried to think of a cutting response that wouldn't get him thrown out. But the next moment, in what passed for an affable tone, she said, 'I expect you will be glad to see your friend when he arrives. Tell me, does he do embroidery too?'

'He lectures and writes books on Cappadocian caves,' Felix replied shortly.

She nodded. 'Ah, I see, one of those *intellectuals*. My brother went to Oxford, but he didn't stay long, found it all rather rarefied. Not to his taste at all. Still, I hope what will be to your taste, Mr Smythe, is the speciality of the house: my cherry flan. Mr Dewthorp always liked it.'

And he died, Felix thought.

At long last the ordeal was over and Felix could retire to bed, where he spent a most disgruntled night. His hostess's tart innuendos had rankled and spoilt his normally unbroken sleep. Intervals of insomnia were punctuated by fractured dreams filled with echoes of her mincing voice and yaps from the beastly dog. The tasteless supper also featured.

At one point he got up to visit the loo. The dreams had faded and mercifully the darkened house was as silent as the grave. But passing her room, he trod on a loose floorboard whose loud creak made him jump and stumble against the door. He saw a beam of light through the keyhole and froze. Oh hell, had he woken the old bat? He had a momentary vision of an irate Peebles standing before him, scowling in curlers. No fear! Thus, unrelieved and holding his breath, he tiptoed back to the refuge of his room where, pulling the blankets over his head and with eyes tightly shut, he promptly fell asleep. He awoke the next morning in the same foetal position, and – not surprisingly in view of the nocturnal change of plan – in some urgent need to spend a penny.

With the mission accomplished he was about to return to the bedroom to fetch his razor, when the air was suddenly rent with blood-curdling shrieks and a violent hammering on the bathroom door. Felix was startled. Admittedly he knew all about the indignity of being taken short, but this was a bit much, surely. He stood irresolute, biting his lip. Should he respond, open the door and confront the batterer? It might not be wise. Had Mrs Peebles gone mad, perhaps? If so, he might be in danger. After all, one could get a nasty knock from a demented woman – especially if she was a good four inches taller than oneself. And even if sane, it would surely be embarrassing to encounter one whose call of nature was causing such anguish. Yes, very embarrassing.

As he debated the matter the hammering increased, but the shrieks were replaced by words: 'Christ almighty! 'Elp!'Elp! She's been done in!' Neither words nor accent suggested the voice of Mrs Peebles and for this Felix was thankful. Cautiously he unlocked and opened the door. He was confronted by a female in a pinafore with wild staring eyes.

'My Gawd,' Elsie the cleaner gasped, 'you took your time! Smothered she is, bleeding smothered!' And without more ado, she had grabbed his arm and dragged him into his hostess's bedroom. At first all he registered was a pair of pink stays draped over an armchair, besides which lay an upturned plant pot, its contents strewn in a dark patch on the carpet. But then, as he lifted his eyes, he saw the rumpled bed in the corner with its heaped pillows and shapeless mound – and a plump and dangling arm.

He swallowed hard. 'I'm not sure if one should—' he stammered.

'Look!' Elsie cried, and advancing to the bed lifted one of the pillows.

A face of putty stared up at them, its nose and cheekbones curiously mottled with purple specks and the tip of a dark tongue protruding coyly. The lady had certainly altered since last seen, and Felix gazed, paralysed.

Hideous, ghastly. He closed his eyes, gulped, took a deep breath and glanced sideways at the gibbering cleaner. Calm, calm – that is what he must be. At all costs he must be cool in the face of Elsie – or indeed in the face of anyone else likely to appear. If only Cedric were with him.

Thinking of Cedric, he gathered himself, cleared his throat, and in a voice of unctuous authority (normally reserved for duchesses when advising them on their flower arrangements) said, 'Go immediately and telephone the police – and when you have done that, summon an ambulance.' Or should it perhaps be the undertaker? He wasn't sure, but they generally said something to that effect in the films. But evidently it did the trick, for without another bleat Elsie had left the room and could be heard pounding downstairs to the telephone in the hall.

Left alone, Felix shot a furtive glance at the bed and its smothered occupant, the head and face framed by a wilderness of straggling grey hair, and felt sick. Rather unsteadily he vacated the bedroom for the bathroom.

Oddly enough, in retrospect it was not so much the image of the dead woman that haunted him, but rather the memory of the armchair and the alarming stays.

CHAPTER FOUR

When the telephone call came through, the Southwold police were ill-prepared. Well, why should they be otherwise? Murder was not an everyday occurrence in that sedate little town, and especially not the despatch of one as starchy as Mrs Mary Peebles. Bert Hill the desk sergeant was, to put it mildly, surprised. What was it the mayor had once said of her? 'A bastion of propriety'? Something daft like that, at any rate. In his view, bastion of bloody-mindedness would be more accurate . . . Still, evidently she had copped it, been done in if you please. A fact that rather eclipsed metaphorical niceties.

'But are you sure?' he asked Elsie as she yelled down the telephone.

'Of course I'm sure!' Elsie screeched. 'I can tell a stiff any day and—'

'Ah, but can you? You see sometimes it's difficult to establish—'

'For Gawd's sake, Bert Hill, just do as I say and send the blooming cops. It's not much to ask!' The line went dead.

Thus goaded, Hill reported the matter to Inspector Jennings who was temporarily in charge of the station while his superior, Chief Inspector Nathan, languished at home with a broken leg; an injury sustained not in pursuit of villains, but by sawing off his own support during some overzealous tree pruning. Jennings was newly promoted, and although in the past such crimes had come his way, his involvement had only been in a junior capacity. So, he seized the moment with both hands. Pausing only to take a final bite of his bacon roll and summon a sergeant and constable, he sped off to the dead lady's house.

At the house itself things were moving at a more leisurely pace. Having issued instructions to call the authorities, Felix felt faint and had to be propped up in the kitchen with the deceased's brandy (an inferior sort and kept for 'medicinal purposes', a class for which the current situation seemed entirely suited). After literally bolstering him up, Elsie joined him in this and together they waited for what seemed a very long ten minutes, before two police cars arrived. During this interval and on their second round, Elsie enquired about Freddie. 'So where's the little perisher gone?' she asked. 'Usually when I arrives he's asleep in his basket – except when I'm late and then he's prancing all over the shop. But he's not here now. I wonder where he is. Have you seen him, Mr Smythe?'

Felix shook his head and closed his eyes. As if he cared where the little sod was – probably sprawled on the compost heap, smothered like its mistress. Fortunately such speculation was curtailed by the appearance of the police, and things began in earnest.

Hardly able to contain himself, Jennings raced up the stairs to take stock of the body and bedroom. He stared down at the thing in the bed and was put in mind of his Aunt Grace, who often looked like that in the morning. But peering closer he realised that the very dead Mary Peebles was a poor imitation of his relative, a ghastly parody, in fact. His eyes swept the room, noting the upturned flower pot, the trampled blooms and the faint glow from the bedside lamp. Why was it on? Had the little chap downstairs touched it? Well, they would soon know once they had taken his and the girl's fingerprints. The girl? It was Elsie Burbage, of course. When younger and new to the area he had enjoyed a brief walk-out with her sister. But he doubted whether 'our Elsie' would have had anything to do with this mess. Far too self-preserving. Squeamish, too. He remembered the god-awful fuss she had made over the family's dead guinea pig. No, Elsie Burbage was not the killer type . . . But what about that lodger? He didn't look very strong, but it was amazing the energy people could muster when stirred. He would need a rigorous questioning: rigorous but gentle. He thought of Nathan's words: 'Kid gloves to begin with. You can take 'em off later.'

Leaving a constable to guard the landing while awaiting the forensics team, Jennings went down to the kitchen where he was met with a haze of cigarette smoke. In the middle of this, with brandy bottle between them, sat the two witnesses. They looked pale and slightly glazed – though whether this was due to shock or cognac it was hard to say. Both presumably.

Clearing his throat and gesturing to the sergeant to open his notebook, Jennings began his initial enquiry. He started with Elsie. What time had she arrived that morning? Why had she gone up to the bedroom? ('I always does, she needs her tea.') When lifting the pillows had she touched the corpse? ('No bloody fear!') Apart from the death of her employer had she noticed anything odd about the house; any sign of a break-in, or anything out of place or missing?

The girl stared blankly, and then said slowly, 'Well, Freddie wasn't here, if that's what you mean.'

Jennings was curious. So who was Freddie, another lodger? He discounted the idea of a lover, handy though that might have been. Still, as Nathan was always telling him, rule nothing out. 'And this Freddie – a friend of hers, was he?'

'Huh, you can say that again. Miserable little so-and-so, always under my feet he is. And if I don't get here pronto in the mornings and shove him outside, he'll pee on the doormat. Does it deliberately.' Elsie frowned and drew heavily on her cigarette.

Jennings sighed. A pity. No lover, of course; merely a missing dog that peed on doormats. He might have guessed. He turned his attention to the other: an unknown stranger, male, and one who had been on the premises overnight. Better potential than Elsie. In the manner of his mentor, firm but affable, he took the witness's details and listened to his account.

Despite shattered nerves, but perhaps braced by the brandy, Felix delivered this with surprising clarity. Asked about the lamp, he stressed that he had touched nothing in the room when summoned by Elsie, but that he had definitely seen a beam of light from the keyhole when he had bumped against the door in the early hours. Yes, he agreed that it was surprising, but could assure the inspector that he hadn't heard a single sound the whole night through. In fact, the first noises he had registered were those of Elsie's screams and violent knocking when he had been engaged in his morning ablutions. 'It practically gave me a heart attack,' he protested indignantly.

Jennings gave a sympathetic nod and thanked him for his co-operation. 'But you will realise, sir, that following the forensics report we shall require a formal statement tomorrow at the police station. So you'll have to remain close. It's just a routine procedure and nothing to worry about.' He gave his version of a benign smile, omitting to mention that in addition to the statement and some further questions, fingerprints would also be taken. It didn't do to rattle them at this stage.

Felix nodded, but then frowned as a thought struck him. 'Actually, Inspector, I don't think I could stand staying another night in this house, I'm not quite sure what I should—'

'Stay here? Oh no, that's out of the question, sir. You will have to find alternative accommodation. This is a crime scene, you see; nobody is allowed in except us. We'll be cordoning it off shortly, so you had better get your things together. The officer here will accompany you to your room.'

Felix was alarmed. Accompanied to his room by a police officer? He didn't fancy the sound of that. Most unbecoming! But he smiled bravely, while at the same time wondering where the hell he was supposed to go – to a cell in the police station? With the hotels being fully booked that might just be his fate. Jennings cut in on his thoughts, saying that doubtless he could try another guest house, and suggested helpfully that there was one down by the pier, which might suit. Felix was not enamoured with the advice. He was tired of cramped quarters, ill-hung pictures and poor food. Besides, who was to say that it too wouldn't contain a corpse.

'You could stay with us,' Elsie said cheerfully, 'and then you could help my mum choose her new marigolds.' She turned to Jennings: 'You see it's flowers with Mr Smythe, he knows all about them. A regular expert he is.' She flashed Felix a matey grin.

Flattered though Felix was with such evident discernment, it was not an offer that had immediate appeal. He was just formulating a tactful response when the obvious solution hit him: Loader in Blythburgh. With Cedric arriving there that evening it would be ideal. Surely they could squeeze him in somewhere? He scuttled into the hall and dialled the number Cedric had given him.

Success. Loader was at home, and on hearing the distinctive nature of Felix's quandary was excited and intrigued. 'By all means stay here,' he said, 'always ready to give sanctuary to a friend of Dillworthy's – especially one in such a sticky hole.' He gave a low chuckle, not echoed by his caller. 'The wife's currently in America gambling her way through Las Vegas, so I'm afraid things are a bit casual. Your pal will be in the spare room but you are welcome to the attic; it's not as bad as it sounds.' Provided it didn't harbour a cadaver, Felix didn't care what it was like.

Much relieved, he returned to the kitchen and told Jennings of his plans and gave the Blythburgh address and telephone number. 'Not that I shall be running away, Inspector,' he joked.

'No, you won't be,' Jennings agreed sternly, and directed Constable Brown to go with him to collect his belongings.

Given the number of shirts, toiletries, assorted footwear and other accoutrements (including the waistcoat), the packing process took some time. There are those for whom packing is a hasty affair: fling 'em in and slam the lid. Felix was not of that kind, and took meticulous care over every item, dividing the folded clothes with multiple sheets of tissue paper – not unlike spreading cream between the layers of a delicate sponge cake. At one point he sensed an impatience in his overseer, but took no notice. After all, since it wasn't he who had killed the old bat, the law could damn well wait. However, such indifference was broken by the sound of a vehicle drawing up and Brown saying cheerfully, 'Ah, here are the ghouls. Thought they'd never get here.'

Felix was startled. 'Ghouls? What do you mean?'

'The forensics, the blokes that mess around with the body and take its temperature and all that stuff. As soon as that's over the other lot can wrap it up and carry it downstairs into the van. Then we can all go home – or leastways back to the station. I haven't had my breakfast yet.'

Since Felix had no desire to be entangled with ghouls and corpse-carriers, his packing accelerated accordingly. Not wishing to delay Constable Brown's breakfast any longer than was necessary, he hauled his suitcase down the stairs and out into the car.

Aimless and confused, Felix drove to the promenade where he parked and gazed morosely at the sea. He shut his eyes and brooded. Why on earth had he suggested coming here? Why hadn't he stayed in Knightsbridge being charming to fashionable hostesses and berating Covent Garden for its slow deliveries? So much safer. It had of course been the flattering invitation to the Aldeburgh party, now only three days away. Suppose this frightful affair put the kybosh on that? The Sandworth being full had been bad enough, but the murder business was simply awful. And it was one thing the police summoning him to make a formal statement, but would that be the end of it? After all, presumably he was what was called a 'key witness' (surely, God forbid, not a suspect), so they might want him again. They might even confine him to the immediate area 'pending further enquiries' or some such bureaucratic phrase. And what about the nice little jaunt into Norfolk he and Cedric had planned – would that be messed up too? He lit a cigarette and scowled at the dashboard. Clearly the Fates were against him.

And then suddenly, inexplicably, a childhood memory

stirred, and he heard his mother's voice. *Oh, do come on, Feelo, don't be such a pancake. Snap out of it! Give 'em the old two-finger and you'll feel better. Trust yer Ma, she knows!* He began to grin and tentatively raised two manicured fingers. And then hastily lowered them as a dog walker passed.

Glancing at his watch he was surprised at the time. Nearly mid-morning. Like Constable Brown, he had missed his breakfast and was now gripped by an imaginary yet insistent hunger. He formulated a programme: food first, collection of the vase and lilies second, find a phone box to call Cedric and then drive to the Loader chap's house at Blythburgh. Somehow the clear agenda plus memory of his mother's injunction had lifted his spirits, and leaving the car, he sauntered casually to forage in the high street. Had he the knack he might have whistled a jaunty tune. Lacking such skill, he instead donned his Bulgari sunglasses and mentally thrust two fingers at the world and its wiles.

CHAPTER FIVE

As the train approached Darsham, Cedric considered what might be in store. Something out of the ordinary most certainly, but what? Just before setting out for Liverpool Street, he had received a telephone call from Felix, evidently speaking from a phone box. The line had been particularly bad and Felix had been gabbling. Although far from deaf, the professor's hearing was not quite as acute as it used to be and he was hard-pressed to glean anything much from the fractured message. The words 'frightful' and 'beastly' featured a number of times and also the fact that Felix was about to drive to Loader's house, but exactly why wasn't clear. Perhaps the Sandworth had telephoned to say that there were definitely no vacancies. The dear boy did tend to overreact. Oh well, all would be revealed shortly . . . Slightly perplexed, Cedric heaved his case from the luggage rack and collected his things, ready to alight.

Needless to say, all was indeed revealed. That evening in the dining room of The Swan, much drink and energy were consumed as the three of them discussed the matter. To compensate for the ruined cod of the night before, Felix indulged himself in a Sole Bay lobster (untainted by ersatz mayonnaise). His thin voice had risen somewhat, as once more, with accompanying gestures, he evoked the grim scenario. His shins received covert kicks from both companions.

Although exhausted by travel and the evening's somewhat bibulous discussions, Cedric spent an unquiet night. In an alien bed and amid bizarrely alien circumstances, far from knitting up the 'ravelled sleeve of care', sleep remained perversely idle. He stared into the darkness, recreating the scene Felix had so graphically described and worried about its effect on his friend. Volatile and nervous, Felix was not fit for such horrors. Might there be a collapse? If the police were too zealous in their questioning it could send him into a spin. A spin? Huh! Felix was always in a spin. If it wasn't his royal patron's ravening corgis, it would be a wilting flower arrangement or the 'disgraceful' triumphs of his arch-rival, the long-established Moyses Stevens. And indeed, compared to the last – and despite its grisly mien – what was a mere corpse? Cedric smiled. No, Felix would survive all right. But not without the usual palaver.

More to the point, would he survive? After a busy time with lectures and some postgraduate examining, the unexpected respite from the Cappadocian article had been most timely and he had fancied the idea of a little trip into East Anglia. Ever since being briefly stationed at Southwold during the war, he had found himself drawn to that part of England. Despite the unsettling nature of a couple of recent visits, its attraction had never palled. So, the present drama was quite a facer and far from what had been planned! Still, it was good to see Miles Loader again and with luck things would work out – i.e. Felix would be free to attend his vital party and their projected jaunt would continue with minimum delay.

His thoughts switched back to the immediate situation. That gift of the vase and lilies had been charming, and what bad luck on the donor that such thoughtfulness should be crowned by so dire an event. He shifted restlessly on the unfamiliar mattress and dwelt on the direness.

But images of the gross were swiftly overlaid by curiosity. What on earth was it all about? Why should such a seemingly uninspiring woman elicit such violence? After all, it was one thing to needle your sensitive lodger, but quite another to be found smothered to death in your bed. Not exactly the sleep of the just. Apart from Felix, to whom then had she been unjust? Intriguing. On the other hand, could it perhaps have been some frightful mistake? The murderer might have stopped by at the wrong house. Inconceivable? Well, such cases had been known . . . hadn't they?

With his mind becoming increasingly hazy, Cedric mused upon that convenient possibility. And eventually recalling its duty, Sleep knitted up the careworn sleeve.

* * *

The next morning, less careworn but even more curious, Cedric joined Miles at breakfast. With Mrs Loader busily engaged in Las Vegas, it was a somewhat humdrum affair at the kitchen table.

'Felix not up yet?' Cedric enquired.

Miles shrugged. 'I did hear stertorous noises from the box room, so I assume he's still sleeping. Best not to disturb, he needs all his wits about him to deal with the heavies.' He grinned and pushed the marmalade in Cedric's direction.

'But are they really so heavy? From what Felix was saying last night they sounded quite mild.'

'Ah,' Miles replied darkly, slicing the top of his egg with neat precision, 'but they hadn't warmed up, had they. Taken by surprise. Since then, they've had more time to think about it, more time to formulate ideas . . . and suspicions. Besides, I daresay by now the forensics will have done their stuff so they'll have a fuller picture. No, I think friend Felix will be given quite a grilling this morning.'

'Well, for God's sake don't tell him that,' Cedric said hastily, 'it'll unsettle the poor chap.'

'Hmm. Forewarned is forearmed.'

'Yes, one might think so, but in this case he may be better armed without the warning. It will jangle his nerves . . . Shh, he's coming!'

Felix appeared at the kitchen door looking spruce in a sharply tailored jacket and hair neatly smoothed. Given the impending interview, Cedric was both relieved and surprised to see him looking almost sprightly. When Miles asked how he had slept, Felix said he couldn't remember but was dying for some coffee, 'The proper stuff, if you have any – I need to keep alert for this morning's show.' He gave an airy smile with little trace of tension.

'Indeed you will,' Cedric said a trifle anxiously, 'it won't be much of a picnic.' As he had observed to Miles, the last thing one wanted was for Felix to be prematurely rattled; nevertheless, such evident calm in the face of trouble was out of character. It was a little worrying and perhaps a casual hint wouldn't be a bad thing after all. 'Uhm, yes – a bit tricky, I imagine. I fear you may find that they—'

'Tricky?' Felix snorted, 'You want to try handling that jumped-up bore Lady Spring-Willis, the one that is always changing her orders and demanding discounts and keeps banging on about her butler being a petunia expert. If she tells me that again I'll shove some bloody petunias down her throat!' For a moment the air of sunny insouciance was replaced by a thunderous scowl as Felix recalled his tiresome client.

'I say, steady on,' his host grinned, 'I shouldn't mention the petunia bit to the inspector, if I were you, he might get the wrong idea. Too close for comfort, if you see what I mean.'

Felix assured him that his relations with the inspector would be most cordial and that naturally he would respond to their enquiries with his customary discretion and diplomacy. He then availed himself of two sausages, two fried eggs, a rasher of bacon and a slice of toast and marmite. Watching this conspicuous consumption, Cedric was glad to think that at least the arch-diplomat could face the interrogation on a full stomach.

Miles Loader was thinking along similar lines, but being

60

a reader of crime fiction the words that came to his mind were: *and the prisoner ate a hearty breakfast.*

At the police station Felix was greeted affably, offered a mug of tea, which he politely declined, and was ushered into Jennings' office.

Like Cedric, the inspector had not spent a particularly restful night. But it was less concern over the killing that had bothered him than the fear that he might not conduct the interview with Nathan's easy dexterity. In Jennings' view his superior broke all the rules in the book and yet, despite the casual approach, generally seemed to get what he wanted from witnesses. Was it the avuncular pipe that disarmed or caught them off their guard? Jennings had once thought of emulating the older man in this respect but had dismissed the idea. He would only burn his fingers stuffing the damn thing, and, besides, was bound to choke at a crucial moment. A cigarette was more his style . . . but then it might look a bit spivvish, the last thing he wanted! No, he would stick to his usual manner: correct and careful. Safer by far.

He regarded the man before him, now looking rather sleek and bearing little resemblance to the wilting figure he had encountered the previous day. The slight frame and delicate hands were not features normally associated with a ravening killer. But you never knew. If the victim had been sleeping soundly and the assailant quiet and quick and knew his business, then doubtless this chap could do the job as well as anyone. A little stiffly, Jennings enquired how Felix was feeling and said he hoped he had managed to get some rest at his temporary abode. Then, addressing the previous day's notes, he asked him to elaborate certain points.

'For example, can you confirm the time you left your room to visit the bathroom? You said yesterday that it was two-thirty. Would that be right?'

'Oh yes,' Felix assured him.

'You seem very certain. Did you check your watch?'

Felix shook his head. 'Didn't need to, there was a large clock in my room on the chest of drawers. I expect you saw it, Inspector.' (Jennings had not seen it, being too occupied with the rumpled bed in the other room and the near effigy of his Aunt Grace.)

'And despite seeing a light from the keyhole you heard absolutely nothing? No snoring or a cough or movement?'

'Well, I wasn't hanging about, exactly – can't say I was that interested. I went back to bed sharpish.'

'Immediately after you came out of the bathroom.'

Felix sighed. 'No, not really. As I explained earlier, I didn't actually get as far as the bathroom. After I had stumbled against her door and realised the light was on, I returned to my room.'

'Why was that?'

Mentally Felix drummed a finger but managed not to. 'Because,' he said tightly, 'I did not wish to be confronted by Mrs Peebles in her night attire.'

Catching the note of distaste and seeing the slightly sour expression, Jennings guessed rightly that mere decorum had little to do with Felix's retreat. He made a note and leant forward. 'And so, what was your relationship with the deceased?'

'Relationship? I am not sure what you mean, Inspector. There was no relationship. I had only met the woman two days ago.'

Jennings regarded him steadily. 'Let me put it another way, sir. How did you get on with the deceased?'

'Get on . . . oh, remarkably well!' Felix lied fulsomely. 'We had much in common.'

'Such as?'

Felix racked his brain. 'Embroidery,' he beamed. 'She was fascinated by my chair covers.'

Jennings blinked. 'I see.' (He didn't.) 'And I gather you had supper together a few hours prior to her death. May I ask if she appeared her usual self? No sign of stress or tension?'

'Absolutely none. Her normal self.' This time Felix spoke the truth and with a grim confidence.

The inspector was just about to probe a little further, when there was a knock on the door and a constable entered holding a note, which he handed to Jennings. He gave a covert wink and withdrew. Jennings glanced down at the scribbled piece of paper. It read:

We've checked Smythe's details, and like he said yesterday he does supply flowers to the Queen Mum – been doing that for about four years. Kid gloves?

Jennings was put out. He supposed it had been too much to hope that the little chap might be a charlatan. But bona fide or not, it still didn't alter the fact that he had spent the night in the victim's house and had been the only other occupant. If nothing else, he had certainly had the opportunity. And even if not the culprit, he must surely have heard or seen something; perhaps so minor that he had forgotten or didn't think worth mentioning. Time might jog his memory. Meanwhile they would keep him in their sights – and take his dabs. He mustered a jovial smile à la Nathan, thanked Felix for his help and said he should remain in the area for the time being.

'Is Aldeburgh of the area?' Felix asked quickly.

Jennings nodded; and then murmured that as a mere formality they would need to take fingerprints. 'Sergeant Harris will do the job in the anteroom, it won't take a minute. Nothing to worry about.'

The gracious smile that had started to cross the witness's face froze. Nothing to worry about? What about his royal patron! Felix was suddenly very rattled. Supposing that HM were to learn that her 'special' florist had been fingerprinted, what then? A fearful vision of his Appointment plaque being torn down by irate palace hitmen flashed before him. It was bad enough being hauled into the police station, but to have to undergo this procedure was too much. The indignity of it! It was all that bloody woman's fault. She should have locked her bedroom door . . . But he knew better than to protest, and meekly allowed the sergeant to do his worst.

At last, settled in the safety of his car, Felix took out his cigarettes and breathed a sigh of relief. He looked ruefully at his still besmudged fingers. Really, the things one had to put up with. Holding the cigarette in one hand and puffing furiously, he thrust the other into his pocket for a handkerchief to wipe the offending marks. The handkerchief emerged, plus something else: a crumpled envelope. He glanced at it casually, and then swore.

H.R. Dagwood Esq., Seaview Avenue, Aldeburgh, the address ran. Felix blinked and gazed in disbelief. But he had already posted the damn thing! He remembered distinctly getting to the post office steps, taking it out and shoving it in. Had he been hallucinating? What nonsense. He had definitely done it. There had been no mistake . . . And then wearily he shut his eyes and sighed. There had been, obviously there had. He cursed and ground out his cigarette.

Well one thing was certain, at least Rosy Gilchrist in London couldn't complain that he hadn't replied to her wedding invitation. That letter had clearly been posted in good time – in place of H.R. Dagwood's. It all came back to him now: Dagwood's envelope in one pocket of his raincoat, Rosy's in the other. With his relief at extricating himself from the Peebles place and eagerness to buy a waistcoat, he had confused the two of them and then promptly forgot about both. His first instinct was to shove it in the nearest pillar box. A few days late of course, but with the sender being dead that hardly mattered. He looked around for a convenient receptacle and gave an impatient sigh: nothing, of course. Hmm. Having just spent a gruelling hour with the coppers he certainly wasn't now going to start traipsing about playing postman. The letter could wait a bit longer.

However, it crossed his mind that he could nip back to

the police station. Let them deal with the wretched thing. Why should he be involved in the woman's affairs? But looking at the building he had just left, he hesitated and then decided against it. He'd had enough questioning for one morning, and if he suddenly reappeared they might want a further statement, or say that his prints hadn't been clear enough and they needed another set. Or any damn thing they could think of.

Without further debate Felix pressed the starter, yanked the gearstick and zoomed off in the direction of Blythburgh. As he passed the large girls' school bearing his own name (but with the saintly appendage) he nervously checked the mirror, half expecting to see a flashing blue light in hot pursuit.

CHAPTER SIX

Emeritus Professor Aldous Phipps stared at the sea. He did not care for it; the Cam was so much prettier – and provided one could avoid the larking undergraduates, much safer. He recalled the German U-boats in the Irish Channel during the war, and the awfulness of Dunkirk, and shuddered. Besides, even in normal times those vast waters were treacherous: one moment placid, the next awash with gargantuan assaults. Frightful! Shifting in his deckchair and adjusting his gaze to the little Norfolk terrier, he murmured, 'Not to your taste at all, Popsie. Much too cold.' The dog seemed to agree and burrowed deeper under her master's rug, her presence signalled merely by a twitching nose.

Phipps continued to contemplate the grey vista and inwardly conceded that one should not look a gift horse in the mouth. After all, it had been very civil of his sister

Isabel to invite him up to Southwold to have, as she had quaintly put it, a 'little break from all that Greek and Latin stuff you are so fond of'. Greek and Latin stuff? Fond of? Didn't she know that he was the best Classical scholar in the business! Really, one's siblings were so ignorant! He screwed up his eyes and brooded bleakly upon his younger brother, proprietor of 'Mayfair Hats', a mere stripling of sixty-five and raking it in designing millinery for dowagers and bespoke sun visors for the followers of Wimbledon. All very lucrative, of course, and it kept that appalling wife of his happy, but hardly a trade likely to add distinction to the family's pedigree. After all, pandering to Mayfair's hoi polloi was not quite the same as being designated emeritus by Cambridge University. The old man gave a complacent smile and contemplated the possibility of a vanilla ice cream. Being at the seaside, one should cultivate seaside habits. He looked around, vaguely expecting to see the equivalent of some Italian gelati man dispensing luscious concoctions.

No such man appeared. Instead, his eye fell on a slightly gaunt figure wearing a trilby and strolling in his direction. Judging from the rather sober suit and measured gait the man did not look like a tripper, more likely a resident – one of those senior town council officials, perhaps. Anyway, with luck he might have some knowledge of ice creams and their acquisition. When close enough he would hail him.

But then as he watched, Phipps experienced a curious sense of déjà vu . . . Hadn't he seen this man before somewhere and in a not dissimilar context? Himself seated on a bench facing a stretch of water, a person approaching, and silence except for the sound of birds – not gulls as in this case, but herons, surely? Ah, of course! On the bank of the Cam, and not so long ago either. A year, maybe.

A sense of Cambridge came upon him and with it the man's name: Dillworthy. Professor Dillworthy, an alumnus of St Cecil's. He remembered he had come up from London to attend some college event. A nice enough fellow . . . a trifle staid, perhaps, but that was hardly a defect in these rough days. What was his specialism? Something to do with caves and rocks, wasn't it? An arid pursuit one would have thought. Still, everyone to his own . . . Phipps patted the selection of Ovid neatly secured in his coat pocket. And then as the figure drew level he said, 'Ah, Professor Dillworthy, I presume. I don't suppose you have encountered an ice cream vendor by any chance? I fear they seem rather thin on the ground.'

Cedric, who had been savouring his solitary walk away from the Peebles drama and unlike the speaker admiring the waters of Sole Bay, stopped and regarded the old man with suspicion. He was unused to being accosted by strangers, even if they did address him by name. And why on earth should the chap assume he knew anything about ice-cream sellers? Absurd. Politely he raised his hat and gave a perfunctory smile. 'I am afraid you have the advantage of me,' he murmured.

And yet, even as he spoke recognition dawned. Oh lord, if it wasn't old Phipps, bane of St Cecil's. He who, during their last encounter, had persisted in addressing Felix not as 'Smythe', but as 'Smith' with a short vowel – a misnomer the latter had bitterly resented. Cedric smiled wryly. But what on earth was the old boy doing here of all places? He doubted St Cecil's had finally dispensed with his presence. Highly unlikely. Aldous Phipps was a permanent college fixture, immovable, and would merely erode like one of its ancient stones.

'I expect you are wondering what I am doing here,' Phipps said brightly. Cedric hesitated. A 'yes' might suggest an intrusive interest, whereas a 'no' could sound churlish. But before he could formulate a suitable response, he was treated to a piquant account of the havoc caused by builders renovating the building adjacent to the professor's own residence in the college mews. 'Barricades everywhere and nothing but noise and wolf whistles,' Phipps complained. 'I couldn't stand it and neither could Popsie. Fortunately, my sister suggested I visit her here for the duration.'

Cedric nodded sympathetically, while at the same time vaguely wondering at whom the wolf whistles had been directed – man or dog.

'Sit down,' Phipps said, graciously gesturing to the vacant space, 'unless of course you are in a hurry, though you don't look as if you are. Communing with the clouds, more likely.' He gave a thin chuckle, and added, '"What is this life if, full of care, / We have no time to stand and stare?" Like so many poetic clichés that one contains a fair element of truth. Wouldn't you say so, Professor?' He gazed quizzically at Cedric.

Cedric hesitated, then did as instructed and sat down beside the old man. 'Er, perhaps that's why they are clichés: we instinctively recognise their truth and then use them ad infinitum until they become vapid with overuse.'

Phipps nodded. 'Very likely. I once had a student preparing a dissertation on just that theme – the prevalence of cliché in the lesser Greek odes. Not the most inspiring of topics.'

'But any good?'

'I've no idea. I only read the first page and sent him away. Too painful.'

'Really? Why?'

Phipps sniffed. 'Nothing but clichés.'

The tone of disdain was then replaced by one of sly animation, 'But let us banish talk of clichés, Professor, I have something much more interesting to address.' It was Cedric's turn to look quizzical.

'Oh yes,' Phipps continued, 'what some in academia might facetiously term a teasing little conundrum, though what others more soberly inclined are likely to regard as a matter of some moment – especially for the unfortunate victim. A very nasty moment indeed, I should imagine. Wouldn't you think so?' The raised eyebrow disclosed an impish glint.

Cedric was bemused. 'Afraid I am not sure what you mean—' he began.

'Oh, but surely you must know. The Clare Bridge hanging, of course! It's the talk of Cambridge. I believe it even featured in the national press. Don't tell me it has escaped your notice?'

Cedric was not a daily reader of newspapers and somehow the item had indeed escaped his notice. He was startled, and dismayed to think that the beauty of Clare's historic bridge should have been besmirched by so morbid an act. Aldous Phipps seemed less dismayed, outlining the details with spirited gusto. 'Anyway,' the narrator concluded, 'I intend to purchase a swordstick.'

'What?'

'Oh yes, an excellent precaution in such circumstances. I mean to say, if Cambridge is to harbour such brigands, one needs to be prepared. Popsie and I live alone, and you never know what frightful things might befall us. However, from what one hears it rather sounds as if the Reverend Hapworth may have invited his own end.' Phipps lowered his voice: 'It seems his habits were a trifle recherché, if you see what I mean' (Cedric didn't particularly). 'Still,' he added briskly, 'forewarned etcetera . . . Uhm, I don't suppose Southwold sells swordsticks? It would save my having to investigate the Cambridge possibilities when I return there.' He stared hopefully at Cedric, and for one unnerving moment the latter feared that ice creams were not the only items he would be required to seek.

Fortunately, the topic of weaponry was dropped. Instead, rather surprisingly, Phipps enquired after Felix. 'I seem to remember that the last time we met you were accompanied by quite a pleasant fellow, a florist I think, by name of Smith. Didn't he have a stall in Camberwell – or was it Peckham? One gets so mixed up with those south London suburbs.'

'An establishment on Sloane Street, actually,' Cedric murmured, wincing at the thought of Felix's reaction should he learn of Phipps's description. 'As it happens, he is here at the moment. But there's been a spot of bother and—'

'He's here in Southwold? Oh, well then, you must bring

him along when you come to supper. My sister grows flowers, lilies principally. Doubtless they'll have something in common, in fact,' he smirked, 'they can talk shop while you and I discuss the Clare Bridge killing. How's that then, how's that?'

Cedric gave a wan smile. He wasn't aware that any such supper had been mentioned; but clearly Phipps had it in mind, for in the next breath he had demanded his telephone number. So be it, Cedric thought, at least it might be a diversion from the current mess. He stood up and was about to go, when the old man said, 'Oh, by the way, Dillworthy, should you chance upon an ice cream seller point him in my direction, would you? There's a good fellow.'

With Felix otherwise engaged, stoutly defending himself at the police station, Cedric had been without transport but had gratefully accepted a lift from his host, as he was keen to revisit Southwold at leisure – and in peace. Loader had business with his solicitors and it was arranged that when finished he would pick Cedric up at the Lord Nelson pub and drive back to Blythburgh. 'You could hitch a lift from our friend after the Stasi have dealt with him,' Miles had joked, 'but who knows how long it will take – ten minutes or in for the night.' Cedric thought this in poor taste but had agreed that the suggestion made good sense. So after his encounter with Aldous Phipps he had continued his stroll, watching the gulls and admiring the colourful little beach huts, before going on to the Lord Nelson for a dry sherry and to await his driver.

* * *

As they neared the house, they saw that Felix's car was already parked. 'Hmm, off the hook, it would seem,' Loader observed.

When they entered the sitting room, it was to find the car's owner laid out on the sofa fast asleep and snoring gently. They tiptoed into the kitchen and made a hasty sandwich, after which Loader announced he intended to go fishing on the Blyth and asked if Cedric would care to come too. Cedric did not care, and said he was perfectly happy to sit quietly and grapple with the crossword.

He managed a couple of clues but was too distracted by the snoring and his own curiosity about the interview. He stood up and briskly tapped Felix's shoulder. 'Wake up,' he said sternly, 'if you go on like that you won't be able to sleep tonight.'

The sleeper awoke, groaned, and said it was all too bad. In answer to the inevitable question, he then proceeded to relate his exhausting experience at the police station and his mix-up over the confounded letter.

'I take it you have opened it?'

'Well, no, not really. It's nothing to do with me . . .' Felix closed his eyes again.

'Except that it was entrusted to you,' Cedric said lightly. 'You never know, it might be important. Maybe it's to her bank manager, or to her solicitor about changing her will or something.'

'Huh! If H.R. Dagwood is the man I saw in the shop, it'll be more like her bookmaker,' Felix said waspishly. 'Do you know, he was actually wearing crêpe soles!'

'Crêpe soles or not, I think we had better check. Come on, where is it?'

Felix waved a languid hand at his discarded raincoat.

Cedric retrieved the envelope and slit it open. The contents read as follows:

Dear Harold,

Since we last spoke you will doubtless be glad to know that matters here have vastly improved, and the adjustment has done much for my roses. In fact, life is proceeding very nicely. All is as it should be with no tiresome complications. Your men were most deft. Their handling of the other problem was also deft; but did it have to be quite so theatrical? Absurd, really. Well anyway, I trust that like mine, your plants are blooming; but if you have any sense, you will cut down that pernicious privet hedge. You know the one I mean – the one in the London garden. Be warned, it is liable to take over.

Incidentally, you were wise to sell the Wapping warehouse (in my opinion always a white elephant), but I fear you have forgotten to send my own share of the proceeds. Even as a teenager you were always tardy in such matters. I trust you will see to it.

With kindly thoughts,

Your sister

Cedric regarded Felix over the rim of his glasses, and murmured, 'This'll wake you up, dear boy: H.R. Dagwood is not the lady's bookmaker but her brother. Here, take a look.'

'Her brother? Oh my God, that's all one needs!' Felix closed his eyes and then, opening them, scanned the proffered note. 'Huh. So what does all that mean?'

Cedric shrugged. 'Apart from the fact that she wants money, I can't see that it says very much. She was evidently keen on her garden. Rather sounds as if the brother had recommended a gardener. What had he done – overpruned her roses or something?'

Felix also shrugged. 'Can't say I noticed any roses. Nothing but annual bedding plants – begonias in serried ranks. Still, I suppose she may have had a wilting rambler somewhere.' He paused, and then added, 'But the tone is typical: tart and bossy.'

'Hmm. It's a personal letter. Perhaps you should send it to the brother with an abject apology saying you had opened it by mistake.'

'I didn't open it,' Felix said indignantly, 'it was you with that smart paperknife I gave you – you just can't resist using it. Besides, I doubt if he would be particularly gracious. You may recall that I was the one in the house when she was murdered. Not exactly the best person to admit to delaying and opening his mail.'

'The police could probably handle it. They might even find it useful – victim's last words and all that. You could take it to them.'

'I may do, but I can't see that it is crucial evidence, exactly. I mean, if it had said: "Between you and me, I think John Brown the grocer is likely to murder me in my bed" it might be of some interest. As it is, it's just a sister being hoity-toity to her brother. They do it all the time.'

At that moment the telephone rang, and once more the letter was thrust aside as Felix leapt from the sofa: 'Quick, that might be the Sandworth with news of my room!' he cried excitedly.

Cedric went to the hall and picked up the receiver. 'Is that you, Miles?' the voice said.

'Afraid not. He's gone fishing. This is Cedric Dillworthy, I'm staying here.'

'Ah, Professor!' Isabel Phipps exclaimed, 'Just the man I want. I gather you met my brother this morning. He is most keen that you and your friend should come to supper – and of course Miles too, if he would like. The only problem is that things are a bit congested in the next few days, so I don't suppose you could manage tonight, could you? Rather short notice, I'm afraid.'

Cedric replied politely that they would be delighted, while at the same time surprised that Aldous had been so quick off the mark. Was the old boy bored already? He remembered Felix talking approvingly of the sister; she sounded fairly civilised, and so with luck the evening could be quite agreeable.

Returning to the sitting room, he told Felix that it had not been the Sandworth but the lily lady. His friend gave a pout of disappointment, but then brightened and said, 'So what do you think I should wear? One of my cream shirts or the blue?'

With practised diplomacy, Cedric assured him he would look charming in either.

CHAPTER SEVEN

A year into his promotion to chief inspector, Ted Tilson of the Cambridge constabulary was feeling rather jaunty. Having successfully wound up their most recent cases – two colourful robberies and one bleak little knifing – and having been suitably complimented by the hierarchy and given a very neat profile in the local press, he was feeling pleased with life. So pleased, in fact, that he was relishing the prospect of the present challenge, confident that he and his team would soon solve the affair and nail the perpetrators. He had a mental picture of the superintendent's grudging offer of whisky as he presented him with yet another successfully concluded case. He could also see the headline in the local newspaper: 'The Clare Bridge Horror: Tilson's Triumph'. It was an enticing little reverie and one that he indulged for a few seconds before being interrupted by the entry of Detective Sergeant Hopkins. He liked Hopkins but there were times when the young man could be an irritant, and this was one of them.

'I don't like the look of this,' Hopkins said gloomily, 'it's going to be one of those jobs that drags on and on and with nothing to give a decent lead.' He sighed and added, 'And the thing being so bizarre doesn't help either – I mean why stun the chap first and then string him up? Why not just bash him to kingdom-come and leave him on the towpath? Much simpler. Treating the poor bugger like this makes it a drama and excites the public, and then with all their damn-fool questions there won't be a moment's peace. So far we haven't got a clue.' He frowned and chewed the top of his pen.

'Nonsense,' Tilson said briskly, 'we do have a clue in that we know that the victim was not all that he should be, leastways not for a vicar. Too fond of the choirboys and with a habit of making "miscalculations" in the church funds: oversights in his own favour, naturally. A bit of a sleaze, it would seem. We can certainly explore that angle.'

'Ah, so you think this was a reprisal, a peevish act of revenge by one of the Church Commissioners or a disgruntled choirboy?' Hopkins' voice held the merest tinge of sarcasm. 'I suppose the commissioners might hold a grudge – I'm told they're a tricky bunch and object to being taken for a ride. Perhaps one of them got shirty. But the choirboys we interviewed just sniggered and called Hapworth a silly old fart. We know the type, well enough: smoothly unsavoury but fairly harmless. Mind you, the ladies seemed to admire him. Maybe one of them liked him too much and was miffed by his lack of interest. They don't like being spurned, ladies don't.' Hopkins gave a knowing wink and added, 'Still, she'd have to be a hefty girl to lay into him like that and—'

'Shut up, Hopkins, and listen!' Tilson snapped. 'You're just like the super, always rabbiting on! You may be in line for promotion, but any more bilge like that and you can forget it.' He glared, the earlier good humour rapidly evaporating. 'Just because he wasn't a first-grade villain doesn't mean his background is of no relevance. A chap like that could have all manner of slippery connections. Find out what he was doing in London before coming to Cambridge. And what about that diary you found at his lodgings – any use?'

Hopkins shrugged. 'It isn't a proper diary, more an appointment book. Boring. Just church stuff ... services, meetings, funerals and whatnot.' He paused and added, 'Although there are a couple of entries that aren't clear, one in January and the other in April. They both say the same: "Off to Orf".'

'What?'

Hopkins repeated the words slowly, and then added, 'A lot of the other stuff is in pencil but those two are in ink. Still, it could be anything I suppose – his auntie or his bookmaker.'

Tilson scowled. 'Let's have a look,' he said curtly.

Hopkins fetched the diary, laid it on the desk with a flourish and retreated for lunch before settling down to his London researches.

Left alone, Tilson munched a sandwich and leafed through the pages. Yes, Hopkins was right: boring. The usual mundane entries that you might expect from a busy cleric. He turned to the months of January and April. As Hopkins had noted, 'Off' to 'Orf.' was clearly inscribed in both. Judging from other items, some of which contained abbreviations, the vicar had been a meticulous writer with even the briefest notes being correctly punctuated. Thus, the full stop after 'Orf' might imply a truncated form of a longer name, a place name perhaps. Discounting Hopkins' helpful suggestion of aunts and bookmakers, he pondered the matter hoping for inspiration. He could think of only one place: Orford near Warrington in Cheshire where his wife's mother came from; an obscure little village set in a heavily industrialised district. Why should Hapworth strike north on an arduous journey to visit a place like that? To admire the scenery? Hardly. Perhaps, like the mother in law, he came from that area and had some local business to deal with.

He continued to study the pages, and then saw that both entries preceded an appointment in Cambridge for the following day, one for a baptism in the early afternoon and the other for some parish meeting in the morning. Getting back in time for those events would certainly require fast driving – and presumably rushed business. Whether leaving the same night or very early in the morning, it must have been quite a scramble. He sighed. Perhaps Hopkins was right, the reference was not to a place but to a person. Yes, that was probably it, some fellow cleric rejoicing in the name of Orfeo – unless it was a nickname, of course. Anyway, he could put the new DC on to it. That'd keep the lad busy!

Yet still the question nagged, and Tilson continued to brood. Then, with sandwich finished, he quarried in his desk for the AA atlas and ran a finger down the 'O' section of the index. Aha, much more likely! It could well be the Suffolk Orford near the coast, not far from Southwold where his old colleague John Nathan operated. Compared with North Cheshire, a drive there from Cambridge would be simple enough and a day trip perfectly doable. In fact, now he came to think of it, he had a couple of friends who motored up regularly to sail and birdwatch. They had sung the praises of its charm, oysters and ancient church . . . Was that what drew Hapworth, something ecclesiastical? Was he a sort of locum vicar, conducting services when the incumbent was away? Possibly. . . But whatever the reason (provided that was his destination), presumably some sort of contact had been made. And so who had he met there and why? Was it conceivable that there was someone in sleepy Orford who knew more about the Clare Bridge killing than they cared to divulge? He gave a rueful smile. Chance would be a fine thing. Talk about clutching at straws in the eastern wind!

Still, he thought more soberly, it needed looking into. Experience had taught him that sometimes the most unlikely conjectures could pay off. With luck, the road to Orford might lead somewhere very interesting. He would telephone Nathan and make a discreet enquiry. His old mate had a nose like a sniffer dog and knew his patch well; he might just have an angle. Besides, it was time they had another chinwag and a good grouse about the powers that be.

Ten minutes later he was still brooding. Not about Orford, or indeed the motive for Hapworth's despatch, but its method. As all had agreed, while the bash on the head could have been done by a lone assassin, the stringing up suggested an accomplice. Someone on their own could hardly have coped. The victim was a big chap, and it would surely have needed another pair of hands to hoist him up like that. But Hopkins had been right: why go to such lengths? Why not just clock him one and be done with it? The more time spent messing with the victim, the more likelihood of being seen. Dog walkers and undergraduates were nocturnal creatures, and the possibility of one suddenly appearing at the crucial moment, though perhaps slim, was hardly remote. Were the perpetrators both thick and lucky, or chancers taking a calculated risk to make a point? But if the latter, what sort of point? The whole thing had a staginess about it that was difficult to explain.

Some days later, having spoken with Southwold's Chief Inspector Nathan, currently immured in his house with a broken leg, Tilson was still curious about the bizarre manner of the vicar's end. However, a more pressing concern was to learn something of the victim's background prior to living in Cambridge, and to this effect, Sergeant Hopkins' earlier research had proved quite effective.

He seemed to have come from a socially 'sound' family living in rural west Berkshire. After boarding school, he had gone up to Oxford, but apparently failed to complete his studies and left without a degree . . . the letters 'M.A.' after his name being what one might call a courtesy appendage, or wishful thinking. It would appear that for a while he had led a somewhat shiftless career, drifting around the inner parts of the capital, living on a small legacy from a relative and taking occasional temporary jobs: assistant librarian in Kensington, shopwalker at Harrods, dogsbody at a West End art gallery, and for a fortnight, stand-in doorkeeper at a popular and not very salubrious establishment in Soho. Whether it was this post that had given him a taste for the shadier side of things was a matter of conjecture. But from what Hopkins had discovered, he had next cropped up among the fringes of London's underworld, enmeshed in its network of petty crooks and post-war profiteers.

Here it would appear he had adopted a couple of aliases; the wildly original name of Bill Brown and the rather more snappy Harry Hepton (a feeling for alliteration perhaps?), and in a minor way was involved in a variety of questionable rackets, including a spot of pimping and blackmail.

Up to this point in his research, Sergeant Hopkins had been able to trace a fairly clear route, but then things petered out and the trail went cold. Cold, that is, until under the quarry's original name of Stephen Hapworth, the man had turned up in Cambridge as a bona fide clergyman.

Initially the transmutation from petty wide boy to respected cleric would seem to have been remarkably successful. (Maybe he had 'seen the light' or whatever it was these converts were supposed to see, Tilson mused). But more recently, as evidenced by the perplexity of church auditors and annoyance of the occasional choirboy, there had been a distinct falling-off and the righteous carapace had begun to show splits. The august air of Cambridge had become tinged with innuendo; unseemly jokes were made, eyebrows raised, rumours started. Indeed, by the more worldly and less gullible, the reverend gentleman was deemed to be distinctly flaky.

In view of that recent history, and reflecting on the London findings, Tilson wondered whether such a development just went to show that, whatever the circumstances, some individuals will eventually revert to type. Hapworth's type being? The chief inspector knew the sort all right: small beer, big ambition. Arrogant but dependent on others, one who might be termed a handy second (or third) fiddler . . . Yes, he was one of thousands. The chap had been accused of petty embezzlement, and the likelihood of a court case mooted. Yet despite the tittering gossip, Hapworth had scorned a lawyer, declaring haughtily that should such a case be brought he would naturally conduct his own defence.

Tilson grimaced and shook his head. Such assurance, such stupidity . . . Well, that little piece of legal theatre had certainly been nipped in the bud – and replaced by a show far more dramatic!

He cogitated, reread the report and then summoned its compiler to offer congratulations. 'A nice piece of work, Hopkins. It's a start, if nothing else. The problem is,' he continued, 'it doesn't exactly narrow the field, does it? Our man had two lives, London and Cambridge, different milieus, same propensities.'

'Ah, but it may be wider than that,' Hopkins replied sombrely. 'What about the Orford area? You suggested that those diary entries might indicate a Suffolk link. So how is your old colleague up in Suffolk coping – made any headway, has he?'

Tilson sighed. 'The chief inspector is laid up with a broken leg and sore head, injuries sustained from inadvertently sawing off the bough he was standing on. It's his deputy, Inspector Jennings, who is pursuing the matter. He's been recently promoted . . . like you will be one day, I suppose.' He paused, and then added drily, 'Let that be a lesson to you. Should you ever reach the status of DCI, avoid climbing trees or mistaking yourself for Tarzan – especially when you are over fifty.'

CHAPTER EIGHT

On his way home to Walberswick, Inspector Jennings dropped in on Chief Inspector Nathan to enquire after the latter's broken leg, to chew the cud over the Peebles drama and to taste some of his superior's homemade cider – a brew that bore no resemblance to any cider Jennings had ever tasted. Yet from past experience he knew that invariably the acrid potion produced an uncanny sense of well-being. And Jennings could do with a bit of well-being. It had been a taxing day, not helped by the uselessness of the Smythe witness. Either the chap was a born liar or as deaf as a post. Besides, just because he supplied the Queen Mother with flowers did not necessarily make him averse to murder. You could never be sure with these Londoners: barrow boy or toff, they were all dubious. Forgetting to ask about the leg now imprisoned in plaster of Paris, these were observations that he bleakly made to Nathan.

The latter regarded him thoughtfully, and then said, 'What you need to do, old son, is to stretch your mind a bit. Shelve the little fellow and look further afield. Orford, for example.'

Jennings was both stung and curious. 'Why Orford?' he muttered.

'You know that Cambridge business under the bridge, the vicar who was strung up there? Well, my old pal Chief Inspector Tilson of the Cambridge force phoned yesterday and told me – quite informally you understand – that he's got a hunch that the victim may have visited our neck of the woods a couple of times, Orford. It's in his diary.'

Relaxed and emboldened by the cider, Jennings said carelessly, 'So what? A lot of people like the place, it's very pretty. I mean to say, my old granny is a regular visitor; it's the oysters, she goes to that nice place that specialises—'

'Your old granny lives in Walberswick, a few miles down the road, not in Cambridge ninety miles away. And unlike Hapworth, I bet she doesn't note it in her diary when she goes there – assuming that's what the reference means.'

Staring blankly at the rigid leg propped on its footstool, Jennings took another sip of cider, and said, 'No, I don't suppose she does. But anyway, what's that got to do with things here?'

'Ah well, that's for you to find out, isn't it, Inspector.' Nathan grinned and made an elaborate show of lighting his pipe.

Jennings sighed. It was half-past six and he wanted his supper. 'Why don't you give me a clue,' he said acidly.

'I take it you have checked her background – habits and all that?'

Jennings nodded. 'It's in hand.'

'Hmm. Well in that case you will know about the prayer meetings.'

'Er . . . not entirely,' Jennings murmured, having no idea what his boss was talking about.

'Ah, so you don't know,' Nathan said briskly. 'In which case, I suggest you take a look, pronto, before the Cambridge crew get going. You wouldn't want to be pipped at the post, would you? I mean they might think we're a bit slow here in Suffolk, you know what these city types are like.'

Jennings sighed and submitted. 'What prayer meetings and what have they got to do with Mary Peebles?'

'The ones she attended in Orford. You might pick up a lead of sorts. They're a bit of a rum bunch, so I hear, but harmless enough it seems. Still, there might be someone there who had a grudge, or at least could shed some light. Besides, like I said, you don't want to be caught napping by Cambridge when they start nosing. They are bound to check Hapworth's reasons for visiting. Maybe he kept a mistress over there , . . Or perhaps his motive was less fun. Perhaps he had some dealings with this lot that Peebles was mixed up with – him being a clergyman and all that. In which case there just might be a link between the two killings. Mere speculation, of course, and our immediate concern is the lady herself, so look into it and find out who her cronies were. You'll feel better.' Nathan grinned and emitted a swirl of pipe smoke.

A little stiffly, Jennings lied that he felt perfectly all right, and asked how the chief inspector was familiar with the group.

'Oh, I am not familiar with it, just picked up one or two local rumours. Can't say I was interested – until now, that is. Why should I be? Society is awash with earnest groups of that sort. But with Mary Peebles being a member, and her being murdered, that makes them a bit more interesting, doesn't it? I suggest you get on to Furblow, the vicar here in Southwold. He'll probably know about them, or know someone who does.'

Jennings nodded, thanked the chief inspector for his advice, and getting up to leave said he hoped the leg would soon mend.

'It had bloody better,' the invalid snorted, 'can't stand the boredom . . . Here, do you want to sign it? That's what they do, isn't it?'

Jennings blinked. 'Sign it? Er, well I . . .' He gazed uneasily at the proffered limb encased in its pristine plaster. 'My pen's broken,' he said, 'besides, surely you'll want a flashier signature than mine. Try the chief constable, he's always ready to sign things; anything will do, even a leg.'

Nathan laughed. 'Be like that, then! But mind you pursue the Orford link, and be quick about it. It could be handy, if only to keep the super happy. You don't want him on your back.'

No, Jennings brooded as he drove home to Walberswick, he didn't want the superintendent on his back – nor anyone else, including Nathan. This was going to be his pigeon! Still, admittedly, the boss's tip about the Orford setup was interesting and with luck could be productive, which was more than the afternoon's interview with the Dagwood fellow had been.

Jennings frowned in recollection of his recent visit to the victim's brother in Aldeburgh. He hadn't liked him particularly; not his sort at all. Brash and patronising, that's what he had been. His frown deepened as he thought of the sod's welcoming words: 'Given these appalling circumstances I am rather surprised not to see Chief Inspector Nathan here. No doubt you and your sergeant are very able, Inspector, but I should have thought that in a ghastly case like this an officer of slightly higher rank would be appointed. Still, naturally I shall do my best to help you.' He had flashed an ingratiating smile.

After expressing sympathy for the man's loss, Jennings had explained evenly that Nathan was indisposed and that he could be assured that the investigation was receiving the police's full attention. This was, he added, merely an initial enquiry pending further developments.

'And let's hope there will be further developments,' Harold Dagwood had replied brusquely. 'It's scandalous that she should have been butchered in this way!'

Ever the pedant, Jennings had murmured that it hadn't been butchery but asphyxiation. It was not the most prudent remark.

'Oh, is that all,' the other said caustically, 'a mere smothering. Quite mild in comparison. Lucky old Mary, cleanly choked to death and spared all the gore.' He glared.

Jennings had made a hasty but reluctant apology, which the latter graciously acknowledged, though added that he hoped their questions wouldn't take up too much time as he was a busy man and couldn't sit around yacking all day. He had paused, perhaps regretting his choice of words, for he said ruefully, 'To quote my dear sister of course – "yacking", it was one of her favourite expressions. Alas, I fear never to be heard again . . .' His pensive gaze swept the room, before returning to the police officers. 'So,' he said briskly, 'what is your particular interest? Where I was at the time of her death, I bet. Isn't that what you bods usually want to know?' He gave a hollow laugh. 'Well, I can tell you; I was in London attending to some of my business interests – and, as it happens, visiting a lady friend. Check it out if you like. Now, what's your next question?'

Refraining from pointing out that, as yet, there had been no questions, Jennings had said it would be useful to know when the gentleman had last seen his sister.

'Friday the sixteenth, three weeks before it happened. She had asked me to tea – worse luck.' Seeing Jennings' surprised look, he explained, 'God-awful cakes she used to make, dry as old bones. Sandwiches stale too. Huh! I don't know how those lodgers coped.' He gave a mirthless laugh, before adding more soberly, 'Still, *nil nisi* and all that.'

'But apart from the cakes, you spent a pleasant time with her? She didn't appear tense or agitated, or hint that she was being threatened in any way?'

'Perfectly normal. We talked about the usual things – her sewing and bridge classes, the Women's Institute, my new premises in London, the government, the bloody dog – all that sort of thing. No, there was nothing to suggest that there was anything wrong or different from usual.'

'And were you close to your sister?'

'Close? Well, we weren't joined at the hip, if that's what you mean. But we certainly rubbed along all right. Oh yes, we were quite matey in our way. Neither of us had any children, you see, and she gave her old man the push years ago. A weedy type, I seem to remember. Got remarried and went to Australia some years back. A pity, really, otherwise you might have pinned it on him. As it is, you've got quite a bit of work on your hands, haven't you, Inspector? Still, I am sure that with your competence you and your sergeant will get the swine in the end.'

The words were said smoothly enough but Jennings had sensed a note of sarcasm. Considering the man's opening gambit, there probably was. Ignoring the probable barb, he said, 'So you don't think she had any enemies?'

Dagwood shrugged. 'Enemies? No more than any of us has ... except perhaps those who had sampled her cooking.' He grinned; and then glancing at his watch, frowned. 'So, I think that's it, Inspector,' he said dismissively. 'As I said, I'm rather busy just now, and as you can imagine, it's hardly the best time for me. It's been one hell of a shock. Terrible. But naturally, if there's anything else I can help you with or I hear of anything, I'll let you know.'

Jennings had nodded curtly. 'Oh yes, we'll call you in if you're needed, sir. You can be sure of that.' He felt piqued; returning to the car he had a vague sense that it had been not he, but Dagwood who had been conducting the interview. He wondered how Nathan would have handled things. 'There's always one, isn't there, Sergeant,' he had muttered frostily to Harris.

'Oh yes,' Harris agreed stoutly, 'they're all buggers, really.' It wasn't something that Jennings could entirely concur with, but it served its purpose and he felt mildly better.

Those had been the bare bones of the interview. And very bare they had been, Jennings thought ruefully as he parked outside his small cottage. In fact, with hindsight the only notable thing was that Dagwood had made no reference to the Orford prayer meetings, which Nathan had been so keen to stress. Her other local interests had been mentioned – the Women's Institute, the bridge circle and so on – but not a word about the religious bit. Had she deliberately been concealing her involvement from her brother? Or had he elected not to mention it?

Jennings pondered, and then shrugged. Well, as far as he was concerned that could all wait. For the time being it was not cider but a draught of Adnams beer and a solid pork pie he was after. And then a relaxing evening with some Agatha Christie. He hadn't read a good Poirot for ages. He entered his cottage and made a beeline for the fridge.

The next morning, following Nathan's instructions, Jennings telephoned the Reverend Mark Furblow, incumbent of St Edmund's, Southwold's ancient wool church.

When asked if he could spare a few minutes, the vicar suggested they meet at the graveyard, the more secluded part at the rear. Jennings was slightly surprised: it seemed an odd place to choose. 'All right—' he began.

'You see it's a question of the sheep,' Furblow explained,

'our groundsman is on leave so I am having to deal with them. They only came yesterday and may not have got the hang of things. Besides, there are a couple of escape routes that need to be plugged, and that's my exciting task for the day. No peace for the pastors of the Lord, ho! ho!'

'Er, no,' Jennings agreed, utterly mystified. 'And these sheep – what can't they get the hang of?'

'Cropping the grass, of course. The diocese bigwigs are mad about the idea, it's all the rage and saves paying for all those lawn mowers. I don't know if the brainchild was Canterbury's but he's certainly very keen. Far be it from me to thwart the hierarchy in such matters, thus I've agreed to give it a go . . . Anyway, Inspector, I shall be at your disposal any time after lunch – sheep willing!'

So that afternoon Jennings strolled up to St Edmund's to see what the vicar might know of the Orford sect and to admire his new-found flock. He wondered if he would find Furblow clad in a chasuble playing panpipes to the munching incomers. Unlikely, of course, but one never knew with these people, and it was as well to be prepared.

He rounded the corner of the church and scanned the area for a sign of sheep or shepherd. Unlike the frontage with its tended graves, ordered paths and shady yews, this part seemed a semi-wilderness: wildflowers aplenty, but also plenty of weeds. Half obscured by the long grass and creeping ivy, the tombs lay gnarled and broken. Yet the air of neglect held a pleasing serenity, and for a brief moment Jennings savoured the stillness, mission forgotten. However, peace was abruptly disturbed by a loud bleating to his left – and then by an even louder noise. 'Oh do shut up, damn you!' a voice exclaimed. 'And get out of the way!'

Jennings swung round, and was confronted by three woolly rumps and a man in shirtsleeves kneeling at a rickety fence wielding a mallet. No sign of a chasuble, but on the ground lay a discarded panama and clerical dog collar. Sidestepping the sheep, Jennings approached the vicar and introduced himself.

The vicar stood up, wiped his forehead and proffered his hand. 'Ah, Inspector,' he said a trifle breathlessly, 'afraid you've caught me at a tricky moment. It's these wretched sheep, they won't leave me alone. They're supposed to be eating the grass, but all they do is gawp and get in the way.' He glared at the creatures and then gestured to a nearby bench. 'We'll sit there quietly and with luck they'll get bored and move off.'

'Perhaps they think the job is too much for them,' Jennings remarked, glancing around. 'I mean, there's only three and this is quite a big space.'

'Ah, but these are just the vanguard. Apparently, we are to expect reinforcements tomorrow. The farmer is delivering them from Woodbridge. Perhaps when their colleagues join them, they'll get the message.' The vicar paused and added, 'A bit like parishioners, really, doubtless they'll respond better en masse. It's the herd mentality.'

Ovine matters disposed of, Jennings hastily raised the question of the Orford sect and Mrs Peebles' attendance there.

'Ah poor, poor Mary Peebles – a frightful business, truly dreadful,' the vicar lamented. 'It's cast quite a shadow over our little town – or at least among the more sensitive souls.

As you might expect, there are a few ghouls who display an unseemly relish, youngsters mainly, but most people are deeply perturbed. As well they might be. For example, old Mrs Brophy who keeps the sweetshop told me she hasn't slept a wink for days and sits up knitting all night with both barrels of her shotgun primed. Well, naturally I said that I trusted she held a licence for the weapon, and that in any case a prayer might be more suitable.'

'And did she agree?' Jennings asked.

Furblow sighed. 'No, not really; her exact words were, "prayers be damned, bullets are better".' He frowned. 'I suppose I should have had a quick answer for that, but do you know I was flummoxed – yes, quite flummoxed. Tell me, do you ever feel like that, Inspector?'

'It has been known,' Jennings replied curtly.

Furblow stared glumly at one of the sheep, and then said, 'So, you wanted to know about those Orford people Mary consorted with. I fear I shan't be of much use to you. I am aware of the group, of course, but we at St Edmund's have little reason to fraternise; they are what you might call pugilistic.' Seeing Jennings' startled expression, he explained, 'Oh I don't mean in any physical sense, but in the sense that they don't mince their words, nor indeed their attitudes. Sin is what drives them.'

'Driven by sin? But I thought they were some sort of Christian group.' Jennings was faintly shocked.

'Ah no, not their own sin, but rather the transgressions of others. It is their mission to expose and stamp it out. And stamp they do, as I know to my own cost.' Furblow gave a bleak laugh.

'Really? In what way?'

'It was a couple of months ago. I was in the middle of my Sunday address and had just reached the point when I was gently reminding the congregation that, alas, we are all sinners and there are times when we must forebear criticism of others, when there was the most awful racket from the side aisle. Three people had stood up waving their arms and banging tambourines. At first I thought to myself, oh lor' it's the Salvation Army! But not at all: it was poor Mary Peebles and two other ladies. "Rubbish," Mary yelled, "it's people like you, Rector, who give the church a bad name. Namby-pamby piffle, that's all you can spout. Sin is sin and cannot be condoned. People must be shown the error of their ways!" And so saying, she and her two adjutants did a left turn and marched out . . . Well, as you can imagine, I was a trifle startled, but managed to retain my composure and continued with my sermon. It didn't work, of course. After that little drama nobody cared a fig what I was saying and were far too busy sniggering and tut-tutting. A total shambles, really.' Furblow gazed up at the church tower in rueful recollection.

'Tricky,' Jennings murmured.

The latter shrugged. 'Ah well, if you join the church you can expect that sort of thing, I suppose. There are always the grumblers and subversives – a bit like the police, I dare say.'

Jennings inwardly agreed but made no comment. Instead, he enquired as to the names of Mary Peebles' fellow protestors.

'Oh, didn't I say? The twins, of course, Joy and Gaye

Goodhart, a surlier pair it would be hard to find. I doubt if you'll get much help from that quarter – though being of the Orford brigade and thus colleagues of the deceased, they may be more co-operative than usual. They live just over by the new RC church. Ironic, really: an irritant for them and a trial for the priest. Still, Father Rupert takes it in good part: says it's a penance to be offered up. Theirs is the white house, number ten I think – though for goodness' sake don't say I told you, they may come and harass the sheep.' Jennings had the impression the vicar wasn't entirely joking.

Leaving the pastor puffing on a cigarette and meditating upon his woolly charges, Jennings made his way back to the police station.

Headway? A little. At least now he knew whom to approach about the Orford setup, and a little more about the victim's personality. Bellicose! As presumably were her two cronies. Perhaps that was the root of the murder: fury fuelled by internal strife. If the bunch were as pugilistic as Furblow suggested, who knew what vicious rivalries it might encourage. Perhaps in her zeal to carry the banner of righteousness, Mary Peebles had overstepped the mark or upstaged one similarly keen. Was that it, a nest of fanatical vipers battling for moral hegemony? Jennings' lively imagination conjured a graphic image, and by the time he reached his office he felt quite perky. Without doubt, he told himself, the 'surly' Goodharts should be approached forthwith.

CHAPTER NINE

At the same time as Jennings had been weathering the interview with Harold Dagwood the victim's brother, with greater ease Cedric had been visualising dinner with the Phipps family. With luck it might be quite a pleasant affair, and certainly good for Felix, who could do with a convivial distraction, however small. The poor boy had certainly gone through it! And thus at seven o'clock, spruced and cheerful, the three friends squeezed into Loader's Morris Mini and set off on the short drive to Southwold.

What had been a somewhat damp and blowy day had turned into a benign evening. The breeze had dropped and Southwold lay becalmed in the rays of a lingering sun. Being a little early for Isabel's supper, Miles parked at the side of South Green and the three of them strolled in the direction of Gun Hill and the six eighteenth century cannons, sentinel on the cliff's edge ready to repel all raiders.

No raids being imminent, they gazed in silence at the docile sea, bathed in a serenity that belied the drama of recent events. Miles found himself pondering the fate of Horace Dewthorp who had stumbled to his death in nearby Dunwich only two or three miles down the coast. It just went to show that safety was never quite what it seemed.

Felix, turning from the guns, contemplated another landmark: the lighthouse rearing up above the roofs of Southwold and also standing firmly sentinel. A symbol of protection? Not entirely. Mary Peebles had slept in its lee and yet some dire fiend had entered and done for her . . . with himself only yards away! He shuddered and hastily dwelt on brighter matters, like the intricacies of floral pillars and his next appointment with the Queen Mother. Compared to his awful ordeal in that fated house, even the corgis took on a kindly aspect.

The evening's calm was broken by a sharp bark. A muscly little Jack Russell scurried across the turf, followed by its owner throwing a toy rabbit. Jolted from admiring the fading sun and pale sickle of a rising moon, Cedric was amused by the creature's jaunty antics as it leapt for the toy and pranced around the guns. But it made him think of another dog, and turning to Felix he said, 'I say, what do you think happened to that miniature Yorkshire terrier you found so annoying? Did the police mention it?'

Felix, his royal reverie broken, frowned. 'No idea,' he replied shortly, 'and they certainly didn't say anything to me about it.' He looked at his watch. 'Come on, it's time we were off. The Phipps lady will be waiting and I'm dying of thirst.'

Sauntering back across the green, they were joined by Reggie Higgs who had evidently been invited to help swell the ranks and disarm the Cambridge house guest. On being introduced to Cedric, Reggie said slyly, 'I trust that bit of fakery your friend bought met with your approval. Rather a pretty little piece, actually.'

Cedric declared he was delighted. 'Provided there is wit and elegance, any bit of fakery has value.'

'Ah, a man after my own heart!' Reggie exclaimed. 'You must visit my shop one day – and who knows, you might even find a few genuine articles amid the elegant dross.' He grinned.

Isabel Phipps proved a lively hostess and to get things going had produced two large jugs of chilled sangria. At first Cedric had been wary of this, his own preference being the austerity of a dry Martini. He had always associated the English version of sangria with garden fetes or boisterous vicars on church outings. But he was reassured by Aldous Phipps, who sidling up murmured, 'Better than it looks. Amidst all that fruit and froth there lurks half a vat of rum and brandy – gin too, I suspect. Taste it and see.' Cedric did as instructed and was happily taken aback.

The preprandial chatter continued into supper where inevitably much of the talk was of the Peebles drama. 'Funny it happening so soon after her ex-lodger had fallen off the cliff,' Miles Loader remarked. 'It's odd the way things can coincide. I remember old Dewthorp once joking that he might come to a sticky end – though I don't suppose he had expected it quite so soon. I doubt if he was sixty.'

'Sixty-one to be precise,' Reggie Higgs said. 'You may recall my telling you I had sold him a small figurine for his birthday.' He paused, and then added, 'Actually I don't think they hit it off particularly – he and Mary, I mean. Or at least, I don't think he was overly enamoured with her. So presumably that was why he decided to rent the flat in Pier Avenue. Still, one thing is certain; it wasn't he who did her in. One less suspect for the police to pester!' He directed a lopsided grin at Felix. It was not appreciated.

Aldous Phipps, who had been about to lift his wine glass, set it down and cleared his throat. 'Dewthorp,' he mused, 'not the most common of names in my experience. In fact, the only one that comes to mind is that of a Horace Dewthorp, a clerical gauleiter at King's who took early retirement last year. By all accounts he had their tax affairs tied up with gold thread. I hear the new man is an awful dud. But then of course these days—'

Doubtless Phipps would have continued his musings had Reggie not interrupted. 'Did you say Horace Dewthorp? And do you mean King's, Cambridge?'

Aldous Phipps looked mildly surprised. 'But of course. I believe that London has such a college and I gather there's one in Newcastle – an offshoot of Durham – but naturally I refer to our great Cambridge institution.' He flashed Reggie an indulgent smile.

'And I refer to our Horace,' the latter said. 'He definitely worked for a Cambridge college in some capacity, although he never said much about it. But it's clearly the same chap. I didn't know he was a tax expert. Had he mentioned it, I'd have asked him to sort out my returns. Still, it's a bit late now.'

'Most things generally are,' Felix muttered dourly. 'If I'd known I was destined to meet that Mary Peebles I would never have gone near the place.' It wasn't the most controversial remark, and other than polite smiles elicited no response.

Phipps continued. 'The same chap, eh? Well, from what you say it would seem so. Same name, same city. Dear me, what an unfortunate falling off, as Shakespeare might say, yes exceedingly unfortunate!' Phipps gave a thin smile pleased with his little quip. He paused, and then warming to his own wit, said, 'The old maxim is right: "Two's company, three is none" . . . although in the present situation perhaps the adjective excessive might be more apt.' He beamed around at the table.

There was a puzzled silence, broken by Isabel protesting, 'Oh really, Aldous, must you be so gnomic! What company are you talking about and why excessive?'

Even as she fired the question, Cedric, a crossword addict, had mentally started to decode the reference. But he needn't have bothered, for Phipps supplied the solution. 'The Company of Coincidence, of course. Firstly, Mrs Peebles' ex-lodger died shortly before her own demise, and in their different ways both deaths were violent; secondly, the gentleman in question was evidently the one I knew of in Cambridge. So far two mild coincidences. But there is a third one, a trifle more unexpected . . .' Phipps broke off and bent down to administer a titbit to Popsie and to ruffle her coat.

'Oh do come on, Aldous, we are agog,' his sister said briskly and with the merest irony.

Hmm, she thought, *nothing changes. Still the drama queen!*

Phipps resumed his position, and carefully adjusting his napkin said, 'As you may have read, though I gather it escaped the eye of our learned friend here' – he nodded towards Cedric – 'Cambridge has recently been afflicted with a most distasteful event. I refer, of course, to the Clare Bridge killing. Well, it just so happens that Horace Dewthorp knew Hapworth.'

'Hapworth who?' asked Felix.

Aldous Phipps sighed. 'The Reverend Stephen Hapworth,' he enunciated slowly, 'the victim of the outrage. Hit, garrotted, and hung on a hook. Not a pretty sight, I imagine.' He shot a mischievous glance at Felix, and added, 'Although whether the degree of gruesomeness matched that of your recent experience, Mr Smith, naturally I couldn't say. Aesthetic judgements are so subjective, wouldn't you agree?'

Felix inwardly seethed and made no reply. Really, would the bugger never get his name right!

Miles Loader was also annoyed. It was one thing to be discussing the Peebles drama (fascinating, in fact), but the Cambridge topic was a different matter. He glanced uneasily at Isabel, worried that she might reveal his relationship with the victim. He regretted ever having mentioned it. It had been a casual comment, and it was only Isabel's sly allusion to possible police interest that later gave him pause for thought. *Bridge Victim's Cousin Denies All Knowledge.* Was that a headline he wished to see? No bloody fear. Almost as bad as the reverse! Consequently, he was relieved when Isabel caught his eye, gave a quick smile and turned her attention to refilling Reggie Higgs's glass.

When her brother had arrived hot from the Cambridge killing with all its attendant speculation, Miles had thought she might have told the old boy of his kinship with the deceased. But evidently nothing had been said, and he was reminded that below the casual exterior Isabel Phipps possessed a canny discretion. It was a canniness that her sibling would seem to share. What was it she had said of him in the pub? Fussy, nosy and tiresome, or something like that . . . Well, that rang true enough; but the watchfulness of the darting eyes and the sharpness of their gaze when stilled, hinted at a brain both alert and shrewd. A nosy fussiness did not make you a fool.

'So how well did you know Dewthorp?' Cedric asked Phipps.

'Oh, I don't think "know" is quite the right word,' Phipps corrected him, 'he was hardly in my professional sphere, if you see what I mean. But I was certainly aware of him. Colleagues from King's would praise his administrative acumen and meticulous accounting. And we were briefly introduced when I was chatting with their bursar one day. He seemed a pleasant enough fellow. I don't forget faces, and I do recall two further sightings. Both times he was in the company of the Reverend Hapworth.' Phipps paused reflectively. 'In fact,' he went on, 'the second occasion I remember with great clarity, great clarity. You see, it was a very hot day, and instead of occupying my usual nook in The Eagle for my luncheon aperitif I had seated myself at one of their al fresco tables beneath the canopy – so much cooler for Popsie.' He cast a fond glance at the little Norfolk asleep at his feet. 'I was just taking the first sip of my gin and bitters – most refreshing in the heat I always find – when I noticed the pair of them a couple of tables away and talking earnestly. That is to say, the vicar was talking earnestly, Dewthorp looked somewhat bored.' Phipps emitted a thin chuckle: 'It occurred to me that Hapworth might be delivering a conversion sermon – these holy zealots never miss a trick, you know! Though I cannot say that his recipient appeared especially inspired.'

Phipps chuckled again, but then frowned, and leaning forward said indignantly, 'But do you know what Hapworth had the gall to do?' Heads were silently shaken. 'He kicked my Popsie!'

'Kicked your what?' Felix asked with interest.

'My little dog. She had wandered over – looking for scraps, I daresay – and was just making a brief reconnaissance, when the great lout lashed out. He was wearing his cassock too. Utterly disgraceful.'

'So what did you do, Aldous?' Isabel asked. 'Clock him one?'

'Certainly not. You may remember, dear sister, that our parents always advised against playing fisticuffs with men of the cloth. One was liable to get hurt . . . No, what I did was to gather her up and retreat into the sanctuary of the bar. But I can tell you, before departing I wagged my finger at him very fiercely, very fiercely indeed.'

'He must have been terrified,' Isabel murmured.

Her brother ignored the sarcasm, and addressing

the table at large, declared, 'You know, in my humble opinion there are two types of clergy: the delightful and the dubious. Plainly Hapworth was of the latter variety – particularly in view of what was beginning to be rumoured about his extracurricular activities. Not entirely savoury, one gathers.'

Phipps had given the merest smile, but Miles Loader flinched. While not sure about the generalisation as a whole, he certainly agreed about the Hapworth bit. He wished to God the old man would change the subject. No such luck. For Felix, his curiosity stirred by the Eagle anecdote, wanted to know if that had been the last time Phipps had seen the vicar.

'No. I had that misfortune a week before his death. It was the early evening, and I was on my way to an event at Pembroke when he literally bumped into me just outside the main entrance.'

'Did he say anything?'

Phipps shrugged. 'Not that I recall. He was somewhat incommoded.

'Incommoded? In what way?'

'In what way?' For a few seconds the professor seemed to reflect, and then replied, 'I should say in the way of being as drunk as a skunk.' The phrase was delivered with a reedy resonance that cut across the general chit-chat and stirred mild surprise. 'Oh yes,' Aldous Phipps continued, 'drunk . . . as a . . . skunk. That's the term the undergraduates use, isn't it? Intriguingly graphic, wouldn't you agree? One of their better inventions – they don't have many.' And then turning to Isabel, and in a tone of unctuous sweetness he said, 'My dear, I trust you won't be too terrified if I ask for another drop of claret. An excellent choice, if I may say, one of your more discerning ones.' The request was accompanied by a dazzling smile.

Grasping his chance to divert matters, Miles Loader hastily enquired after Cedric's latest publication, details of which the professor was always ready to supply. Reggie Higgs chatted to Felix Smythe about antiques and flowers, while Isabel tactfully occupied her brother with talk of canines and of Popsie in particular. Swordsticks were also mentioned. Unlike the Peebles pudding, her cherry dessert was a masterpiece and relished by all – Felix going so far as to graciously accept a third helping.

CHAPTER TEN

Miles Loader had suffered an unfortunate session with his dentist in Southwold. Unfortunate, because contrary to expectation, it had resulted in one of his molars being removed. Miles was a poor patient (his wife frequently accusing him of hypochondria) and the assault on his mouth had left him feeling both frail and indignant. The dentist had assured him that 'all was for the best', but the client was less sure. His immediate urge had been to drive home to the safety of Blythburgh and commiserate quietly with the absent tooth. But recalling the presence of the two guests, he changed tack and drove instead to the edge of the common where he could park and recover in peace from the recent trauma. (There had been no trauma; he had merely been unnerved.)

Gingerly, Loader put tongue to unaccustomed gap,

and for no obvious reason winced. He wound down the window, sniffed the air and decided that the outside world was a better place of recovery than the cramped car seat. He got out and strolled a few yards; and then enticed by the warmth and the silence, lay down and sprawled his length on the grass.

The air felt sultry, rare for that part of Suffolk, and he almost drifted off. But not quite, for once more his mind returned to the past – to that day among the corn stooks and the amorous afternoon spoilt by Cousin Stephen. An age away, or so it seemed. He thought about the aftermath. The girl of course had scuttled away flushed and giggling; but Stephen had hung around loitering coyly, and then days later had slyly requested 'a little settlement'. Well, he'd got his settlement all right! Miles grinned at the memory, even now experiencing a frisson of satisfaction as he recalled that perfectly landed punch.

Yet despite the lesson of a bloodied nose and the later surprising discovery of a religious 'vocation', had blackmail perhaps become Stephen's forte, his secular skill and pleasure? Were love of God and love of Mammon juxtaposed, or were they conveniently fused, the one reinforcing or excusing the other? Had he persuaded himself that blackmail was the Lord's work bringing sinners to their knees . . . Or was he just a hypocritical self-serving bastard? Loader suspected the latter.

Sordid though they were, tampering with choirboys and church funds hardly warranted so dire a punishment as death. Surely something bigger, more serious, must have been the goad. And if indeed Stephen had developed a penchant for blackmail, might that have accounted for his dreadful end? Years previously he had received his comeuppance from himself, the incensed younger cousin. Had that little skirmish been a foretaste of something far worse? A prelude to a grotesque reckoning from one with more to hide than a saucy fling in a cornfield?

Loader continued to muse and began to think that perhaps, after all, the Cambridge police should be apprised of that early event. If he was right, and it had indeed been a foretaste of Stephen's later activity, might not such a tip help extend their profile of the victim, and thus suggest a motive? After all, he wouldn't need to reveal his own involvement. He could always say he had been a pal of the pestered youth (name of course conveniently forgotten) and thus privy to the matter: an amused confidant who only now recalled the incident. Yes, he could try that line perhaps.

He lit a cigarette and contemplated the azure sky arched endlessly above the tracts of gorse. No golden corn sheaves here; yet the common's lazy warmth seemed to echo the idle mood of that earlier time. It was too late in the season to hear much birdsong other than the ubiquitous wood pigeon, but a single lark could be spied whirling and twirling miles above. An enviable sight – though far too high to catch a sound, and in any case no match for the rhythmic cooing a few yards away. It was a soothing noise, and the watcher closed his eyes recalling the childhood chant of *Who killed poor Polly? Who killed poor Polly?* . . . But then with a start he opened them, for to his adult ear the cooing now seemed to have slid into a different phrase.

Who's mad, you silly boy, then? Who's mad, you silly boy, then? Who-o-s... And so the damn bird went moaning on. *Yes*, he thought irritably, *I've got the message, thank you.* To go to the police would indeed be madness: they would be bound to suss him out and he would look a fool. And worse still, he could well be subjected to questions about his family and their link to bloody Stephen.

The past vanished, and the present with all its vexations confronted him. He sighed and lit another cigarette. Shakespeare had been right: so much of human angst revolved around the need for public respect. 'Reputation, reputation, reputation! O, I have lost my reputation!' poor old Cassio had wailed. Well yes, the chap had a point: the ego was a fragile thing and easily dented – or at least his was. Did he really want to acknowledge kinship with a sleazy swindler and petty pervert (and now according to the Phipps fellow, a drunkard and kicker of harmless dogs)? No fear! It was bad enough that Stephen's death had been so public and gross; but that he should also be a pastor of 'peculiar' habits and possibly a regular blackmailer, was frightful. No, it was not something to shout about ... nor to whisper quietly to a police officer. After all, it was amazing how easily things got about – and out of hand.

And it was with such thoughts that Miles Loader justified his decision not to play the upright citizen eager to help the law catch those responsible for murdering his relation. Doubtless some might accuse him of cowardice, and they could be right. But Miles had also been right in his reflection on Cassio's concern for his precious reputation.

It isn't only 'conscience that makes cowards of us all', but also embarrassment and fear of loss of face. Pride makes us fallible – and vulnerable.

Knowing that and tired of the afternoon, Loader stood up and wandered back to the car. Yet even as he went, he was still engrossed in thoughts of Stephen: nothing to do with his own dilemma, but a detached perplexity regarding the murder itself. It really was the most extraordinary business. But then so was the Peebles affair; much closer to home and mercifully not something with which he was remotely connected. Unless, of course, Dillworthy's chum, friend Felix, turned out to be the assassin, after all. Were that the case, one might be had up for harbouring a criminal. He grinned and pushed the starter.

Arriving home, he found 'friend Felix' in high spirits. The Sandworth had telephoned to say that yes, a room could be made available the following day, just in time for the party. 'It has a balcony,' Felix chortled, 'and large too, not just some converted broom cupboard. Most agreeable. How nice to be in civilised surroundings at last,' he crowed, 'and with the hotel being right on the front I can take morning strolls along the beach.'.

'But you don't like pebbles,' Cedric said woodenly, 'you always say they hurt your feet.'

'Sorry about the attic,' Loader murmured, 'given the unusual circumstances it was the best we could do.' He winked at Cedric.

Felix ignored Cedric's remark but had the grace to look abashed by Loader's. 'Don't worry, dear chap,' he said

114

hastily, 'it's the best attic I have ever encountered. Superb views over the marshes! Now, I suggest that tonight, as celebration of my good fortune, we hurtle down to one of Southwold's superlative hostelries where naturally I shall be in the chair.' He beamed and waved a regal hand.

Thanking him for the generous offer, his host retired upstairs with *The Times* to gather strength for the evening's gaieties and to inspect the lacuna left by the dentist. Having carefully incised that paper's crossword, Cedric remained in his chair sipping black coffee and cursing the clues, while Felix stretched his ease on the sofa.

The news from the Sandworth had sent him into a happy spin and for a brief spell the Peebles nightmare and the indignity of the fingerprinting might never have been. The sun shone and life looked sane again. He began to make mental preparations – not just sartorial but also musical. At the original meeting he had felt too ignorant to try joining in the musical discussions, and had confined himself to nodding tactfully. But with this second invitation he felt emboldened to contribute at least a passing comment. Thus, distracting Cedric from the crossword, he started to pick his brains about some of the composer's major works. 'Confine yourself to three,' Cedric told him sternly, 'otherwise you will get muddled and look a fool.'

Felix was stung but had to admit that his friend had a point. Taking the advice, he memorised Cedric's recommendations: titles that he could casually drop at a suitable moment. 'And, er, what about the vocalist,' he grinned, 'what's his speciality?'

Cedric reflected. 'Well, he's good with English folk

songs, and you could always shatter his nerves with your execrable rendition of "The Foggy, Foggy Dew". But I suggest you stick with Schubert – yes, the big song-cycle, that should do. Tell him that his interpretation of the third piece is the most exquisite display of thwarted desire you have ever heard.' Cedric paused, before adding hastily, 'But frankly, you would be wiser to stick to flowers and foliage – that's your métier, dear boy. Leave the delights of Schubert to others. Much safer.'

'And talking of flowers,' said Loader from the doorway (now evidently sufficiently rested to face the rigours of the evening) 'there's the making of a mimosa in the fridge, just enough champagne and Cointreau left. We can line our stomachs in readiness for Felix's lavish treat in Southwold.' This was deemed an agreeable idea and the appropriate measures were taken.

A little later Felix's generosity knew no bounds, and he did his friends proud with Sole Bay fish and Adnams wines.

Dinner over, they were about to return to Blythburgh when Loader suggested they might like to nip over to Dunwich. 'It's OK', he assured them, 'I may be mellow but I'm perfectly sober.'

'Why?' Felix asked.

Loader said cheerfully that it was probably because he was so used to the stuff.

'Not the drink, Dunwich. Why go?'

The other explained that there were two reasons. One was that it seemed a shame not to take advantage of a beautiful evening to enjoy a beautiful place, and the other was that they could check the spot where Dewthorp had met his death. Felix was hesitant, feeling the second part of the proposal a trifle morbid. But Cedric seemed keen. 'It will give us a chance to walk off that excellent meal, and then we shall sleep all the better.'

Thus, having parked the car and walked across the turf to the cliff's edge, the three of them gazed down in silence at the rocky escarpment, pondering the man's last moments.

'Frightful,' Felix murmured.

'Hmm. But a trifle curious, surely?' Cedric said, frowning. 'I mean, I know he was dashing after the dog, but you'd think he would have had the instinct to pull back in time.'

'Ah,' said Felix acidly, 'but being in charge of the Peebles dog may have stifled instinct. If the creature had gone over, the recriminations would have been dire.' He spoke with feeling.

Loader pointed to a large, jagged piece of chalk protruding from a clump of gorse. 'He is supposed to have tripped there. The locals say that forty years ago someone did just that, so I suppose that's the assumption – or at least the police seemed to think so. Mind you, that was in the dark and the fellow blind drunk. Dewthorp was a teetotaller and it was daylight. Still, according to Reggie Higgs he was always pretty clumsy. I gather he once collided with a pram on North Green outside the library and left the occupant spreadeagled on the pavement. Said he hadn't noticed it. There was an awful shindig.'

'So, no question of suicide?'

Loader shrugged. 'The police have discounted that, and

from what I recall he seemed perfectly content – not that one can tell, of course. God knows what goes on in people's minds. We don't know the half of it.'

They nodded in solemn agreement; and then, tired of their exercise, moved from the cliff's dark edge to regain the car and the safety of Blythburgh.

After the previous day's demanding events of pulled teeth and lavish entertainment, the next morning was spent in peaceful inertia. Cedric stayed in bed, Felix spent a long time pottering in the bathroom and Loader lolled on the sofa reading the newspaper and telephoning his wife in Las Vegas. 'I have won three hundred dollars!' the faint voice announced. 'Isn't that splendid?' Her husband agreed that it was indeed excellent; but when he enquired how much she had lost, the line crackled and the response was rendered inaudible. Better not to know these things, he thought philosophically, and returned to *The Times* and an enlivening little article on debt and insolvency.

The morning's languor gave way to a brisk and busy afternoon: Felix was poised to set off to Aldeburgh. The police had to be notified of his new temporary address, the Hillman's tyres and battery carefully checked (only a half-hour's drive but a breakdown would have been catastrophic!), and suitcases packed and loaded. It was a taxing business, but at last all was ready and fond farewells made.

As the departing guest drove off in a flurry of hand-waving and exhaust, Loader remarked, 'I suppose he'll be all right over there, will he?

'Oh yes, in his element,' Cedric assured him, 'or at least, provided there is no corpse to encounter. No, he will take to the musicians' party like a duck to water. Doesn't know a note, of course, but that won't stop anything.' He paused and frowned. 'Mind you, the last time we were in the Aldeburgh area he did have an altercation with a coypu.'

'With a coypu? You mean those peculiar marsh creatures like peevish beavers?'

'That's it. He was driving back to Aldeburgh from Southwold one night when he was violently attacked, or so he says. He had stopped to answer a call of nature, when the beast came at him with all cylinders firing.' The normally decorous Cedric began to giggle. 'Yes, quite a little drama it was. Still, he survived to tell the tale – and tell it he does. In fact, I am rather surprised he hasn't mentioned it to you.'

'Hmm, probably got other things on his mind: the Peebles experience, not to mention the police interest. Can't say I'd want to be in his shoes.' Bad enough, Loader thought gloomily, being related to the hanged Hapworth.

Cedric seemed to reflect; and then said soberly, 'Difficult to know which would be worse: being confronted by a smothered landlady of the Peebles ilk or by an irate coypu. Both liable to induce nightmares.

CHAPTER ELEVEN

Currently Felix was far from enduring nightmares. In fact, he was feeling particularly chipper. His drive over to Aldeburgh had been smooth, his reception at the Sandworth welcoming, and his large bedroom much to his satisfaction. He unpacked carefully, swaggered into his evening clothes and went down to the bar for a pre-party drink. At that early hour few people were there, but this was no loss, for it gave him a chance to mentally rehearse the list of opera titles that Cedric had given him. Occasional hobnobbing with the Queen Mother had taught him that preparation was key . . . Then with drink finished and music repertoire carefully memorised, he set off for the Jubilee Hall.

As he walked up its steps among strangers, he heard his name called. He turned, to see a familiar face. It was Dick Cottle, someone he had met in Aldeburgh on that first occasion and who had been so decent in inviting him to the earlier soirée on Crag Path. Then, as now, he wasn't quite sure what Cottle's status was in the social hierarchy, but he seemed to know everybody and clearly played an important part in the town's musical life. Probably some vital committee member, Felix surmised. The point was that he rather liked the chap and was glad to see a familiar face.

He was even more glad when, once inside, Cottle summoned a waiter and saw that the newcomer was supplied with a glass of champagne and a plate of shrimp canapés. 'My wife makes these,' he whispered, 'so I can vouch for their safety. They're miles better than those others.' He gestured disparagingly at an array of pineapple segments harpooned with sticks of cocktail onions. 'Tell her you like them, and I can snaffle some more.'

Earnestly they discussed the finer points of the canapés. And then just as Cottle was politely enquiring about the Sloane Street flower business, there was a sudden collision and Felix spilled his champagne and nearly choked. A man pushed past, toting a small canine on a lead. 'Whoops! So sorry. Silly me,' the man murmured, and moved on.

'Who's that?' Felix asked irritably, smoothing his lapels and gesturing towards the drink-spiller (shorter than himself, he noted with satisfaction). He drew up to his full height of five foot six-and-a half, and glared at the departing back.

'Oh, that's Ezra, Ezra Simmonds,' Cottle explained, 'plays the flute in his spare time, which is why he's here. And when he's not spare, he does the gardening for Harold Dagwood, the local property bigwig whose sister was murdered, and for certain others – provided they pay enough.' He winked, and nodded in the direction of their two distinguished hosts. The hosts were being charming amid a circle of friends and admirers. The Ezra person was not among them, but stood apart, sipping whisky and feeding cheese straws to the dog.

Felix received two jolts, and felt quite weak. The first jolt was the name of Harold Dagwood, the intended recipient of the letter he had failed to post and, as it had turned out, the victim's brother – the same man he had encountered in the Southwold draper's shop. The second jolt was the dog. Surely to God it was that little pest Freddie or Teddy, or whatever she had called it! He stared at the creature, noting its undershot jaw, the slight kink in the right ear and the way it wriggled its rump. Yes, he was sure that was the creature: the one that hadn't barked on that fateful night and then mysteriously disappeared. Not that he had cared, at the time he had assumed it had gone the same way as its mistress. Dead in a corner somewhere. Yet here it was as right as rain and gobbling disgustingly.

'Fond of dogs, are you?' Cottle asked, seeing Felix's interest.

'What? Oh, no . . . I, er, just thought I had seen it before somewhere. In Southwold, perhaps,' Felix replied vaguely.

'You probably had. That's where Ezra found it. Picked it up a few days ago, scampering all over the place. Totally lost, apparently, and with no collar or name tag. Ezra said it seemed to take to him immediately and showed a particular penchant for his trouser leg.' (Oh yes, that's definitely the little beast, Felix thought.) 'Anyway,' Cottle continued, 'he brought it back here; said that if the owners couldn't be bothered to take care of him, then he would.' He laughed. 'He's soft like that, Ezra. Loves animals! Here, I'll introduce you, and he can apologise for spilling your drink.' Felix had no desire to meet the diminutive Ezra and even less the wretched dog. But it was too late, for the pair had already been hailed.

Cradling the little thing in his arms, Ezra Simmonds waggled the dog's paw and urged it to say 'Hello' to the nice gentleman.

Anyone would think it was a bloody parrot, Felix seethed. He mustered the pretence of a smile. The dog gazed at him impassively before emitting a petulant shriek – presumably of recognition. Ignoring this and polishing his tarnished smile, Felix addressed Ezra: 'Mr Cottle tells me you play the flute – it must give you so much pleasure. I wish I had such a talent.' He was about to expatiate upon the delights of musicianship of which he knew nothing, when Cottle interrupted:

'Oh, indeed he does, and with such gusto. I don't know where he gets the breath from! Our composer thinks very highly of him' – he nodded towards the elegant shoulders of a dinner jacket encircled by admirers – 'which is why he uses him as a merciful stand-in should the regular flautist be sick or tight.'

The merciful stand-in seemed unimpressed with the endorsement and muttered something to the effect that gusto only came into it when demanded by the score, and that most of the time he liked to think he played with a subtle finesse. Turning to Felix, he murmured silkily, 'As doubtless you exercise the same sort of finesse in your flower arrangements for our esteemed Queen Mother.'

The smirk of modest deprecation, which Felix reserved for such allusions, wavered. He was startled. How did this total stranger know who he was? 'Oh indeed,' he replied, 'one has to be very subtle – the palace loathes any hint of ostentation.' He cleared his throat and added, 'But, er, I am surprised you would know that I—'

'Ah, but we in Suffolk are a gossipy lot and it's amazing what the grapevine yields.' Ezra tapped the side of his nose and gave a slithering smile. Then, giving the dog's paw a farewell wag, melted into the crowd. Felix pursed his lips. For some reason the encounter had unsettled him, but he couldn't think why.

But his unease was broken by a stifled chuckle from Cottle. 'I say,' he whispered, 'the "Profile" approaches.'

'What?'

'The tenor. He's making a beeline over here. I'll leave you to it.' And Cottle too slipped away among the throng.

Instantly, unease vanished. Felix grasped the proffered hand, and in answer to the genial enquiry, exclaimed, 'Oh yes, indeed I am – and how clever of you to recognise me after this time. And what a pleasure it is to be back in musical Aldeburgh. A treat indeed!' He beamed at the handsome features and sensed that the precious waistcoat had not gone unremarked . . . or unapproved.

There followed an exhilarating exchange of pleasantries. Or at least the guest was exhilarated, though who is to say what the other may have felt. In the course of these pleasantries Felix made passing reference to St-Jean-Cap-

Ferrat and its famous author: 'We go there from time to time' (they had been once) 'and have that pleasure again this September. His villa is delightful, and he of course fascinating. Such a charming host.'

This information struck the right note, for apparently the writer was one of the tenor's favourites. Enthusing about the acerbic prose with its razor-sharp insight, he mentioned a couple of titles – a cue that Felix immediately grasped. 'Ah,' he exclaimed, 'what splendid material for an opera! Has that ever been considered, I wonder? Perhaps when we are there, my friend and I could whisper the idea into the great man's ear.' He gave a sprightly smile.

The other also smiled, not so much in a sprightly way as with veiled scepticism. He said something about his colleague hating to be accused of touting for trade, adding that fun though the idea sounded, the composer was absolutely drowning in projects and thus such a thing simply not feasible. 'Try Tippet,' he suggested helpfully.

Not knowing who Tippet was, Felix dropped the subject and was about to speak glowingly of the other's role in a Henry James adaptation (one of those works Cedric had apprised him of), when he was forestalled by the reappearance of Ezra Simmonds. The man had sidled up and stood hovering, still holding the wretched dog.

'So sorry to barge in,' the interloper said, not showing a glimpse of sorrow, 'but we have all been summoned for photographs on the beach. Apparently, we are required to assemble before the light fades.' And so saying, he grasped Felix's arm and whispered, 'Come with me and I'll show you the best place to stand.'

Felix was all in favour of procuring the best place but would have preferred another guide. However, bidding a hasty farewell to his host, he submitted to being hustled outside on to the shingle and nudged into an elevated position close to the spaces for the VIPs. When all were assembled and the cameras poised, Ezra gave a conspiratorial wink (unreturned) and muttered, 'Raise your glass and look towards Their Nibs.' Dutifully, Felix struck the pose while the photographers snapped.

There is a limit to how long one can balance on a lobster pot, but Felix coped with elegant dexterity. When the picture later appeared in the press, the result was really rather good . . . though it might have been even better had he not been shown crammed next to Ezra Simmonds and Freddie's intrusive snout.

Festivities over, Felix returned to the hotel, but not before being invited by the Cottles to join them and a small group for cocktails in the lounge the following evening. Naturally the prospect found favour and Felix happily accepted.

Climbing the stairs to his room, he felt a warm glow. How well things were going! The current evening had been a resounding success and very nearly compensated for the fearful Peebles business. Once he had got over his initial shyness and been greeted by faces half remembered from the earlier occasion , he had been able to relax and mingle. In this respect the affable Cottle had been especially useful: making new introductions and gaily referring to him as 'the Queen Mother's special florist.' The highlight, of course, was the warm reception given him by the two 'top brass'.

Such charming chaps. So elegant and urbane – and what a contrast to that awful Peebles brother, the Dagwood person. Although an Aldeburgh resident, mercifully he hadn't featured in such a refined gathering. Probably couldn't tell a flute from a cello. Felix gave a superior smile.

But any such smugness was quickly dashed by the idea of a flute, for it brought to mind his encounter with Ezra Simmonds. There was something about that slick little flautist that he hadn't liked, though he was blowed if he knew why. He frowned, hearing again the yapping dog and the silky tone of its now master. He also saw the latter's sleekly brushed hair; and catching sight in the mirror of his own wayward spikes, made a mental note to order more 'taming oil' from Trumpers in Jermyn Street the minute he was back in London. Fortunately, he still had some left for present needs.

His mind returned to the Jubilee Hall and the cause of his irritation. According to Cottle, apart from playing the flute the man was also employed by Dagwood as an occasional gardener. So perhaps that was it – an association of distasteful ideas: dog, Dagwood, Peebles. Freud could have explained matters. As might Cedric, had he been with him. For a few moments Felix thought fondly of Cedric, then changing into his pyjamas, opened the window and sniffed the cool night air.

He gazed at the starlit sky, the expanse of glimmering water and the will-o'-the-wisp gleams from distant fishing smacks, and enjoyed what he saw. The scene put him in mind of a line from some poem he had been forced to learn as a schoolboy: 'It is a beauteous evening, calm and free, /

The holy time is quiet as a nun . . .' Well, the evening was beautiful and quiet all right – but as to nuns, he wasn't so sure. He recalled himself as a youngster being faced with a gaggle of them on the pier at Southend. They had been making an unholy racket and chewing sticks of peppermint rock; probably been let out on a rare spree. Briefly Felix dwelt on the memory. But then banishing all thoughts of roistering nuns, and resuming his pleasurable images of the party, he got into bed, turned off the light and fell instantly asleep.

Some hours later he awoke in a muck sweat and enveloped in a blinding light. He seemed to sense a presence, but dazzled by the light could see nothing. He heard a voice; then the light went out and he was returned to a silent darkness. For a few seconds Felix lay rigid, heart pounding, shocked out of his mind. And then gradually, and emboldened by the silence, he gathered his wits and fumbled cautiously for the bedside lamp. The room was reassuringly the same as before, its elegance only slightly marred by discarded garments.

He was puzzled and still somewhat unnerved. The experience had been so vivid, so real! Maybe some fellow guest had mistaken the room number and blundered in, and then realising his mistake made a quick exit. Yes, that was probably it, some fuddled idiot without a clue what he was doing. But had he also been a fuddled idiot in forgetting to lock the door? Cursing, Felix scrambled out of bed . . . The little bolt was firmly in place. Clearly no one had entered: it had just been a bloody dream!

And yet it was a dream that wouldn't go away, and despite an excellent breakfast it continued to nag. It pestered him as he strolled in the sunshine beside the shingle and the fishermen's nets, and then later intruded upon his mid-morning coffee at the White Lion. The experience had been so tangible that he wondered if it hadn't been a dream at all; an hallucination, perhaps – a vision, even! But Felix was not given to visions (except perhaps those of marauding corgis) and such an oddity seemed unlikely – unless he was going batty, of course. He lit a comforting Sobranie and had just begun to form a reflective smoke ring, when, with a gasp that nearly made him choke, he stopped abruptly. Mechanically he stubbed out the smouldering cigarette and stared into space.

The pub's cosy lounge bar faded, as another scene confronted his eyes. The radiant light shone again, but this time with clear details: a mantelpiece dubiously graced by a pair of portly china cherubs; ill-sewn floral curtains; a lumpy mattress; the creak of a door and a voice that muttered *fuck!* The images were sharp and the sound unmistakable. Mentally Felix was back in familiar surroundings: his bedroom at the Peebles establishment. He ran quivering fingers through his hair. So that's what it had been about! A dream, after all. But a dream of a memory – a memory deeply buried, and then partially disinterred in the stylish safety of the Sandworth.

The original scenario was only too clear. Despite what he had assured the police, he now realised that he had indeed seen and heard something in that fearful night: yes – that sudden blaze of overhead light, the merest squeak of a

129

door handle, a vague form and the whispered oath. Thus, he reasoned, in all likelihood it had not been the prompting of his bladder that had woken him, but the sudden intrusion. But then why on earth hadn't he remembered the incident when interviewed by Jennings and his cohorts? They would probably have been quite interested. Perhaps when stirred from sleep his brain had been befogged and less retentive. Besides, given the shocking discovery the following morning it was little wonder that his mind had seized up; a sort of temporary amnesia. Yes, as Cedric would doubtless say, it had been a classic example of memory playing tricks and suppressing the unwanted.

Felix sighed: well, in this case it was not so much a trick as a game of ruddy hide-and-seek. He drummed agitated fingers on the table and was about to ask for the bill, when the awful implications struck. His fingers froze and he suddenly felt sick.

Whoever had stealthily entered the house that night and smothered Mary Peebles had also been within feet of himself, even perhaps stood above him with pillow poised to bring it down on his blissfully sleeping face. Clearly the intruder had mistaken the guest room for hers: realised his error, cursed, and then crept across the landing to do his worst. Christ! It had been bad enough knowing he had been under the same roof as the killer, but to think the fiend had been there in his bedroom was simply ghastly! Felix shut his eyes and shuddered, his imagination in riot conjuring the hovering form and malevolent stare.

'Are you all right, then?' a voice said. 'You don't look too good to me. Can I get you another coffee?'

Startled, Felix looked up at the concerned face of a plump waitress, and hastily thanking her for the offer, murmured that he was perfectly all right but merely a little tired. He paused and added, 'Actually, if you don't mind, I think a small brandy would be in order.' He gave a brave smile, convinced he had escaped extinction by a hair's breadth.

'Righty-O. One brandy coming up,' was the cheerful response. 'That'll do you good.'

It didn't particularly; but at least he felt mildly soothed and was grateful for the waitress's homely words, a comforting reminder that not everyone harboured sinister intent.

He dwelt further on the disagreeable Mary Peebles and her brazen despatcher. Unless the man was a lunatic, it had not been a random attack. They must have known each other and her death carefully planned. Known each other? Yes, but not so well that he knew her bedroom. Still, well enough to gain entry to the house without having to break in (according to the police there had been no signs). Very likely he had had a key. Stolen. Or had she given him one? Either way, it surely suggested a degree of closeness. Felix frowned and brooded.

Although not aware of the mistaken room incident, the police had reached similar conclusions. But Felix was not to know this, and he now saw himself as a latter-day Sherlock Holmes and felt rather pleased; so much so, that responding to the waitress's kindly query he very nearly ordered another brandy. But for some reason the monitory face of Cedric intervened, and he declined.

Settling the bill and leaving a grateful tip, he left the

White Lion and wandered back to the hotel. On the way he prepared a schedule. He would telephone Cedric immediately and tell him of the lost memory and the fact that his dear friend had been within an inch of losing his life. And then after delivering that bombshell he would rest quietly on the veranda in readiness for the evening's rendezvous with Cottle and other charming persons. He debated whether to wear the waistcoat again. Maybe something casual would be more suitable, something slicker – even a tinge raffish, perhaps! Hmm. It was quite a problem really and would need careful thought.

CHAPTER TWELVE

While Felix was debating his sartorial problems, Inspector Jennings was also pondering. His initial confidence in approaching the Goodhart twins had waned slightly, for he kept remembering the vicar's adjective of 'surly'. At the time he had assumed it was another example of the cleric's colourful embroidery, but he was now starting to feel a mite tense. Suppose they turned out difficult as the vicar had implied: aggressive, tart and uncooperative. What then? How should he play it? Nathan would have known of course – oh yes, doubtless he would!

He had taken Sergeant Harris with him as backup. But even so, as they approached the Goodharts' door Jennings braced himself, preparing for the worst. But the worst was not immediately apparent, for the door was opened by a bespectacled lady beaming in pink – pink pinafore over a pink skirt and feet clad in matching galoshes. Though slightly fazed by the footwear, Jennings maintained his official look and politely introduced himself and the sergeant.

'Ah,' she said, 'I was just about to make a nice pot of tea. You must be the officer who telephoned yesterday. I told my dear sister, Gaye, that we might expect you and she is busy preparing; she won't be long.'

They were ushered into a small sitting room unnervingly bereft of all pictures, books or interest. Except for one thing of startling horror. Pinned drunkenly to one wall was a large piece of material, which looked like something left out for the dustmen. It appeared to have been knitted, and displayed greying patches of various hues and in shapes of no discernible design or point. On one side there ran a yellow border, but on the other the frayed edges hung listless and fatigued.

Their hostess must have seen Jennings eyeing it, for she said, 'Ah that's our little tapestry, everyone remarks on it. Rather daring, don't you think? My sister and I attended an exhibition of wall-hangings in Ipswich, which we quite enjoyed. But afterwards Gaye said to me: "You know, Joy, I think we could produce something as good as those, don't you?" I assured her that we most certainly could! And so straightaway we took out our needles and set about it – and this is the result.' She gestured proudly.

'Very nice,' Jennings said soberly. After she had bustled from the room, he hastily averted his eyes.

While they waited, and with nothing else to distract his attention, Jennings wondered about the sister and hoped she wouldn't be long. He was eager to get things going.

Joy had said the other was 'preparing'. Preparing what? Herself? Yes, doubtless hastily daubing her face to meet the gaze of the police inquisitors. Women did that; even his Aunt Grace was known to apply a swirl of lipstick on special occasions (crooked).

However, Jennings was wrong in his assumption. For when she appeared, Gaye Goodhart's face was daubed with merely a frown, but her hands were full.

She carried a sheaf of papers, pencil box and a large briefcase. These she dumped on the table, and turning to the officers said, 'Now, which of you is in charge? I am the treasurer, you see, and it's imperative that this matter be dealt with before anything else.'

Jennings blinked, cleared his throat and began to say 'I am Inspector—'

'Ah yes, the inspector,' she said briskly, 'Jennings is the name, isn't it? Or at least that's what my sister said – mind you, she's getting so deaf these days, it might have been Lenin.' She emitted a rasping laugh.

'It was not Lenin!' her sister exclaimed. 'My hearing is impeccable, as well you know. Why, only the other day I was complimented by the scoutmaster on my sharp—'

'Shut up,' the other snapped. 'Now, Mr Jennings, I'd be obliged if you could check my calculations. I have been doing the monthly tally and I am far from satisfied. I'll show you the ledger.' She opened the briefcase and withdrew an accounts book.

Jennings gazed sombrely at the tweed-clad woman before him (no pink galoshes, but like her sister with grey bobbed hair and assertive spectacles), and wondered if she took him to be an auditor or an inspector from the Inland Revenue. She could, of course, just be batty.

'Actually, madam, we are here to enquire about the case of Mrs Peebles, the lady who was unfortunately murdered, and so I should be obliged if—'

'Yes, yes, of course you are. We know all about that,' Gaye Goodhart said impatiently. 'But first things first. You see, she is in arrears.'

'No she's not,' Joy Goodhart sniggered, 'she is dead.'

The other cast her a withering look. 'Dead or alive, Mary Peebles' subscription to the society is two months overdue, not to mention the three shillings and fourpence owed for the cream tea we held last month. She was always tight-fisted. She said she would bring it the next day, but never did.'

Boldly, Sergeant Harris intervened, echoing the pink one's point: 'Well she certainly can't now.'

Jennings shot him a warning look, and Gaye Goodhart scowled. 'No, but the sum total can come out of the estate, and if the executors fail to cooperate, I shall expect the police to take action. People are so slack these days.'

Jennings was about to say that the victim's parsimony was incidental to the enquiry and that anyway it was a job for a solicitor, when there was a pained sigh from Joy. 'Didn't I tell you, Gaye. I said it wasn't a police matter, but of course you wouldn't listen – you rarely do.' The words were softly said, but Jennings caught the note of smug triumph.

However, such triumph cut no ice with the other, for with an indifferent shrug she turned to Harris and said,

'It's so wearying to be put in the wrong all the time, don't you find? My sister is an expert in these things, as is that meddlesome priest over the road. Always has to have the last word!' She sniffed, and gesturing towards the door despatched her sister to fetch the tea. 'If the inspector is averse to talking finance, then let us dissect Peebles' death over a cuppa. A most stimulating topic.'

'Oh yes, do let's,' Joy replied eagerly. 'I won't be a min!' She scuttled out.

In the ensuing silence Gaye Goodhart stared fixedly at the wall with pursed mouth. Jennings – wishing he was elsewhere – consulted his notebook, while Sergeant Harris pondered why the woman should assume he was invariably put in the wrong. He had always thought his relations with his boss were moderately good, or so it had seemed . . . She was a tartar all right, this one! But then the other was a bit off too: where the hell had she got those pink galoshes from? They would make a nice Christmas present for the kiddie. He must remember to ask her before they left.

Such musings were curtailed by the return of Joy Goodhart bearing a teapot and a plate of buns. Setting these down on the table she announced firmly that she would be mother. 'It's my turn,' she reminded her sister.

'It's not, actually, but please yourself,' the other said carelessly, 'my mind is on higher things.'

When rather diffidently Jennings enquired what those might be, she replied: 'God. And whether the unsavoury mode of Mary Peebles' passing will persuade Him to overlook her many shortcomings. It is to be fervently hoped.' She reached for the largest bun and took a good bite, then glancing at Joy gave a nod of approval. The tension between the pair seemed to ease and for a few moments they chewed happily. Unenticed by bun or tea, Jennings took the bull by the horns and boldly began to make enquiries.

Apparently, the sect had been holding its meetings in a private house at Orford for the past ten years. It had been formed by a small group of worried locals who, rightly or wrongly, felt that modern mores were becoming intolerably loose, and pastors of the major Christian churches no longer up to the job.

'The job being?' Jennings had asked vaguely.

'To rout out sin and confront the Devil, of course,' Gaye had answered. 'As a police officer, Inspector, I am sure that is your mission too – and indeed your sergeant's here.' She waved a hand with its segment of bun at Harris, who, nodding vigorously, agreed that it was his daily concern.

'You bet!' he exclaimed, 'Ruffians, car thieves, road hogs, bovver boys, shoplifters, sheep-shaggers . . . If you ask me, they could all do with a kick up the arse. But these days, of course, we're not allowed to do anything which might—' Catching the look of fury on his boss's face, Harris stopped abruptly, and lowering his eyes, stared meekly at the galoshes.

'And these shortcomings of Mrs Peebles that you mention, how would you describe them?' Jennings hastily asked, his features resuming a look of earnest enquiry.

'Manifold.'

'What?'

138

'What I said: manifold. She was afflicted by many and various.' Gaye turned to her sister for confirmation. 'Wouldn't you say so, Joy?'

'Oh yes, dear, but you have already made that point. What the inspector wants is a few concrete examples. Am I not right, Mr Jennings?' Before Jennings could answer or Gaye rise to the snub, the other produced an impressive list of items, which she ticked off on nimble fingers: 'Vanity, greed, rudeness, impatience, sloth – she never rose before eight-thirty – bossiness, obstinacy, pride. In short, all the usual vices.' She rested the busy fingers in her lap and gave a serene smile. 'Still, one shouldn't speak ill of the dead – or so one is told. Though frankly, if it's the truth, why not?' It wasn't vitriol, merely the twittering of a fractious starling.

'You've omitted the obvious,' Gaye Goodhart said severely.

'Oh, have I, dear? Well, I am sure you can supply that.' The serene smile widened.

For a couple of seconds her sister glared at the ceiling; but then, leaning towards Jennings, she said darkly: 'Ambition, that was her problem, Inspector, ambition. In my view Mary Peebles was driven by it. When she first arrived from London, we were most welcoming and invited her to join our little group at Orford. She seemed very interested and fitted in well and became a keen member. Indeed, I would go so far as to say a zealous one. Wouldn't you agree, Joy?'

'Oh yes, dear, zealous – that's the word. I couldn't have put it better myself.'

'No, possibly not,' was the dry response. 'Anyway, Mr Jennings, it gradually became clear that she was getting ideas above her station. She became overbearing and kept insisting that our efforts to convert the impious should be more vigorous. We needed to take a firmer line, inject ourselves with a robust militancy . . . It wasn't an entirely bad idea, and some of the members agreed. She could be quite persuasive and—'

'Oh yes, exceedingly so,' Joy interrupted, 'Do you remember the time when she insisted that we went with her to disrupt the vicar's sermon in St Edmund's? As a matter of fact, I thought it was rather fun, and it certainly worked a treat.' She giggled.

'It did,' her sister said acidly, 'until you put a fist through your tambourine. Those things are very expensive, we can't afford to have them vandalised.'

Joy shrugged. 'Ah well, good causes cost money. After all, what's five shillings when souls are to be saved? That's what I say.' She beamed at Harris. 'Wouldn't you agree, Sergeant?' The latter opened and then quickly shut his mouth.

Ignoring this, Gaye continued: 'Upsetting that bore Furblow might well have been a good idea. But I could see exactly what she was angling at: the society's chairmanship. That's what she was after; the office that was to be mine at the end of this current term. Well, as you can imagine, I wasn't having that. Disgraceful! Oh no. Such ambition had to be nipped in the bud . . . no, not just nipped, incised.' She glowered at Jennings, narrowed her eyes and looked distinctly frightening.

Seeing the furious face and hearing those words, Jennings experienced a pang of excitement. Oh my God, he thought, is the old trout going to admit to the Peebles murder? She obviously had the motive: jealousy. She also had the will and pugnacity. Had he been right all along: vicious battles within the sect's hierarchy? . . . Was this going to be his lucky day? He took a deep breath. And then in his smoothest, most coaxing tone à la Nathan, he asked affably what had happened next.

'Next?' Gaye asked, evidently puzzled. 'Well . . . she died, didn't she. I have to say, Inspector, it was extremely frustrating. I had various plans afoot to stop her little game, and so naturally I couldn't implement any of them, could I?' The corners of her mouth went down and she stared fixedly at the wall with its awful tapestry.

Jennings sighed. 'No,' he replied gloomily, 'no, you couldn't.'

He was about to signal their departure to Harris, when Joy suddenly said: 'My sister is right. I fear the deceased was not an easy person. She could be so disparaging. Such a pity. I mean to say, we all have to exercise a little forbearance in our personal relations, do we not? It's what makes the world go round!' She flashed a smile of dazzling benevolence, before adding, 'Fortunately, Gaye and I have learnt to be a little more understanding about the shortcomings of others, but poor Mary never quite developed the knack. She could be very harsh at times.' She glanced at her sister, still engrossed in the tapestry (presumably brooding upon the frustrated plans). 'Am I not right, Gaye?'

'What? Oh yes, yes indeed. She had become extremely disdainful of certain people – including, I believe, ourselves, though I can't think why – and latterly of some of her lodgers. Admittedly she had doted on that rather boring Dew person who fell off the cliff, but there were others of whom she was less enamoured, especially that last one. Smith or Smy or whatever his name was. She telephoned me the day after he arrived to apologise for not being at the previous meeting – something to do with having to write a letter to that loud brother of hers in Aldeburgh – and was most scathing of the man. Said he was suave and shifty, and had he been a character in a film she wouldn't have trusted him an inch. Apparently, he had started to give her some very funny looks which she didn't like at all.' Gaye, shrugged. 'Naturally, one wouldn't know about that. But I mean to say, if you take in lodgers you can expect the worst. It was her own fault.'

Joy nodded vigorously. 'And then of course there was Mr Hepton, not that he was a lodger, but she was very snooty about him as well. Do you remember?'

'You mean that gentleman from Oxford who she brought to two of our meetings? No, she wasn't too keen, said he was pretentious and—'

'Cambridge,' Joy corrected.

'What?'

'Cambridge, that's where Mr Hepton came from.'

'No, it was definitely Oxford. I remember clearly,' Gaye retorted. 'However, it really doesn't matter, one of those places, anyway. Really Joy, must you always interrupt?'

Sensing the onset of further altercation, and feeling rather weary, Jennings terminated the interview. Rather to his surprise the sisters seemed disappointed, and they pressed the officers to stay to lunch. 'Joy makes an excellent dish of boiled brisket and pickled tripe,' Gaye said, 'we serve it to all our friends.' Alas, the kind offer was regretfully declined and the visitors took their leave.

'Christ!' Harris muttered in the porch, 'that was a narrow squeak.' He had evidently forgotten to ask about the galoshes. Or gone off the idea, perhaps.

As they returned along the gravel path by the open window, Joy Goodhart's breathy voice was heard to say, 'Gaye dear, what *is* a shop-shagger?'

CHAPTER THIRTEEN

After they left, Jennings was silent for a while. And then he said, 'Peculiar. There's something not quite right there. An odd couple.'

'You could have fooled me,' Harris agreed helpfully, 'they're both round the twist.'

'Hmm. Not entirely, Sergeant. They may be sharper than you think, but I can't quite make out . . . Look, you go and have a sandwich in the King's Head or somewhere. But mind you're back by two o'clock sharp and not a minute later.' Without a word Harris took off, making a beeline for chips and stout. The prospect of normality beckoned.

Left alone, and also with a bit of time to spare, Jennings decided to 'take a turn on the front' as his old granny would say. He hadn't seen the sea for a number of days and he needed to check it was still there. Avoiding the high street's bustle, he walked slowly into Victoria Street with its comforting smell of brewery fumes, and on towards the Sailors' Reading Room. He might have taken his ease on the bench outside, but noting the two children using it for a gun turret or similar, hastily moved to a seat further down nearer the beach. Here, away from the sound of children's voices mimicking machine guns, he relaxed in the sun's warmth. Lighting a cigarette, he contemplated the incoming tide, its waves challenged by a solitary surfer.

It was a funny old business, he thought, that was for sure. The victim had met a lurid end: smothered in her own house and in her own bed. She had been a pillar of the community, ostensibly at any rate, and though not necessarily liked, seemingly eminently respectable. She had belonged to the Ladies Guild and the local bridge club. A bit eccentric in her dislike of things Anglican and her espousal of some oddball alternative – but then surely everyone had their quirks and preferences, especially in religion. She had kept a guest house, plain and sober and not something to attract gossip or rumour. Jennings gave a wry smile and flicked his ash. Oh yes, a guest house, not a bawdy house. A pity. The latter might have given a useful lead.

Inevitably thoughts of the guest house brought to mind its final visitor, and what Gaye Goodhart had said about his effect on the hostess . . . What was it Mary Peebles was supposed to have said? Something about him being like a cinema villain and that he had kept giving her peculiar looks. Yes, that was the gist; doubtless Harris would have noted the exact words in his notebook. He could check when he got back to the office.

Jennings loosened his tie, stretched his legs and reflected on Felix Smythe. A funny little fellow and not especially to his taste either: a bit too smooth and 'Londoney' for his liking. Still, he had been cooperative enough at the interview – though most murderers were unless caught on the wrong foot. But why should he want to kill Mary Peebles? It didn't sound as if she had known him previously. Perhaps he was a funny bugger and had tried to proposition her, made overtures which she had rejected. Fuelled with fury, had he gone berserk, barged into her room and in a frenzy of frustration attacked her before he knew what he was doing? One did hear of such things – or so Nathan was always reminding him. He gazed at the surfer battling defiantly with the breakers. He looked a puny chap too. Hmm . . . perhaps Mr Smythe should be recalled for further questioning.

His mind returned to the morning's interview and he winced. Furblow had been right: the ladies were not the easiest pair to deal with and their family name surely a bit of a misnomer. The abrasive Gaye had been quite formidable, but was it the simpering pink one that was the subtly dominant? One thing was clear, though: they had both resented the victim, and in their different ways been happy to put the boot in (or in Joy's case the galosh). But maybe such pungency was simply their habitual mode. The world was full of misfits who, bored with themselves, took to picking at others as a means of spicing their empty lives. Jennings recalled the sitting room, barren except for the unaesthetic wall-hanging.

All the same, he mused, their views on the victim had

been far from barren – indeed, starkly trenchant. He suspected that although no doubt jaundiced, their shared assessment may have held a substantial truth: Mary Peebles could antagonise people, possibly even enjoyed it. But were character defects in themselves enough to prompt murder? Or had some sort of fear been the motive? Jennings contemplated the clear horizon, wishing his own thoughts could match its clarity.

So, he pondered, besides the twins' impressions and the victim's comments on the Smythe chap, what else had emerged from the interview? Two things: that despite being critical of a number of her lodgers, apparently Mary Peebles had looked with favour on Horace Dewthorp, the old boy who had fatally missed his footing when exercising her dog. In fact, according to the caustic Gaye, she had 'doted' on him. An exaggeration? Or perhaps suggestive of a softer side, after all. Conversely, she had been scathing of the Hepton fellow who had appeared at two of the sect's meetings, saying he had been pretentious and tedious. The Goodharts had disputed his provenance – Oxford or Cambridge. But whether—'

Such ruminations were interrupted by a woman's voice: 'So this is where you sneak off to when no one's looking, Inspector Jennings,' Elsie Burbage chuckled. 'Having a quiet think about poor old Peebles, I bet. Cor, a nasty job that was! I still haven't recovered,' she declared cheerfully and looking remarkably hale. 'Here, budge up and then I can cadge one of your fags. I could do with a puff after cleaning Father Rupert's kitchen. Gawd knows what he cooks there, but he makes a right old mess! It's him being a bachelor, I suppose.'

Jennings felt mildly affronted. 'But I am a bachelor,' he replied stiffly, 'and there's nothing wrong with my kitchen.' He did as commanded, budged up and offered her a cigarette.

'Oh no? I'd need to see your floor with my own eyes before I believed that,' she said, and winked. It wasn't a pass, merely a merry quip. And as if to reassure, she thrust out her left hand. On the engagement finger there glistened a large diamond.

'What cracker did you get that out of?' Jennings asked.

She tossed her head. 'If you want to know, it's best-quality paste – none of that cheap stuff like Ada Wainwright wears. Ben Bugle gave it me because we are going to get married. So there!'

Jennings gave a sombre whistle. 'You don't say. Phew, he was always a brave lad, poor old Ben.'

She took no offence, and lowering her voice, said, 'So how's the case going – got any suspects? Or is it all wrapped up?'

Jennings resumed a po-face and said sternly that he couldn't possibly divulge official data. (The fact that he had scant data was naturally irrelevant.) However, it struck him that, in a relaxed off-duty fashion, he might be able to glean a little more from Elsie. When he had officially interviewed her and taken a statement, the girl had been understandably het up, and other than saying there was no sign of a break-in or disturbance, she had been of little use. But as Nathan was fond of saying, hindsight could yield dividends: 'It's surprising what comes to them once they've calmed down and gained their equilibrium, old son. Give 'em a breather, and the stuff they dredge up can be quite illuminating. A gentle nudge usually does it.'

'As a matter of fact, Elsie, it is a very nice ring and I am sure you will be extremely happy,' Jennings told her earnestly (and sincerely). Then clearing his throat, and after a suitable pause, he delivered the gentle nudge: 'I don't suppose there's anything else you recall about that shocking morning, is there – any small thing that might just have slipped your memory?' He flicked a careless pebble at a scavenging gull.

At first she was silent, evidently absorbed by the expanse of sea before them. And then in a dark voice she muttered, 'If he's not careful he'll come a cropper, he will.'

Jennings felt a flash of excitement. 'Really?' he prompted her. 'Who will?'

'That berk on the surfboard. Hasn't got a clue. You should see my Ben – now he's really good at it.'

Jennings closed his eyes and bit his lip. Useless!

But then, berk dismissed, Elsie turned to him and in a puzzled tone said, 'Now you mention it, there was something different. Funny, really, because—'

The studied casualness vanished. 'In what way?' he demanded.

'It was them Penguin biscuits – those nice milk chocolate ones with shiny wrappers. Freddie loved them, greedy little hound.'

If Jennings had hoped for some shattering revelation to clinch the case, this was not exactly it. He enquired what was so special about the biscuits.

'They've got two layers, one crunchy and one soft – ever so nice.'

'No, Elsie,' he said patiently, rather wishing he were back with the Goodharts, 'I mean what was it you thought odd?'

She explained that when she arrived in the early morning to get her employer's tea, she had noticed a couple of the biscuits on the floor; the foil was torn open and the contents obviously chewed or trodden on. 'There was an awful mess, so I swept up the bits pronto because Mrs P. was fussy like that, and I knew she'd be tetchy if she saw them when she came down.'

Jennings shrugged and said that presumably the dog had enjoyed a midnight feast before escaping into the night.

'Not unless it had used a stepladder,' Elsie replied, 'the tin was kept on a shelf.'

'Well then, in that case maybe Mrs Peebles had fancied a midnight feast. I'll ask forensics if they found any remains when they—'

'Shouldn't think so, the biscuits were only kept for visitors and the dog. She couldn't abide them, thought they were common.' Elsie sniffed. 'But then she thought that about a lot of things.'

'I see. Now tell me, Elsie, as far as you know how many keys were there to the kitchen door? The intruder didn't use the front as that was bolted from the inside, so the only means of access would have been by the back. Apart from your own, what others were there?'

Elsie shrugged. 'Well, she had her own set, of course, front and back. There was a special one with a red ribbon for the lodgers, and one other, which she kept on a hook in the pantry. I told your sergeant about that when you was talking to Mr Smythe. It was in there when he checked it.'

'Hmm. And are you absolutely sure that you had to unlock the back door when you arrived?'

Elsie gave a caustic laugh. 'I suppose you want me to say it was blooming wide open and blowing in the wind. But I can tell you, it wasn't. It was shut and locked, and I had to use my key – like I said at the time.' She glanced at her watch and leapt to her feet, exclaiming that she couldn't sit gossiping all day as she had to go to the Market Place drapers to select a corsage for her 'going away' outfit. 'If you're a good boy, I'll send you a wedding invitation,' she yelled, as she bounded off up the slope.

'Can't wait,' Jennings murmured, and then made a mental note to instruct Harris to inspect the kitchen for a biscuit tin.

Alone once more, he continued to ponder. What also seemed odd was that if the murderer had indeed possessed a key, why – having just executed that horrific thing – did he bother to relock the door on exiting the place? Most people surely would have scarpered pretty damn quick and not wasted time fiddling around. He certainly would have! Unless, he reflected, it had been an inside job after all . . . A surmise which naturally brought him back to Mr Felix Smythe. Yes, he really would have to examine the chap again. Supposing that, having done the deed, and exhausted by the exertion, he had simply returned to his room and collapsed into blissful sleep. Or maybe he was one of those people given to a bizarre form of sleepwalking in which subliminal desires could be unconsciously enacted. Such things were not unknown. There was of, course, another possibility: that Mrs Peebles herself had let the man in at the front (assuming it was a man), rebolted the door and invited him up to her bedroom, where instead of amorous ardour she had been sent to kingdom come. But then that still didn't explain why he should have locked up after himself. Perhaps he was just fussy.

Jennings scowled and stood up. He had taken time off in the hope of clearing his mind and seeing a glimmer of light. As it was, owing to Elsie Burbage he now felt more bemused than before. It was too bad. Moodily he walked back to the police station where the desk sergeant told him that the deceased's brother had just telephoned demanding a progress report. 'He sounded a bit huffy,' Bert Hill said cheerfully.

The news did not enhance Jennings' mood. The prospect of a huffy Harold Dagwood was tiresome. In itself the state of the man's mind was of little importance; what would be irksome was if he started to intrude himself into the investigation. It rather looked as if he might. Just because he was the victim's brother hardly gave him the right to a detailed report whenever he pleased. Who did he think he was – the superintendent? If the man imagined he was going to return his call he could think again. Jennings' sense of protocol was offended and he had no intention of dancing to the tune of some minor local tycoon – or a major one, for that matter. It was a bit much!

Huffily, like his caller, the inspector sat down at his

desk, signed some papers and then summoned Harris to investigate the Peebles kitchen in search of a biscuit tin. Asked if he was feeling especially hungry, Jennings scowled and explained what Elsie Burbage had told him about the mess of crumbs she had found under the table. 'A useless piece of information,' he observed, 'but it might just be worth checking for fingerprints, I suppose.'

'Oh yes, sir,' Harris replied brightly, 'leave no stone unturned. That's the motto, isn't it?' As an attempt at tactful support, it didn't work terribly well. The inspector's scowl deepened, and dismissing the sergeant he began to prepare questions for a second interview with Felix Smythe. This time he really must screw something out of the chap.

He hadn't got very far when the phone rang. 'It's him again,' Bert Hill said sepulchrally, 'shall I put him through?' Jennings sighed and braced himself.

'Ah, glad you're back at work again, Inspector,' the brusque voice began, 'as there are just a couple of things I need to settle with you.' Jennings bridled at the refence to being back at work, but politely asked what they were.

'Well, to begin with, perhaps you would let me know when my sister's house will be available. I say my sister's house, but in fact technically it's mine. And now that the poor girl is dead, I propose to do it up and put it on the market. There's quite a bit of work to do, so the sooner things start rolling, the better. And naturally there are also a few mementos and family heirlooms I should like to recover.' The brisk voice paused, and then added more lightly, 'I daresay your boys with their deerstalkers and magnifying glasses will have crawled all over the place by now and given it a proper casing. One likes to think their efforts have been productive and that you are on the bastard's trail . . . So tell me,' he added, 'when will it be free?'

Jennings wished the other bastard would shut up and allow him to get on with the Smythe interview notes, but patiently assured him that he would be alerted as soon as possible. 'These house examinations take longer than the public thinks,' he murmured.

'Evidently,' was the dry response. 'Now, my second question is to do with that lodger. I take it that he has been eliminated from your enquiries? I mean to say, if anyone had a prime opportunity then it was him, though why he should want to attack Mary I can't imagine. Still, I expect you are pursuing all of that, aren't you?'

Gently seething, Jennings told him that matters were well in hand, but that unfortunately he wasn't in a position to discuss the details of the case with outsiders.

'Outsiders?' Dagwood expostulated, 'I'm her bloody brother!'

With seeming sympathy Jennings explained that the term had applied to all those not actually in the Force, and that naturally the authorities were giving the crime their maximum attention and he could be assured that when appropriate he would be informed of fresh developments.

'Hmm, I should think so,' Dagwood said grudgingly. And then in a kindlier voice, asked, 'And how is Chief Inspector Nathan? Please give him my best wishes for a speedy recovery. A very bright cove, in my view, and what bad luck being incapacitated at such a time as this. I expect you could do with him.' He rang off.

If that last remark was intended to rile the inspector, it succeeded. 'Sod,' he breathed to himself.

Relieved of Dagwood, Jennings returned to compiling his list of questions for the Smythe interview, reading some edict from the superintendent and waiting to hear from Harris about the biscuit tin. Eventually the latter appeared.

'Did you find anything?'

'Yes and no,' was the answer.

'And what's that supposed to mean?' Jennings asked irritably.

'It means that we did find a tin – as you said, on an upper shelf. But apart from a few crumbs and an empty wrapping paper there was nothing in it.'

'Well now, that's what I call really illuminating,' Jennings said with heavy sarcasm.

'Ah, but you see, sir, what is interesting is that there wasn't a mark on it – leastways, a bit of smear but not a single print. It strikes me that if the deceased kept that tin of biscuits for the guests and to give treats to her dog, you would think she'd be using it quite a lot. I mean, according to what Elsie said to you, Mrs P might not have liked them but others did. So, you would expect it to have been in fairly frequent use.'

'Hmm. And what about other things on the shelf, did they have fingerprints?'

'Oh yes. There was a tea caddy and some pots of jam, all smothered in them – hers, mostly, and from what one can make out, some of Elsie's too. But like I said, nothing on the tin.'

'I see . . . Well, Sergeant, is your conclusion the same as mine?'

'What – that the prints were deliberately polished off?'

Jennings nodded. 'It would seem so. Somebody scoffed the biscuits, or perhaps shared them with the dog, and then went to great pains to erase the traces. Why should they bother to do that, unless they were in the kitchen illicitly?'

'You mean like hanging about prior to doing her in, or had just done it and was feeling peckish?'

Jennings winced. 'Rather baldly put, Sergeant, but something like that, perhaps.'

After Harris had withdrawn, Jennings refilled his fountain pen and studied his list of questions for Felix and added another: ask if he likes Penguin biscuits.

CHAPTER FOURTEEN

Back in Aldeburgh, Felix's morning trauma was largely dispelled by his sojourn on the hotel veranda and Cedric's emollient words on the telephone. He was now all poised to join the musical coterie in the lounge. He doubted if the two VIPs would be there (doubtless exhausted after the party or rehearsing gently in some intimate drawing room) but it would be most agreeable to mingle with a few of the cognoscenti and be included in their dissection of the previous night's gathering . Yes, most agreeable. Felix smiled at the mirror, gave a final sleek to his hair and set off on parade.

Downstairs all was mellow, warm and welcoming. In a secluded corner a pianist played softly; attentive waiters flitted among smartly dressed guests, and from the bar area came the low murmur of convivial chat. Taking his bearings,

Felix hesitated. At first he saw no one he recognised, and was just about to approach the bar for a dry Martini when he glimpsed a little group clustered in a far alcove. Ah yes, there were the Cottles talking to John Drew, one of the organisers, and some other familiar faces. About to drift over, he then thought it would look better if he already had a drink in hand.

He was in the middle of giving the barman some very precise instructions ('No, kindly do not shake it. And I only want a smidgeon of peel, not half the lemon!') when a soft voice said, 'Oh, it's Felix, isn't it! Are you going to join the others? I've just left them – alas a tiresome business engagement. So, I fear we shall have to be ships that pass in the night.' Ezra Simmonds smiled winsomely.

Felix smiled back, distinctly miffed. There was a familiarity about the man's tone which grated. Just because he had secured him a good place in that press photograph didn't mean to say they were bosom pals. Still, fortunately the chap was about to leave, so that was all right. He relaxed. But he was too soon, and it was not all right. For in the next instant Ezra had whipped out his wallet, and signalling to the barman said, 'This one's on me, Tony. Keep the change.' Before Felix could gather his wits let alone decline, Ezra had made a pert little bow, breathed the words 'Bottoms up', and departed for the foyer.

Felix stared indignantly at the retreating figure. And down your effing hatch! he mouthed inwardly. Really, to be patronised by that little whippet was a bit much. Talk about taking liberties! Irritably he turned back to the bar and seized the now impeccably prepared Martini and took a sip. Delicious – and he hadn't even had to pay for the damn thing.

Thus fortified, he sauntered over to the corner alcove and joined the group. Here he was greeted most cordially, invited to share a sofa with a spry little lady with hair dressed in a wayward bun, and who, to his embarrassment and secret delight, assured him that his ten-minute talk with the tenor had been much enjoyed.

It was all very affable and amusing. And Felix was just wondering if it would look out of place if he offered to stand more drinks, when he was distracted. 'I say,' someone said, 'old Ezra was on form tonight, full of merry quips. Must be the new flute. Either that or the Dagwood chap has commissioned him to landscape those two big properties he's buying. Going to convert them into flats, I hear. Another eyesore for Aldeburgh to bear, I suppose.'

Mrs Cottle giggled, saying that landscapes were likely to be slightly out of Ezra's reach but he was a dab hand with daffodils and tulips. 'I'm serious,' she said, 'Harold Dagwood's garden always has the finest tulip display in Aldeburgh, masses of them and all varieties. Delightful.' Had that been all that was said on the subject Felix would merely have felt mild distaste: he had no wish to hear about Ezra's tulip fixation, and even less about the swaggering Dagwood, especially in such congenial company. But alas, it was not all, and he was made to feel acute embarrassment.

'Can't say I like the man,' someone else said, 'but I don't imagine it's much fun having your sister smothered like that. A frightful business. Glad I don't live in Southwold, must feel very eerie.'

'Oh, but the Southwold denizens are a tough bunch, not sensitive souls like us in Aldeburgh. They're bound to cope,' John Drew declared. 'Besides, I've always thought there was something sinister about that little town. It probably harbours all manner of assassins.' There was general laughter.

His wife told him to be quiet and that it was no laughing matter. 'It's simply ghastly,' she exclaimed. 'That poor woman, all alone and—'

'But she wasn't alone,' Drew said, 'I gather there was a lodger.'

'Goodness,' the lady with the bun exclaimed, 'one shouldn't like to be in his shoes. Very uncomfortable – especially if one were the murderer!' Turning to Felix she said, 'Wouldn't you think so, Mr Smythe?'

Felix paled, nodded and said nothing. For a few seconds he almost felt faint. Usually he rather relished being centre stage, but certainly not for this reason! It would be appalling to have all eyes turned on him, avid with curiosity, and quite possibly horror. There flashed through his mind an image of polite consternation, the exchange of covert glances, falsely hearty laughs, a blank embarrassed silence. Hell on earth, how should he play it? Brazen lie or sheepish truth? 'Er, actually,' he began. And then stopped, apparently coping with a cough.

'Weren't you billeted in Blythburgh? I think you said you had motored over from there,' John Drew cut in. 'A bit close for comfort, I should say. Still, I expect you—'

What John Drew expected was never known, for at the moment a young man appeared waving a piece of paper, and in excited tones announced: 'I've got him. I've got Richter! He will definitely come to us next year and says he can't wait. How's that!'

The effect was electric, even prompting a refined cheer. All eyes were riveted on the grinning newcomer. Cottle stood up and thumped him on the back: 'Congratulations, Paul, you've certainly won your spurs as new secretary. What'll you have?'

In the ensuing jollity, Felix Smythe was mercifully forgotten. As was the poor Mrs Peebles.

Back in his room, Felix lay on his bed reviewing matters. In some respects the evening had been most agreeable, just as he had envisaged. In other ways it had been decidedly iffy. The initial encounter with Ezra was merely annoying, but that last bit had been fearful! Thank God for the Richter person. He had no idea who the man was (some performer, presumably – Cedric would know) but he had certainly saved his bacon. Apart from a hasty farewell to the Cottles and a wave to the Drews, he had quietly removed himself. He would like to have said goodbye to his sofa companion, but she had been in animated talk with the messenger. Just as well; it might have prompted further probing. She was perfectly right, of course. Given the current situation his shoes were definitely pinching. That wretched Mary Peebles had a lot to answer for.

Such had been Felix's keen anticipation of the party and his relief in securing the Sandworth, that he had overlooked the singularity of his own position. That his recent companions might see him as a questionable curiosity had not really impinged. It did now. Though mercifully diverted, their interest in the Southwold drama had been unnerving. It had also been salutary. For the time being, he mused, it might be prudent to keep a low profile (a personal feature he was rather proud of). After all, it was one thing being known as 'Felix Smythe, the Knightsbridge florist,' but did he really like the sound of 'Smythe, the sinister lodger'? Not exactly.

He was about to light a cigarette, when he realised that he was hungry. Normally he would have gone down to the dining room, but he suspected that some of the group may already have drifted in. Supposing he were invited to join a table? Tricky. The prospect of further jovial enquiry was not enticing. He looked at his watch. Perhaps there was a nearby pub that did food. The White Lion was a possibility, but it would be just his luck to see a face from the night before. Somewhere less obvious would be better; there was bound to be something.

Slipping quickly past the dining room and with coat collar turned up ostensibly against the gathering mist, Felix left the brightly lit hotel and made for the centre. He did not often wear a hat but on a whim had included a trilby in his luggage. To help lower the profile he now put this on. It did not enhance anonymity, if anything it made him look like a hoodlum's sidekick, or a shorter version of the Third Man. Oblivious of that effect, he wandered in the direction of the Moot Hall, savouring the night air, the distant slap of breaking surf and the brooding stillness of a community swaddled in its ancient past.

He wandered past the war memorial into Crabbe

Street and beyond. But the area seemed bereft of anything suitable – certainly nothing displaying a warm light or signs of bar food, however rudimentary. Had the Brudenell Hotel been open he might have ventured there and risked encountering another familiar face. But since it wasn't, he was spared both walk and risk.

He was just thinking that the sensible thing would be to return to the Sandworth and persuade them to send a tray to his room, when the air was suddenly filled with a heart-warming aroma: the smell of sizzling chips. Felix's nostrils flared as he sniffed the tantalising odour. And suddenly he felt not just hungry, but ravenous. Eagerly he scanned a side alley, but other than a strolling cat it yielded nothing. He hesitated, thinking that perhaps the smell had wafted over from the high street. Would that be a better bet? He stood unsure, debating directions. And then he heard his mother's impatient voice: *'For goodness' sake, don't dither, Feelo – just follow yer blooming nose!'* He did as he was bid, and his nose led him down a narrow lane on to Crag Path next to the shingle. Other than strewn lobster pots, fishermen's nets and upturned boats, there was nothing.

And then of course he saw it, a large white van with the words KEN'S COCKLES & CHIPS painted on its side. He could see the narrow counter with its bottles of sauce and vinegar, the cheerful light, the outline of Ken (?) serving a couple of youths, and above all, he could smell the merchandise. For Felix the scene was a glittering cynosure, a beacon of hope; he was drawn to the van as a pin to a magnet. Gratefully he ordered a bag of cockles and two lots of chips wrapped in time-honoured newspaper. Preferring to enjoy his feast in comfort rather than to stand about loitering, he looked for somewhere to sit. Close to the roadside was a handy lobster pot – in fact, it may have been the one Ezra had directed him to stand on for the photograph. He eased himself onto it and began to indulge.

The indulgence went on for some time, during which he admired the now moonlit sea and pondered its vastness. How different from London's landlocked Serpentine, or indeed Southend's cheery waters. He smiled, recalling that the last time he had sat in the open air gobbling cockles it had been at that seaside mecca with his ma on one of their special day trips. What treats they had been – ice cream, ginger pop, silly hat and a go on the big slide. A life away! Indeed, not so many years after the ending of the Great War . . . And now here he was in 1961, the proprietor of a fashionable flower shop (or emporium, as he preferred to call it) graced by Her Majesty the Queen Mother; living in a bijou flat off Sloane Street; mentioned by Beverley Nichols in the *Tatler* and enjoying the close companionship of a distinguished professor. What more could a boy from Bermondsey want?

At last the final chip and cockle were demolished; but with their loss went the nostalgic mood. Returned to the present, Felix grimaced and answered his own question: such a boy would like to be free of the Peebles entanglement and all its rotten ramifications. Apart from that last hiccup and the intrusive Ezra, the Aldeburgh interlude had been fun and worth the journey. But the next day he would be in Southwold again and confronting who knew what. The inspector had graciously granted him leave of absence but that didn't mean there wouldn't be more interrogation – though for the life of him he couldn't think why. But they were a persistent bunch the police, and it wouldn't surprise him if they had something else up their sleeve to agitate his nerves.

He was just wondering whether to telephone Cedric and Loader to see if they knew anything, when there was the sound of crunching tyres and the purr of a running engine. The noise stopped. He turned and saw a large Rover parked a few yards from where he was sitting. The driver's window was wound down and he could see the glow of a cigar. Evidently here was someone else in need of twilight sustenance. There was the banging of a car door and faint footsteps, and from the interior a voice shouted, 'Hold on! Get me some shrimps, if they've got any. I'm not too keen on those cockle things . . . Oh, and mind you put sauce on the chips, vinegar doesn't agree with me.'

Felix was in the middle of thinking how remarkably faddy some people were, when he froze on his lobster pot. He was sure he recognised the hectoring tone. And he certainly recognised the small figure of Ezra Simmonds, now approaching the van. He groaned. Not twice in one evening, surely! And could it really be that Dagwood character in the driver's seat? Quite possibly. Ezra had said something about keeping a business appointment, so maybe that was it: an urgent talk to do with landscaping the new properties mentioned by one of the music group, or the question of tulips for that 'delightful' spring display. Doubtless something of vital import.

Felix scowled and debated his next move – though

whether movement was a good idea, he wasn't sure. To stand and walk off briskly might attract as much attention as a leisurely saunter. To do either might risk recognition. Better to stay where he was; they were bound to leave once Dagwood had got his fodder. With head down he took a covert look at the figure of Ezra waiting to be served at the van, and upon noting that the fellow's shoulders barely reached the counter, he felt a tinge of smugness. Yes, no doubt about it, he was definitely taller than that little squirt!

He remained stock-still as Ezra returned to the car with his purchase. He had expected to hear the sound of the car door opening, but there was nothing, and he sensed that the man was still lounging about outside. Then he did hear a click, but realised it was the driver's door and that the other had also got out. Holding his breath and bending lower (tying his shoelace should anyone ask), Felix could hear a murmured conversation.

The murmur increased as a voice – clearly not Ezra's – said distinctly: 'Well, I'm off to London at the end of the week; got to check one or two things with the boys. Dexter – or the 'Pernicious Privet' as my sister used to call him – is playing up again. The girl was right, he's a liability. She was always nagging me about him; said I was a fool not to notice. Huh! You need eyes in the back of your head in this game. You settle one thing and another bleeding thing comes along. I suppose my beloved sibling would have said it was all grist to God's mill.' He gave a loud laugh, and the next moment a cigar butt landed within inches of Felix's feet.

Felix stared at it with distaste. Just get back in the sodding car will you, and buzz off, he thought. Obligingly this is what they did, for at the next moment there was a slamming of doors, and to his relief, the sound of the engine firing. The Rover trundled off and Felix was left in peace.

Peace? Well only partial, for he felt shaken. The ubiquitous Ezra was an irritant, but the thought of Dagwood – and he was sure that had been the guy – was unnerving. The encounter in the draper's still rankled, and hearing the voice again had rekindled his dislike. He knew the type: arrogant and bombastic. A troublemaker if ever there was one. The recent awkwardness at the hotel had been bad enough, but the last thing he wanted was for the bereaved brother to know he had been in the Peebles house that awful night. But supposing Jennings had already told him? They must have discussed matters, so presumably he might know there had been a lodger. Still, one liked to think the police were discreet enough not to drop names. But one couldn't be sure, damn it. And besides, with all the local shindig and curiosity, Dagwood could easily hear it from some other quarter: in such cases gossip spread like wildfire. It was all very disturbing and the sooner he and Cedric could distance themselves from the whole area and continue their original itinerary, the better.

Moodily and rather stiffly, Felix detached himself from the lobster pot and started to go back the way he had come. As he walked by where the Rover had been parked, he noticed a bundle of greasy wrappings discarded at the kerbside. Typical! Fastidiously folding his own empty chip paper, he tossed it primly into the nearby waste bin and continued on his way.

CHAPTER FIFTEEN

Reggie Higgs had been busy dusting and sprucing up his display shelves, when Miles Loader entered looking rather pleased with himself. 'I say' he crowed, 'I'm in the money!'

Reggie sniffed. 'I'm glad to hear somebody is. Why? Have you cleaned out Newmarket or won the football pools?'

Loader explained that it wasn't quite as magnificent as that, far from it; nevertheless, he had just received some excellent royalties from his latest publication, *The Strategy and Tactics of Cromwell's New Model Army*. 'I gather that Old Ironsides is back in fashion on the GCE syllabus,' he explained, 'and apparently bellicose schoolmasters and mistresses, of which there plenty, are boning up on it like mad. It just goes to show there's a lot to be said for war.' He grinned.

'Congratulations,' Higgs said drily, wishing to God that he could flog the Coalport plates in his window. They had been there for ages. Perhaps if he substituted a set of reproduction Louis Wain cat drawings or some flying geese there might be a better response. The punters were a funny lot.

'Ah, I see we are in a merry mood,' Loader mocked. 'Tell you what, come and celebrate my coup in The Crown – unless, of course, you are expecting hordes of tourists – that'll put roses in your cheeks.'

Reggie Higgs quicky assured him that the bank holiday being over, the likelihood of tourists was bleak and that a lunchtime drink would set him up to no end, especially at his friend's expense.

Thus, they adjourned to an old haunt; the womb-like back bar of The Crown.

'So how are your guests?' Reggie enquired. 'Smythe must have had a nasty shock over the Peebles business, though he seemed all right the other night at Isabel's supper. Still, I wouldn't want to be in his position. A bit worrying, I imagine.'

Loader explained that Felix had been absent for a couple of days being 'musical' at Aldeburgh, but was likely to return at any moment. 'Dillworthy seems to think he may be questioned again. Bad luck, really, I doubt if he would hurt a fly.'

Reggie Higgs supped his ale and observed sagely that luck, whether good or bad, was invariably the result of being in a certain place at a certain time, and that when conjoined the oddest things could ensue. 'I mean to say,' he remarked, 'take the fate of Horace Dewthorp. Admittedly he had a dicky ticker, but if he hadn't been on those Dunwich cliffs and running after that damn dog, he might have lived for another twenty years. A rotten fluke, if you ask me.'

Loader frowned and said he had been thinking about that only recently, and still felt it was rather strange. 'I mean, I can't quite envisage Dewthorp running anywhere. From what I recall, being a bit clumsy he moved fairly carefully – presumably in case he put his foot in it, if you see what I mean. But in any case, he was a steady sort of chap, staid really, and not one to rush about, even after an escaping dog.'

Reggie grinned and said that he had been neither steady nor staid the last time he had seen him. 'Almost doubled up with mirth he was. I meant to tell you.'

'Why, what was the joke?'

'I never found out, but it was something to do with a pile of old *Lilliput*s and vintage *Men Only* magazines, which I had on a side table; they are becoming very collectable, you know – all part of the nostalgia kick. It was the day I sold him that Punchinello figure for his birthday. He had been casually leafing through them, when some photo must have caught his eye, as at the next instant he had snapped up one of the tattered *Men Only*s and was chuckling like hell. "Good lord, that's a turn up for the books," he had spluttered, "I'd recognise her any day, and the same distinctive earrings! I'll give you double the price." I'd never seen him like that before, but didn't get a chance to ask what was so funny as just then a mob of St Felix girls came in wanting to buy a gift for one of their housemistresses. I assumed that *Men Only* wouldn't be quite to the lady's taste and showed them something more appropriate: china bulldogs. When they had gone, so had Dewthorp. A pity, really, I'd have liked to share the joke.' Reggie cast a regretful look at his now empty glass.

It was a glance that Loader noted and suggested the other half. His companion said that although he didn't usually drink at lunchtime, in the circumstances he was sure he could manage it. Other than his own publishing windfall, Loader wasn't entirely clear what those circumstances were, but dutifully went to the bar. As he waited for the barman to emerge from the main lounge, the side door was pushed open and a figure slipped in.

It was Aldous Phipps plus the canine accomplice, Popsie. Dog and master cast an appraising eye around the small space and then approached the counter. Loader greeted the old man and asked what he could get him. Phipps beamed but declined, saying that his order might take some time as he and Popsie had rather particular requirements; however, they would be delighted to join his table once those had been dealt with. Respectively, these requirements appeared to be a complex amalgam of cherry liqueur, cognac and bitters swirled in a large sherry glass, and some Schweppes tonic in a bowl with a slice of lemon.

Replete with these libations, Phipps and his dog then joined the other two, where they sipped and lapped appreciatively.

'Funny you should come in just now, Professor,' Loader said, 'as we were in the middle of discussing Horace

Dewthorp and that disastrous fall. Such bad luck. Didn't you say the other night that you had known him in Cambridge?'

Phipps shook his head. 'No. What I said was that I had known of him and had spoken very briefly a couple of times. No more than that. But he struck me as a decent fellow – albeit a trifle earnest. Not among the madcap classes, if I may put it that way; no sense of fun. I did make a merry quip at our second encounter, but he remained totally po-faced . . . Mind you, as my bon mots had been in Greek, he may not have grasped the essence of the wit. A pleasant type, but I doubt if one of the liveliest.' The old man smiled indulgently.

'Ah, so not one to buy a copy of *Men Only* and laugh like a gurgling drain?' Reggie enquired.

Phipps stared blankly, then said, 'Dear me, do you mean that rather outré publication the college porters used to read, the one featuring scantily clothed young ladies? Goodness, I didn't know it was still around. Are you saying that Dewthorp was an aficionado? You do surprise me.' He emitted a thin laugh and gave Popsie a dig in the ribs. Full of Schweppes, the little dog burped loudly.

'An aficionado? No, I shouldn't have thought so. As I explained to Miles, he was just glancing at them idly while I wrapped the figurine. But clearly some picture must have struck a note with him.' Reggie expanded on the incident, telling Phipps what he had told Loader.

Silently the professor scrutinised his drink, a murky shade of puce, and then said, 'You say he was taken aback, astounded eh? A reaction which surely signifies one of two things: either he had known the subject in the past but was surprised to see her featured in that sort of journal; or he had never seen her in the past but deduced her identity from what he had observed of a present-day acquaintance. But whichever the case, the context evidently afforded much drollery. Well, it's cheering to think that Dewthorp had a few moments of gaiety before his unfortunate demise . . . Hmm, I wonder if the sitter was clad or unclad.' Phipps cleared his throat, adding primly that his query was based not on prurience but merely intellectual curiosity.

Loader grinned. 'Really?'

'Oh yes. You see, if the subject was mainly clad, one could assume that she was simply a cheeky miss who enjoyed dabbling in the risqué. Perhaps a former girlfriend. On the other hand, a total nude would imply professionalism – a commercial tart using the magazine as a handy sideline. Ah well, tart or mere totty, she clearly had a penchant for memorable appendages.'

His views delivered, Aldous Phipps stood up, thrust Popsie into her harness, and thanking them for their company, said he must rush to be in time for lunch. 'My dear sister is most punctilious – serves it on the dot, and to be late brings penance. One will be expected to grapple all afternoon with that fiendish jigsaw puzzle.' He raised his eyes to heaven, gave a tired sigh, and muttering 'Fearful, fearful,' exited the bar.

Reggie Higgs gazed after him, and in a puzzled voice remarked, 'Funny these ancient scholarly types; curious the things they know . . . I mean, do you know a tart from a totty?'

'Er, no not exactly.' Loader glanced at his watch and exclaimed, 'Oops! I'll have to go. I think friend Felix is nigh this evening, so I'd better be off. Got to put his room to rights and shove something in a vase – flowers will do. Cheerio for now.'

Left alone, his companion finished his beer while pondering certain distinctions.

Felix Smythe was indeed nigh and Cedric had telephoned the Sandworth to report that, as feared, Inspector Jennings would like another word with him. Thus, when Loader got home grasping a bunch of slightly wilting larkspur, Cedric announced that the inspector would come to talk to Felix the following morning.

'But why here and not at the police station again?' Loader demanded.

Cedric shrugged. 'I had the impression he wants to keep it fairly low-key, doesn't want to intimidate the dear boy. Probably thinks the interview will be more productive if kept on a casual level. Sensible, really, I mean to say . . .'

'In that case let's hope he doesn't appear in a socking-great police van. The neighbours will love that!' He scanned the somewhat dishevelled state of the sitting room and added ruefully, 'It also means this place needs tidying: we've got books and stuff everywhere and the hall is crammed with my gumboots and angling gear, and there's an enormous trail of cigarette ash on the bottom stair.'

'Nothing to do with me, old fellow,' Cedric protested, 'I always use an ashtray. Didn't the char come yesterday? You did say she's a heavy smoker.'

'Yes, that's as maybe, but we still need to get things shipshape. From what I know of Jennings he's a bit of a prissy type and it might make a better impression if the place looks orderly. And after all, Felix is bound to feel more relaxed against a stage set. It's a pity I don't have a portrait of the Queen Mother to display; it would give comfort to him and be a reminder to the inspector of the witness's connections.' Loader winked and went into the hall to throw boots and fishing rods into a cupboard.

After making a few cursory adjustments to the cushions and rearranging his own reading material, Cedric removed himself to his bedroom. He was reluctant to play housemaid when he could be spending his time more profitably: i.e. rereading the Peebles letter which Felix had omitted to send to Dagwood – or indeed present to the police. On the face of it, the content had seemed prosaic enough and of little interest. Still, conceivably, it might just supply a lead, however tenuous. Despite his indifference, perhaps Felix really should pass it on to Jennings. Legally, withholding evidence was almost as bad as tampering with it, wasn't it? But then, Cedric reasoned to himself, who said anything about the thing being evidence? Evidence of what? As Felix himself had said, merely a few commonplaces written by any sister to any brother. Oh well, he would take another look and then mention it to Felix on his return and see what he thought. After all, it had been Felix who had nearly been murdered, not himself. He put on his spectacles and opened his attaché case.

The second time around the letter didn't really yield much more than the first. As before, he noted its stiff, colourless style and wondered if the recipient mightn't have found a telephone call more engaging. And yet he couldn't help feeling that more was being said than appeared, almost as if something were being deliberately withheld. Was he being unduly fanciful? Probably. He tossed it aside, closed his eyes and rested quietly until the return of the wandering Felix.

CHAPTER SIXTEEN

As Felix drove back to Blythburgh he was both pleased and disgruntled. In one respect he was delighted by the success of his time with the musicians and their circle, and indeed by his inclusion in the group photograph on the beach. In future years might it be reproduced in some august musical biography, with names of all participants clearly listed? It was a nice idea. But he was also disturbed by Cedric's message that he was again to be questioned by the Southwold police. The news was what he had feared, and he could have done without it. It was all very well being told he wouldn't have to report to the station itself, and that the inspector would instead make a 'home visit', but he would prefer it not to happen at all. It was a bit much!

Little had he known when driving up from London that he would be placed in such a distasteful and embarrassing situation. The less he saw of the police the better. The last thing he wanted was to undergo further probings and to have to relive the experience of that fearful night and that fearful woman. He had a fleeting vision of the bloodless gothic face on its crumpled pillows, and nearly winged a meandering cyclist.

However, once back at Miles Loader's house and able to regale its occupants with the success of his visit, he felt more robust. He was further fortified when, on mentioning that he had much enjoyed chatting with the little lady with the wispy bun, Cedric had clearly been impressed. 'Was she thin and with bright eyes?' he had asked. Felix nodded, saying she had seemed to know a good deal about orchestras and such. 'Naturally, she would,' Cedric had replied, adding that for the daughter of an eminent composer, and herself a major figure in the musical world, such knowledge was quite likely.

Felix was both pleased and startled, but his eager query as to her name was interrupted by his host coming in to announce that the police had rung to check if Mr Smythe would be available for the inspector's visit the following morning. Felix grimaced. Once more plunging into gloom, temporarily forgot about his bright-eyed sofa companion.

Felix's nonchalance on the morning of his first interview was not replicated on the morning of the second. This time no gargantuan breakfast was consumed and other than strong coffee he barely touched a thing. The two friends did their best to reassure him but he remained tense and fidgety.

'He will want to know if you've remembered anything significant, some small detail which may have easily slipped your mind,' Loader said, 'so I suggest that—'

'What, you mean like the small detail of that thug coming into my room and nearly strangling me?' Felix said sarcastically.

'Yes, exactly. But lay it on thick. He'll like that, it will give him a new scenario to think about. But tell him about your dream at the Sandworth and why you must have suppressed the real thing. That'll make it more convincing.'

'But I am convinced,' Felix protested.

'Yes, but it's not your conviction that matters; it's his. And if I were you, I'd stress how charming she was . . . mind you, not too much or he might think you had fancied her and made a pass. But do try to sound really sympathetic, if you can.' Loader grinned and Felix closed his eyes. With advice like that how could he go wrong?

'The big question is the letter you forgot to post,' Cedric reminded him. 'How are you going to handle that?'

Felix replied that he had no intention of handling it at all. 'If I give it to him now, he is bound to think I was remiss not producing it earlier – or that my mind is defective.' He waved a weary hand. 'Besides, I told you, it's clearly of no significance. Why stir things up unnecessarily? He'll only get excited and start asking even more questions. Pointless.'

On that dismissive note the witness retired to his upper room – the attic – to collect his thoughts and practise his responses.

By the time Jennings and Harris arrived he was sufficiently calm to welcome them in himself, Miles and Cedric having withdrawn to the garden, and to offer coffee and cigarettes. The latter were declined but the coffee gratefully accepted. Having carefully arranged the furniture so that the comfy chairs were facing the window, he sat opposite the officers with his back to the light. It was another piece of Loader's expert advice. 'These third-degree fellows always like to see their victim's faces, the eyes especially,' he had told Felix helpfully, 'they learn a lot that way.' Thus, feeling safely shaded, the witness beamed and asked brightly how he could help them.

'Like biscuits, do you?' Sergeant Harris asked.

To say that Felix's beam wavered would be a modest understatement; the smile vanished and he stared blankly at Harris. It passed through his mind that perhaps the man was hinting he would like an accompaniment to his coffee. If that was so, he was out of luck; his host didn't have any. Alternatively, perhaps it was some fatuous attempt at casual chit-chat to make him more receptive. Clearing his throat, he replied, 'An occasional Bath Oliver is pleasant enough, but I'm afraid if you want—'

'So you don't like Penguins?' Harris persisted.

Felix swallowed and fiddled nervously with his cufflink. Effing penguins? Who was this berk – some mad ornithologist? He glanced at the inspector. The inspector's face was rigidly set, as if fighting pain with stoic endurance. But the pain appeared to ease and he said apologetically: 'I am afraid my sergeant puts things rather bluntly. What we need to check is whether during the night of the murder you happened to have consumed a few Penguin biscuits in the kitchen. Some people suffer from nocturnal hunger pangs and can't resist the odd nibble.' Noting Felix's frosty look, he went on to explain about the heap of biscuit crumbs and wrappers that Elsie had found under the table.

Felix assured him that he was not one afflicted by such cravings, and that in any case he had a particular aversion to the type, finding them overly sweet. 'So, what else would you like to know?' he enquired evenly. (He had nearly suggested that the sergeant should make a special note of his biscuit preference, but stopped just in time. On no account must they be antagonised!)

While confident on the subject of biscuit consumption, Felix was less at ease regarding Mrs Peebles' letter. Consequently, when asked if he had seen much of the victim or spoken with her on the day of their supper together, he was blandly vague, explaining he had spent a very busy time and really hadn't seen much of her at all.

'Not even at breakfast?' Jennings asked.

Felix hesitated, and then with a light laugh confessed about his brush with Freddie. 'I was going out and hadn't seen the little chap on the stairs, and nearly tripped over him. Mrs Peebles was just coming out of the kitchen and heard him yelp. She was awfully good about it, and said he was a naughty boy for getting in the way, and asked if I had slept well. But frankly, I felt a bit embarrassed at having upset the dog like that and so left the house smartish. Silly, really.' Felix gave a neatly contrived sheepish smile.

Jennings nodded, evidently satisfied. And then returning to the night's central event, he remarked that it still seemed odd that Felix had heard nothing during those fatal hours, and asked if there was anything he could add to his previous account.

The witness relaxed. Clearly this was his cue to acquaint the inspector of the strange dream at the Sandworth and the incident of the killer in his room at Southwold – an experience so shocking as, alas, to have been temporarily erased from his memory. With Loader's advice in mind, he would give it all it was worth. Thus, leaning forward in his chair, he began: 'Now as it happens, Inspector, I think I may be able to help you there. You see . . .'

Out in the garden – Cedric in a deckchair and his companion crouched weeding a flower bed – the two friends spoke quietly to each other. 'How long do you think they will take?' Miles asked.

Cedric shrugged. 'It all depends on Felix. If he co-operates and adopts his Queen Mother style, that is, charming and attentive, they could be finished quite soon. On the other hand, if he gets rattled and nervy things may take longer.'

'You mean if he gets sulky.'

'I do. They'll get suspicious and see it as a challenge.'

'Hmm. I take it he is not going to show them the letter.'

'No. I think he feels a fool not having given it to them earlier; thinks it will show him in a poor light. The dear boy is a bit sensitive like that. But in any case, he's genuinely convinced it is worthless and will only muddy the waters. But you know,' Cedric added thoughtfully, 'it may be more than it seems. Not quite sure why I say that, but it's almost as if it were a kind of code, and—' He broke off, as from the front of the house there came the sound of a vehicle starting up; and the next moment the French window opened and Felix stepped onto the lawn. He looked rather smug.

'Go all right, did it?' Miles asked a trifle anxiously.

'Oh yes,' the other replied. 'Once they stopped mumbling about biscuits they became quite coherent.'

'And were you?' Cedric asked.

'Was I what?'

'Coherent.'

'Of course I bloody was! A damn good witness, that's what.'

As they drove away, Jennings said grimly to Harris, 'The next time we do an interview, I'll thank you to keep your mouth shut until I have had the first word. I know you've been on a course about the use of shock tactics in interviews, but you don't want to believe everything they tell you. Ridiculous!'

'Ah but I thought that if—'

'You've thought enough, Sergeant,' Jennings snapped.

CHAPTER SEVENTEEN

Jennings' mood was not the best. Despite his hopes, the visit to Blythburgh to reinterview the Smythe fellow had been largely unproductive, and certainly wearing. Smythe had responded in a way both fulsome and cagey; at times seemingly open and co-operative, at others distinctly shifty. As Nathan would sometimes remark, dealing with witnesses or suspects and listening to their accounts was all a question of sifting fact from fantasy, significant detail from fanciful dross. Often it was the unsaid rather than the said which gave a clue.

As it was, quite a bit had been said. But was that simply to mask some underlying anxiety or unease? Did that business of the dream amount to anything at all? Just how far was bloody Smythe a reliable witness? Irritably, Jennings drummed his fingers on the desk, and then drew a stupid face of the chief constable on his blotting pad before turning to the racing section of the local paper. Of the two species, human and horse, the latter was the more reliable.

There was a knock on his door, and thrusting the paper aside to pick up his fountain pen, he struck a pose of alert enquiry.

Bert Hill entered. 'It's the vicar. He's on the blower and says he's got something that may be of interest to you.'

'Really? What sort of thing – a Bible?'

'I couldn't rightly say, though it might be, I suppose. Something to do with books, anyway; but I couldn't catch what exactly. It's the same in church – lowers his voice just when he gets to an interesting bit. So, what do you want me to tell him?'

'Hmm. I'm busy just now. Tell him to drop in this afternoon. Late.'

Doubtful whether the Reverend Furblow had anything of interest to produce (other than a pet lamb, perhaps), Jennings returned to the racing results.

When the vicar arrived, he deposited a slim packet on the inspector's desk. Looking slightly embarrassed, he said, 'Uhm, it's not the sort of thing I normally carry about with me, but in the circumstances, I thought it might be of some relevance to your investigations.' He gave a rueful smile.

From the packet Jennings withdrew a worn copy of *Men Only*, its cover adorned by a robust girl in a diminutive swimsuit. For a moment he regarded it in silence, not quite sure what he was supposed to say. 'Er . . . I see—' he began.

'Actually, I don't suppose you do see but I thought it

might be helpful to you,' Furblow said earnestly. Jennings blinked, wondering if his manhood was being impugned.

The other started to elaborate. 'It was among a pile of books and other bits and pieces belonging to the late Mr Dewthorp. Originally, of course, he used to stay with Mrs Peebles but after that he had been renting a couple of rooms in Pier Avenue and the owner, Mrs Dingle, gave them to me yesterday. She thought I might find them useful for our next bring-and-buy sale. I gather that after his death she had naturally cleared his rooms ready for a new tenant but kept the books in case anyone wanted them. It was only just now that she remembered she still had them. The other stuff was the usual debris – pencils, rubbers, razor blades, old socks, all that sort of thing. But some of the books are most interesting, most interesting – and very saleable, I like to think. I mean to say, there's a nice John Buchan, a handsome copy of Gibbon's *Decline and Fall*, a catalogue of Suffolk's flora and fauna, an excellent Collins dictionary, the commentaries of Marcus Aurelius, *Jane Eyre* and uhm . . .'

'And *Men Only*,' Jennings said.

'Ah yes. I was coming to that. Between you and me, Inspector, I don't think that item would be entirely to the liking of our little flock at St Edmund's and—'

'You mean the sheep would disapprove?'

'What?' For a moment Furblow looked puzzled, and then smiled, 'Ah, you joke, I see! But you get my drift, I'm sure: some might think it wasn't quite the proper article for a church bazaar. You know, "lowering the tone" and all that. The Vestry Committee is rather pernickety in these matters . . . quite right, probably. There are enough rude things said about the Church as it is, and it would be foolish to offer a hostage to Fortune, wouldn't it.'

And what do you want me to do about it? Jennings thought irritably. Why, for God's sake, bring it in here? Really, as if he hadn't enough on his plate without vicars wasting police time bringing in trashy magazines. In an even tone he enquired the significance of Furblow's offering.

'The significance is what is inside.' Furblow leant towards the desk and leafed through some of the pages, retrieving a piece of folded foolscap. 'I was going to throw the thing away, but this slipped out and I thought it might be pertinent.' He sat back in his chair, folded his hands and waited while Jennings perused the contents.

It appeared to be an unfinished draft of a letter to a young niece, rather smudged and with a couple of crossings-out and amendments. The tone was genial and indulgently avuncular.

My dear Lily,

I trust you are enjoying your American sojourn and that the journalism course is being useful. Investigative journalism is the branch to cultivate and I suspect you would make an excellent 'sleuth'. I look forward to seeing you on your return to Cambridge when we can have a good old chinwag. But meanwhile, many congratulations on your first novel, a most imaginative tale – and for one of your tender years, rather racy! How fortunate I am to have both a journalist and an author for a niece. It was a good read and made me chuckle. Keep at it, my dear, and you will soon stir the envy of Agatha Christie.

To that effect, I venture to suggest a scenario for your next plot – loosely based on a few bare facts which I have recently chanced upon, and which I think you could profitably embellish. Its essential theme is righteous hypocrisy and concerns two disparate characters, who, despite their differences, would seem to be linked by that same trait. This may sound a trifle 'heavy', but I have to admit that the apparent situation has afforded me some amusement, and in the right hands (yours) would make a good yarn.

As you know, I have been visiting Southwold over the past year and staying at a guest house run by a very strait-laced lady about whom I have made a most startling discovery, both intriguing and funny. You see what I have discovered is—

At this point the writer had broken off, presumably either to scrap the letter altogether, or perhaps to embark on a longer one. Either way, Jennings was curious. Clearly the owner of the guest house could only have been Mrs Peebles, but who was the other – the one who, according to Dewthorp, shared her flawed rectitude? Someone in Southwold or further afield? And if so, how much further?

He looked up to see the vicar watching him closely. 'Rather tantalising, wouldn't you say? When you spoke to me last week you were keen to discover something of the victim's background. Alas, I fear I wasn't of much help except to refer you to the Goodhart sisters – oh, and incidentally, I trust they were pliable, they aren't always – but when I read this piece it occurred to me it might be of some value to your researches. I mean to say, the letter seems to hint that the good lady wasn't all that she purported to be – mind you, that can be said of many, I fear – but I wonder why Dewthorp kept it in this particular publication? Don't get me wrong, Inspector, I make no judgement regarding his recreational interests . . . after all, this magazine is merely saucy, not gross as one hears some are these days. However, the fact that they were filed together might suggest some kind of link.' He paused, and standing up to leave added, 'Or not.'

Jennings nodded thoughtfully, thanked him for the information, and then politely enquired after the grass-croppers.

At once the vicar's face lit up. 'Absolutely splendid!' he enthused. 'We've just taken another consignment and they are doing a grand job, a grand job! You must come back soon and I'll introduce you to some of my stalwarts.'

Jennings wasn't sure if he wished to be introduced to a stalwart sheep, but intrigued by the unexpected revelations, thanked the pastor for his kind offer.

After the vicar had left, Jennings reread the letter, flipped through the predictable pages of bald jokes and coy pictures, and brooded. Sod's Law being in sound operation, Dewthorp's letter broke off just at the point of interest.

Assuming it had ever been completed, it might provide a handy lead into the victim's private life: a life whose alleged blemishes could have precipitated her death. But had it been completed? Had the fair copy ever been sent? If so, where was the recipient, the niece Lily. Still in America or back in Cambridge? Or any blooming where!

Jennings scowled and turned his mind to Horace Dewthorp, so eager to provide grist for the girl's inventive mill. Well, he was out of the picture all right. Another shaft from Sod. If it hadn't been for that fall, the chap might have been a valuable source of information. He had evidently had some tale to tell, or thought he had. Jennings indulged in a momentary vision of Dewthorp coming to the station and laying before them some wondrous revelation, which would solve the whole mystery, result in the murderer being caught and Detective Inspector W.R. Jennings garlanded in wreaths of laurels. The vision lasted for two seconds.

Back in reality he decided to telephone Chief Inspector Nathan, still off duty in invalid mode. He would drop in on him on the way home, see how he was and pick his brains. Not obviously of course, just the casual query. After all, one didn't want to look too beholden. Not, of course, that he was beholden, he thought hastily, but it was always useful to mull things over with another – especially with one who currently had nothing better to do. He cast a rueful glance at the pile of paperwork filling his in-tray.

Before setting off to Nathan's house in Field Stile Road, Jennings drove into High Street to get cigarettes and to forage for a nice bit of pie for his supper. He was able to park just outside the grocer's and was about to alight, when there was a tap on the nearside window.

He looked up and saw the insistent face of one of the Goodhart twins. It could have been Gaye but on the whole he thought it was Joy. A correct assumption. She saw him looking and tapped again, making gestures that clearly indicated he should open the passenger door. Unwillingly, he leant over and let her in. He was mildly relieved that being in so public a place, she was clad not in the pink apparel and galoshes, but in something vaguely grey and tweedy and that her gumboots were reassuringly black. The fringe and thick-rimmed glasses remained the same.

Settling herself into the passenger seat, she exclaimed rather breathlessly, 'Ah, how nice to see you again, Inspector. I had been thinking I might come to the police station to clarify my point; but as it is, you have saved me the trouble.' She beamed, and scrabbling in her handbag offered him a toffee, which he mechanically accepted. Politely he enquired what her point had been.

'The point which my sister so rudely contradicted, the point about the man Mary Peebles brought to our Orford meeting on those two occasions. As I was trying to tell you at the time, the gentleman came from Cambridge, not Oxford as Gaye insisted. His name was definitely Hepton, Stephen Hepton, I recall. He was tallish and a bit bulky, and' – she lowered her voice conspiratorially – 'I think he may have worn a false moustache.'

Jennings studied the seemingly guileless face, and wondered uneasily if the old bat was having him on. He felt slightly affronted. 'Why do you say that?' he asked curtly.

For a moment she paused, and then said, 'Well you see,

Inspector, I did note that although his hair and eyebrows were a grizzled black, the bristles on his upper lip were definitely brown, brown with ginger flecks, a sort of auburn. Although I say it myself, I have a perceptive mind – not that dear Gaye would agree – and it struck me that black and auburn was a curious combination. Mind you,' she twittered, 'we did once have a cat with some very odd fur. He was called Monty and . . . Still, I don't suppose you want to hear about him just now, another time perhaps. Anyway, as I was saying, I also observed that he would occasionally tap his mouth as if brushing off an insect or removing a crumb. Of course, that may have been merely a nervous habit; on the other hand, perhaps it was to ensure that the manly tache wasn't dislodged. I mentioned the unusual colouring to Gaye, but she was rather dismissive and said I needed stronger glasses. She's full of helpful advice like that.' Joy smiled sweetly.

Jennings also mustered a smile, but out of the corner of his eye noticed that the grocer's blinds were being slowly lowered and its outside sign removed. Evidently no pie for supper. Politely he thanked her for the invaluable information and was just wondering how he could courteously eject the old trout, when she thrust another toffee towards him and announced that she must be off in time to heckle the vicar's choir practice. 'Such fun!' she exclaimed, easing herself back on to the pavement.

Toffee discarded and with dour face, Jennings pressed the starter, reversed rashly, and drove back towards Field Stile Road.

* * *

Mrs Nathan was delighted to see him. 'Thank God,' she exclaimed, 'he's been awful today – bored out of his mind, tetchy but full of silly jokes. I don't know which is worse, the jokes or the complaints. He'll be glad to see you all right!'

She hustled him into the sitting room where her husband was engrossed in watching television, an early version of *Fabian of the Yard*. 'Total bilge,' he grumbled, 'give me *Blue Peter* any day.' Signalling to Jennings to switch it off, he said, 'Well now, Inspector, and how's life with you? Making a better job of it than Fabian, I hope.' He grinned and, pointing to his plastered leg, now inscribed with a number of names since Jennings' last visit, informed him that this was his last chance. 'It comes off tomorrow,' he said, 'so if you don't sign now, your scrawl will be conspicuous by its absence. You wouldn't want that, would you?'

Tactfully, Jennings shook his head. And then taking out his biro dutifully etched his name into the greying plaster. Task performed, he cleared his throat and waited for the inevitable next question, which, as predicted, came quick as a bullet. 'So, old son, case all wrapped up, is it? Villains in custody and the super in heaven?'

Jennings saw the sadistic glint in his eye and muttered something to the effect that it was all rather complex and baffling, but that certain things were beginning to emerge.

'Such as?'

'Well, so far we've established that—'

'I take it you've got the Hepton reference, have you?'

Jennings was startled. Hepton? Wasn't that the man the Goodhart twin had mentioned – the one she said had worn a false moustache and whose first name she had insisted was Stephen?

'Funny you should say that, sir, because . . .' And he went on to describe his encounter with Joy Goodhart that very evening; plus other sundry items of the case, including the tricky lodger, his interview with the aggressive Dagwood, and the Reverend Furblow's recent revelation about the interior life of Mary Peebles.

Nathan listened intently; his jovial mockery replaced by a thoughtful frown. 'Hmm, funny that. You know I told you that the Cambridge lot thought there was a remote chance that their murder victim – the vicar hanged on the bridge – had some connection with Orford? It so happens that Chief Inspector Tilson rang yesterday to say that since we last talked, they have been looking into his earlier life. Apparently, it's not what you would call picturesque. According to their latest enquiries, after the war and before he became a cleric, Stephen Hapworth had moved in some very shady circles in London; sufficiently shady it seems for him to require an alias. One of those aliases had been the name Harry Hepton.'

Nathan leant forward to knock his pipe out on the chimney breast. It wasn't the deftest of movements and ash scattered liberally on the carpet. Reaching for his tobacco pouch, he began to make a clumsy job of re-stuffing the pipe. Strands of tobacco joined the ash on the floor. Process completed, he said musingly, 'I know that Goodhart pair: they're a Southwold fixture, a bit like the brewery or the lighthouse. Of the two, Joy Goodhart is the sharper – though you mightn't think so. But if she said that chap came up from Cambridge and was called Stephen Hepton, then she's probably right.' He looked up and fixed Jennings with a quizzical stare. 'So what do you think, Inspector?'

Jennings stared back, and then said slowly: 'Stephen Hapworth, Harry Hepton, Stephen Hepton – they're one and the same aren't they?'

Nathan nodded. 'It's often the case. People get attached to their names, and even when adopting others, tend to cling to a vestige of the original. Doesn't always happen but it's common enough. I should say it fits pretty well: Hapworth leads a rackety life in London; temporally adopts the name of Harry Hepton; for some reason moves to Cambridge as a bent cleric; visits Suffolk incognito, and specifically Orford – this time using the variant name of Stephen Hepton – returns to Cambridge where he blots his copybook and has a nasty end under a college bridge. The question is, was he murdered by those in Cambridge or in Suffolk? Who had he most displeased?'

For a few moments there was silence until broken by Mrs Nathan entering to suggest that perhaps the inspector would like a nice glass of cider. 'No, he wouldn't,' her husband said firmly. 'He would like a large tumbler of whisky, and so would I.'

After she had left to perform her mission, Jennings asked if the other thought the Goodhart tale of the false moustache was likely.

Nathan grinned. 'Could be. It may sound like a Whitehall farce but it's amazing what these coves will do in extremity. Take that Herr Voigt, for example.'

Jennings wasn't quite sure who Herr Voigt was, but he nodded thoughtfully.

CHAPTER EIGHTEEN

Sipping a cup of thin black tea and puffing an Abdulla cigarette, Aldous Phipps sat in his sister's conservatory savouring its warmth and the scent of lilies. The waft of tobacco smoke mingling with the heady aroma of flowers gave to the place an almost oriental air, which, reminding him of his Cairo days, soothed and amused the basking occupant. But it was not just the past that was absorbing the old man, but the present.

On the whole, he mused, the visit to Isabel was turning out considerably better than he had expected. Not, of course, that he had expected it to be really bad. And besides, anything would be better than being immured at home, his nerves jangled by the incessant noise of workmen's drills and the jovial cries and curses of their operators. He flinched, recalling the giant cement mixer being installed outside his front door on the day he had left. He wondered if it was still there. Bound to be, he thought grimly. The municipal authorities never did anything by halves – or at least, not those things that disturbed the peace of the ratepayers and professors (or their little dogs).

He adjusted his mind to dwell on Isabel and his present situation. Other than the appalling jigsaw puzzle, which she would insist on their sharing, and the glutinous cakes at tea, his time with her and in Southwold was proving quite congenial. Indeed, he might go so far as to say refreshingly stimulating! Fortunately, murder was not an everyday event – or at least not in his sphere – but it had to be admitted that a touch of it now and again gave a surprising fillip to an elderly life, which, despite the benison of books, was becoming a trifle bland. Caustic spats with academic colleagues were of course always pleasurable. But to be cast in the midst of murder was surely a real shot in the arm. Phipps smiled guiltily and addressed the dog. 'Wouldn't you agree, Popsie? A shot in the arm, eh!' Obediently the dog wagged its tail.

In the midst of murder? Most certainly. Cambridge's extraordinary event had been highly diverting, but now to be in Southwold where only recently another gruesome eclipse had occurred was indeed to be in media res! Phipps glanced again at his companion: 'Dogged by assassins, that's what I am,' he chuckled. The creature replied with a sleepy grunt and this time with only the merest tail twitch.

Her master continued to reflect on the Peebles affair. Not only was he staying in the vicinity of the victim's house, but most of those he had met since his arrival had known something about her. Isabel, of course, but also that Dr Loader and the fellow who owned the antiques shop; and then there was Dillworthy's friend, Felix the Floral One, he who had been present on the night it happened. Well, he had certainly been in the thick of things all right, and was presumably by now more than on nodding terms with the police. Still, Phipps conceded, one couldn't dislike the little chap and it was to be hoped he would cope.

Thinking of Felix, naturally brought Cedric to mind. He was glad to have met the professor again for he had struck him as being sane and sound; a little severe, perhaps, but one whose civilised company he had rather enjoyed. Of course, Isabel was a pleasant enough companion and she could still mix a good cocktail; but she had her flowers to attend to and other activities, and their choices in reading were not entirely at one. She seemed keen on someone called James Bond of whom he had never heard; whereas when he had tried to introduce her to Aeschylus or Edgar Wallace, she had laughed like a drain.

He frowned and reflected more upon Cedric Dillworthy, and wondered if he could engineer another meeting. Difficult. Being based in some outlying village (Blythburgh or Blissborough, wasn't it?) and without a car, the chance of their renewing acquaintance might pose problems. Oh well, he would have a word with Isabel – the girl could be quite thoughtful sometimes.

While Aldous Phipps mused on the chance of seeing Cedric again, the latter was also thinking: not about Aldous Phipps, but where to go next. He had been presented with a dilemma. After Felix's interview with the police, they had said that he was free to return to London should he want, albeit to remain available. Felix had been concerned about Bountiful Blooms, and although he had telephoned a couple of times to check that all was in order, he still felt the need to go back and show his face. 'Can't trust them an inch,' he had grumbled to Cedric, 'and if I don't look in, they'll become slack and idle. Besides, you never know, HM might have left a message.'

Cedric rather doubted the latter, but agreed that it was a sensible idea. Despite the current drama, he was happy to remain *in situ* and await Felix's return, when they could then embark on their planned tour of Norfolk. However, his host's wife had telegrammed from Las Vegas joyfully announcing that she had again profited at the gaming tables. Her husband had immediately telegrammed back with an anguished ultimatum:

FOR CHRISTS SAKE RETURN FORTHWITH BEFORE YOU BLOW THE LOT STOP ANY HESITATION AND I SHALL DIVORCE YOU STOP I MEAN IT STOP

The upshot was that the arch-gambler was due to arrive at any moment – suitably loaded.

Given these circumstances, Cedric felt that a tactful withdrawal was indicated, and had contemplated moving to The Swan for a few days until Felix returned. His host appreciated his discretion but had another suggestion: 'Why don't I get on to Isabel Phipps? That house has got three or four bedrooms. I'm sure she would be happy to have you there for a while. It could be company for the old brother; in fact, she would probably be only too glad. But take my advice, keep your door locked – we don't want any more nocturnal attacks!'

There were times, Cedric thought, when Miles Loader's humour was not of the most couth. Still, such an idea wasn't bad. He had liked Isabel and he could probably handle the professor's quirks. If she was willing, so was he.

Isabel was more than willing and greeted his proposal with relief. Her brother's presence, though welcome, was nevertheless proving a bit of a strain. She had feared it might, and there were times when sisterly duty began to falter. Difference in age, temperament and interests had always made their relationship somewhat wobbly, and fond though she was of him, a little went a long way. What he needed was a diversion: a playmate other than the dog. 'Oh, by all means,' she cooed to Miles Loader, 'that would be lovely! Bring him down at once, there's bags of room here. With two professors in the same house there'll be plenty to talk about; they can go for thoughtful walks along the promenade . . . And beyond,' she added.

The arrangement was made, and Cedric's switch from Blythburgh to Southwold seamless. He was accorded a grateful welcome by the two siblings and settled in quickly. Much as he had enjoyed the Loader household, the greater space of his new surroundings and the lily-scented conservatory was much to his liking.

Losing no time, his hostess murmured about the delights of coastal walks. However, her brother had other ideas. He had become a trifle wearied of the coast and its constant breeze; and the sight of the sea, although initially interesting, had begun to pall. Thus, when Isabel suggested that the two visitors should take a pre-lunch stroll along the front, Aldous had drawn Cedric aside and whispered firmly, 'On no account. I have a much better plan.'

The better plan was the high street with its bookshop and the conveniently placed café next door. 'We'll browse the books first, and then exhausted by the excitement of it all repair to that charming tea shop for recuperation and doughnuts.' Phipps spoke with relish, and knowing both the bookshop and the café, Cedric was happy to oblige. Thoughtfully leaving Popsie snoozing among the lilies, the two professors set out across the green.

They pottered among the bookshelves and each found something to his liking: Phipps a fat anthology of Edgar Wallace, and Cedric – with Felix and his kind gift in mind – two recent biographies, one of the Queen Mother and the other of Imogen Holst. Pleased with their selection, they proceeded to the tea shop.

Inside, Phipps pointed to its little inner sanctum at the far end. 'A refuge from holiday hoi polloi,' he chuckled. 'We shan't be overheard there.' Cedric was slightly startled by his companion's words. Not overheard? Were they about to hatch a conspiracy?

But if that had been Phipps's hope it was dashed; for the 'refuge' was populated with Southwold denizens evidently similarly drawn. Cedric suspected that such a gathering was prompted by the Peebles affair. The local press had talked of a 'shadow' being cast over Southwold. Judging from the present crowd it was a shadow of some liveliness. Not that the voices were loud, but there was a cosy hum and a number of faces wore expressions of genteel excitement.

Despite the moderately low tone of the sound, Phipps removed his hearing aid and dropped it in his pocket. 'Such a bore,' he grumbled, 'in a crowd the confounded thing magnifies every noise, even the clatter of teaspoons. But then without it one can't hear one's own voice. It just shows, there's a flaw in every gadget. Do you wear one, Professor?'

Cedric shook his head absently, scanning the room for a table. Fortunately, just as they were about to retreat, two ladies stood up to leave, and the newcomers quickly took their place. The table was in the centre and Phipps grimaced at its prominent position. 'Ah well, beggars such as we cannot be choosers,' he murmured philosophically, then grasped the menu and began to examine it with discerning eye.

Their order given, he leant towards Cedric, and in a tone, which he imagined to be quiet, said, 'Now, Professor, what is your theory?'

'My theory?' Cedric asked vaguely.

'Oh, come now, you must have one, especially as it was your friend who was with her on that frightful night! One feels so sorry for him, so sorry.' He paused to ask a passing waitress to bring a large napkin (evidently in readiness for the imminent doughnut), and then continued. 'However, one must not allow sorrow to inhibit detection. Mind before emotion, that has always been my motto, something I have tried to instil into my students – not that many have listened. It's the pull of the river and the rugger field, they get so confused poor things.' For a moment the sharp eyes looked pensive. But the next moment he had tapped Cedric's wrist and said briskly, 'Now come on, Dillworthy, spill the beans and give me your views.'

Cedric's mind leapt back forty years to when he had been a shy undergraduate being interrogated by an impatient tutor. He felt slightly piqued by the old man's insistence and yet at the same time oddly drawn. He cleared his throat, and before committing himself guardedly enquired if his interrogator had any views himself.

Phipps was vague, saying there was some small matter, which had struck him as curious and which might have a bearing, but that until now he hadn't bothered to raise it, preferring to wait for the right company. He nodded politely at Cedric. 'I enjoy talking to my sister, but she is rather assertive and doesn't always listen. One favours more measured discussions.' At that moment the doughnuts arrived, and he turned his attention to their consumption, shelving all measured discussions.

Cedric sipped his lapsang and watched the process with interest. For an elderly man, Phipps's appetite seemed remarkably virile. Noting a pause in proceedings, he said, 'Well, now that you mention it, there is something that I've been thinking about.' Cupping his ear, Phipps told him to speak up. Obediently Cedric raised his voice and said it again.

Phipps's eyes twinkled. 'Thought there might be,' he said.

'It's a letter from Mrs Peebles to her brother, which she

had asked Felix to post. I fear he forgot all about it and never did. Frankly, I think he should take it to the police. He thinks it's nonsense and of no account. But having studied the thing, I can't help feeling that there is something vaguely contrived about it, as if it were not quite what it seems. It has an obliqueness, if you see what I mean.'

Scoffing more doughnut, Phipps replied that he could not possibly know what Cedric meant unless he saw the letter. 'However,' he added, 'you could be right. It is ironic how sometimes the said can mean so little and the unsaid so much. Macbeth spoke of "sound and fury signifying nothing". But who knows, in this case it may be a quiet temperance signifying much. Do you have access to it?'

'Oh yes, it's in my briefcase. Felix left it when he went dashing off to London and I brought it with me.'

'Hmm. I agree about the police, they like that sort of thing. Yes, he should definitely take it to them. It's quite likely to be the victim's last written words and they may find it valuable.' He gave a smart tap on the table, which rattled the cups: 'And who knows, Dillworthy, it might reveal a great deal about the woman's life and contacts – a key to the killing, one might say. Yes, a veritable key!' Phipps's thin voice rose and he spoke with a sly relish. However, given the letter's muted style, Cedric very much doubted if it was a veritable key, but said the other was welcome to look at it.

'Excellent,' Phipps beamed, 'we shall peruse it together this evening; a restful antidote to the awful jigsaw . . . Now, dear fellow, I don't know about you, but I could manage one of their ice creams. What do you think?'

As they stood up to go, pleased with their books and their burgeoning friendship, they failed to notice the occupant of the adjacent table, his nose in the music section of the *Suffolk Times* and holding a miniature Yorkshire on his knee. Neither were they aware of the man's eyes following them as they moved to the door.

CHAPTER NINETEEN

At home in Walberswick that evening, Jennings lit an unseasonal fire, sprawled in his favourite chair and brooded on biscuits.

Clearly their reference in the interview had made no impression on Smythe; or if it had, he was a damn good actor. But he had seemed to be genuinely bemused. No hesitation, no guilty start, no specious explanation. Merely a shrug and a look of blank indifference. So if the little chap had an aversion to Penguins as he said, and the victim thought them 'common', who the hell had taken down the tin and wiped it clean of their fingerprints?

According to Elsie, Mrs Peebles had kept them for her guests and her dog. That perishing elusive dog! Well, as Harris had so intelligently deduced, the creature couldn't have reached the tin; but he could have gobbled the biscuits all right – biscuits which someone had fed to him. Was that someone his mistress? No. She would have had no reason to wipe the tin afterwards (unless a hygiene fetishist). There could be only one person who had indulged the blighter that night: Chummy the intruder. The question was, before or after the attack? Surely before. Afterwards would hardly be a good time to hang about indulging the appetites of pet terriers.

He conjured the scene: killer enters house via kitchen door (with own or purloined key); the dog yaps and starts to make a din, or perhaps greets him with yelps of canine euphoria. Either way it needs to be quieted. A brisk bash on the head? A stranger or one not expecting its presence, might do just that. But there had been no body, either inside or out. And the idea of the corpse being carried off in a sack was the stuff of dreams. No, it was far more likely that dog and killer knew each other, and the latter au fait not only with its tastes but also the location of the biscuits. Jennings saw it plainly, or thought he did.

Obviously, the cache of Penguins had been used as a sop to Cerberus – a way of keeping the little bugger occupied while his friend sneaked up the stairs and smothered the creature's mistress (albeit not before stopping off en route to put the fear of God in the lodger). The deed done, the man left the room, upsetting the flower vase in his haste, and crept back down to the kitchen . . .

At this point the dramatist paused in his narrative. So, what then? He frowned, visualising the likely scene. The dog still guzzling the biscuits, or possibly sated and snoozing; or maybe alert and ready to welcome its soft-footed friend in the hope of more treats. Yet supposing the door was ajar, might it have scampered into the garden? Jennings pondered. Hmm, if the dog had escaped into the night, then surely the following day it would have been seen roaming about the Southwold paths and alleyways, but so far no stray had been reported. Presumably it had been content to remain in the kitchen until . . . until scooped up and carried away by the murderer. Perhaps the chap thought he could show it at Crufts!

His thoughts turned from dog to door. Why had it been relocked? Jennings stared at the flickering fire and shrugged. No obvious reason – some people just had tidy habits, habits that even a brutal killing couldn't change. Anyway, doubtless the shrinks would have an answer, they always did . . . some ingenious theory about needing to lock away the horror and embrace the normal . . . Well, personally he wouldn't mind embracing some of the whisky his old granny had brought over for his birthday. She was very thoughtful like that; some grandmothers would knit you bedsocks or buy a tie or produce something 'useful' like a potato peeler. No, Gran was a savvy one and knew her arse from her elbow. The grandson grinned and sleepily reached for his present.

As Inspector Jennings imbibed whisky by his fireside while musing upon the anomalies of dogs and locked doors, Professors Aldous Phipps and Cedric Dillworthy grappled manfully with the bottom half of their hostess's jigsaw puzzle. 'You do realise,' Phipps whispered, 'that until we get that side bit in place there won't be any supper, or it will be late and dull.'

'And if we succeed?' Cedric queried.

'Ah, then it will be bang on time and most agreeable. Now come on, Dillworthy, pull your weight!'

The two scholars gazed in anguished perplexity at the garish labyrinth before them. Silence reigned, as peering and frowning they manoeuvred the pieces. Eventually Phipps said, 'I don't suppose you happen to carry a penknife, do you?'

Cedric shook his head and asked why he wanted one.

'To cut some of the shapes of course. If we could shave off one or two corners here and there, we might be able to cobble something together.'

Cedric was shocked. 'But that would be cheating, not to mention vandalism!'

'My dear Dillworthy, harsh situations require harsh measures. When in a tight hole expedience is all. But in this case, you are probably right. I fear Isabel would be bound to notice, however subtly done. She generally does,' he murmured ruefully.

His companion said nothing but rather primly continued to sift the pieces. His efforts paid off, for he was able to find six bits that actually fitted together.

'Congratulations, that's a happy blessing,' Phipps remarked. 'With luck, supper should be most palatable. However, before we have that pleasure, I suggest we look at that letter you mentioned, the one Mr Smith omitted to post.'

'Smythe,' Cedric mechanically corrected him. 'It's upstairs, I'll fetch it.'

* * *

When he returned, Phipps was smoking an Abdulla and holding a propelling pencil. 'Old habits,' he smiled, 'I can't read anything these days without one of these at the ready.' Cedric thought it looked like some sort of weapon.

The pencil went to work, marking this, underlining that. Then, his scrutiny finished, the professor looked up and observed sternly, 'Frankly, if Isabel were ever to address me in that way there would be fisticuffs! Not the sort of tone to endear one. Chilly and bossy, that's what. Chilly and bossy!' He pursed his lips and gave the paper a smart rap. 'If you ask my opinion, the brother must be very docile to accept that kind of drubbing. Mind you, from what you were saying, owing to your friend's oversight he never received it. Nevertheless, I rather doubt if this is an isolated example of the lady's style.'

Cedric nodded and said that Felix would probably agree, having also had a dose of that style. 'Apart from the money angle and the sale of the London warehouse, she sounds to be mainly concerned with the state of their gardens. Pretty keen on her roses too, as if they were quite a feature . . . yet not according to Felix. He was very dismissive and says he wasn't aware that she had any.'

'Really? Well, if they had escaped your friend's discerning eye, then I doubt if she had. People with professional interests are very observant regarding their own specialist field – as doubtless you yourself are with those bits of Cappadocian stone and rubble.'

Cedric was incensed. Rubble? What the hell did he mean! He was just about to formulate some polite but frosty response, when he saw the merest glint of amusement in the old man's eye, and relaxed. 'But if she didn't have any roses,' he said slowly, 'why is she writing about them?'

Aldous Phipps formed a church steeple with his thin fingers and contemplated the appalling jigsaw. Raising his eyes he said, 'I imagine because she was talking about something else – the reference to the roses being merely metaphorical.'

'Hmm.' Cedric stretched over for the letter and took another look. 'You think that the allusion to roses equals something in her life, and that others had been helpful in removing obstacles to make it run more smoothly – helpers presumably directed by her brother?'

Phipps frowned. 'Yes, that's about it. But you will note that she goes on to refer to his horticultural interests, not simply her own – "I trust that like mine your plants are blooming". A further metaphor perhaps, and just as with "roses", the word "plants" is merely a vehicle for the underlying tenor – whatever that might be.' He sniffed, and then added drily, 'I like to think that despite her gardening pursuits, Isabel would never prattle on to me about privet hedges and their destruction, or indeed privet hedges at all. Not the most riveting topic for a letter, I shouldn't think. Unless of course one were using . . .'

The point was left unfinished, for at that moment Isabel appeared with cocktails and the prancing Popsie, and his face lit up. 'Isabel, my dear, we were just saying how clever you are with those splendid lilies. Oh, and just see what our dear friend has achieved with the puzzle – almost a whole corner. Not bad, eh? Not bad at all. Now, what libations are we to enjoy this evening? Something special, I trust, to welcome our guest with!'

211

He stroked the dog and generated an air of benignity rarely observed by the Fellows of St Cecil's Senior Common Room.

Isabel must have approved the adjustments to the jigsaw, for their supper was indeed palatable. No cook himself, Cedric wished that Felix was there to quiz her about the finer points of the fish mousse. Perhaps he should ask for the recipe. On second thought, perhaps not. Felix was pernickety about other people's culinary skills and in the nicest way might hint at the superiority of his own version.

Isabel enquired if they would care to watch some television later. 'There's a fascinating programme all about the Swiss Alps and their flora and fauna.' She asked Cedric if he knew it.

He was about to say that he rarely watched as he found the twelve-inch screen a bit small compared with that of the cinema, when he was interrupted by Phipps announcing that since he suffered both from the cold and from vertigo, he feared the topic would give him nightmares. 'Popsie and I don't have one of these televisions, but since staying here I have become acquainted with something called *Perry Mason* – one of those Yankee legal dramas. Crude, of course, but quite invigorating. A much safer bet than those perilous Alps, I should think.' He turned to Cedric: 'Wouldn't you agree, Dillworthy?'

Cedric gave a wan smile and glanced at Isabel who made a face. 'Ah, the oracle has spoken,' she said, only semi-jovially. 'So, Mason it is. I'll fetch you the chocolates. But personally, I shall retire to bed with Suetonius.'

'Disgraceful,' her brother sighed.

* * *

Later that night – and to his surprise having rather enjoyed the crime drama – Cedric lay awake thinking. Before getting into bed he had again read and cogitated over the letter, and was pretty sure that Aldous Phipps was right. While the last paragraph had been merely curt and bossy, the first part had held a whiff of contrivance. Roses, plants, privet hedge, people: nothing and nobody were actually defined. Did Mrs Peebles usually adopt so brief and guarded a style or was it intentional? He suspected the latter. And what about those comments on the humble privet? Admittedly a prosaic garden feature but it had its uses. Yet from the way she spoke, one would think it had sinister triffid qualities! Surely an exaggeration. And yet here she was presenting it as a pernicious threat, and something to be not merely trimmed but firmly executed.

And what about this London garden in which it was apparently so invasive? Was it Dagwood's own or was it attached to one of his commercial properties? Or even some municipal park with which he had a link or interest? Or, like the roses, was it in fact a term for something else? Again, the reference had been cursory with no elaboration. He recalled Aldous Phipps's words when interrupted by Isabel with the drinks. He had been saying something about a privet hedge being a dull topic for a letter, and had continued: 'unless of course one were using . . .' As Cedric stared into the dark, he mentally concocted the end of the sentence: unless of course one were using a code.

Yes, a code of sorts: he was sure that was what Phipps had been about to suggest. And if so, it certainly accorded with his own instinct. A tacit, covert message, that's what

Mrs Peebles had intended for her brother – an intention foiled by the forgetful Felix. Cedric grinned into the dark. Just as well the lady was in the grave; she would never have forgiven him! A cruel thought, perhaps, but it sent him to sleep immediately.

After breakfast the following morning, Cedric took Phipps aside and casually asked if he had any further thoughts on the letter. 'I think you may have been going to suggest it was in code.'

The old man looked blank, 'In code, Professor? Oh, I wouldn't go so far as that. It may have codish qualities, but that is not the same as actually being in code.' Phipps regarded the other over the rims of his spectacles, and with a kindly smile added, 'I think we need to be precise in our terminology, don't you?'

Once more, the sixty-year-old Cedric was made to feel like a callow undergraduate.

'Er, well—' he began.

'No, not code as such. But as you rightly said, a studied obliqueness. Clearly she is using terms, metaphors, which her brother could be expected to grasp. No embroidery was needed. It's the sort of inconsequential note that many would dismiss, but which for people like ourselves alerts suspicion.'

The last word seemed almost savoured and Cedric wondered if the old boy was still digesting the previous night's crime drama. 'I take your point,' he said, 'but suspicion of what?'

Phipps gave a Gallic shrug and spread his hands. 'Ah

well, that's for the police to discover. We old buffers are merely outsiders exercising our curiosity. We are engaging in what I believe is now termed a spectator sport. Now, if you will excuse me, my Popsie is getting restless and it's time she and I had a little twirl around Market Place to see what titbits we can find.'

Cedric watched them go feeling mildly amused yet more than a little peeved. Was he really at the buffer stage? Surely not. He drew himself up, thrust back his shoulders and set off at military pace for the newsagent.

CHAPTER TWENTY

Back in Cambridge, Chief Inspector Ted Tilson had begun to feel more upbeat. His hunch about Hapworth and the Orford connection would seem to be right. Nathan had telephoned with some interesting news. The inspector handling the Southwold case had unearthed facts indicating that the murdered vicar may well have visited that area. A member of the Orford sect had mentioned a man calling himself Stephen Hepton being seen at two of their meetings. He had been accompanied by the woman subsequently attacked and smothered in her bed.

In itself the surname Hepton was unremarkable; nevertheless, it was a pleasing coincidence that it just happened to have been one of Hapworth's aliases from his London days.

From his high office window Tilson gazed down at the

slowly moving traffic in St Andrew's Street, and smiled. According to the Southwold inspector's informant, the stranger had hailed from Cambridge.

When Sergeant Hopkins entered a few minutes later with a mug of tea, the chief inspector was looking almost benign – smug, anyway. Hopkins put the tea down on his boss's desk and gave him an enquiring look. He cleared his throat. 'The super's happy with that robbery report, is he sir?'

'Robbery report?' Tilson said vaguely. 'Oh yes, Sergeant . . . yes, perfectly happy, as far as I'm aware. No doubt we should have heard were it otherwise,' he added grimly. 'But frankly we have a more pressing matter on our hands, do we not. I refer, of course, to the Hapworth case.'

Hopkins nodded. 'Any news on that front, sir?'

'As it happens, yes. Thanks to your researches and my thoughtful conjectures about the Orford link, it seems we have moved a pace forward.'

'Oh yes, so where are we now, then?'

Tilson proceeded to tell him what he had learnt from Nathan. When he had finished, Hopkins said, 'So, sir, two victims sighted together from different angles – what you might call a left and a right!'

'No, Hopkins,' Tilson replied gruffly, 'not being one addicted to the grouse moor or to clay pigeons, the term is not in my vocabulary. If you mean that we have managed to establish a definite link between Cambridge and Suffolk, Hapworth and Peebles, then you are right.'

'Not if he wasn't wearing a dog collar.'

'What?' Tilson snapped.

'Well, you say that he was in mufti: ordinary jacket and tie and he wore a moustache – which may or may not have been fake. Now, had he been clean shaven and in normal clerical kit we would have been on a stronger wicket. As it is, it strikes me that things are a bit . . .' Hopkins broke off, searching for the right word – 'uncertain,' he beamed.

The chief inspector regarded his sergeant narrowly, and then said, 'Tell me, Hopkins, when you were a kid playing party games did you often find you were the last one to be picked for a team?'

The other gave the question serious thought, and then said: 'On the whole, no. Both sides seemed to want me because I was good at being obstructive.'

In Southwold, meanwhile, Inspector Jennings was grappling with *Men Only* and Horace Dewthorp's drafted letter to his niece. It certainly suggested something fishy about Peebles' life, or at least surprising. He wondered again if the original had been completed and posted. The girl had been on a journalism course in America; if only the writer had mentioned where in America, they could probably have checked. As it was, there were probably hundreds of such courses: New York, Boston, Chicago, anywhere really. Besides, it didn't help not knowing her full name. Lily who? Dewthorp? Or was the relationship from the female side?

Jennings scowled, and then brightened. But by now she could well have returned to Cambridge as her uncle had evidently expected her to, he had been hoping to meet her there. Compared to the United States Cambridge was tiny, so surely to God they could find some track in that cosy milieu. She had sounded bright – so a postgraduate maybe at Newnham or Girton, or with luck already working on a newspaper.

Once more Jennings indulged in one of his fanciful reveries: they would find Lily, she would produce the full text of the letter and thus the details of Mrs Peebles' other life would be helpfully revealed. Like most dreams it quickly vanished. Nevertheless, he still felt the niece was worth pursuing. A long shot, but it might yield something. He would get Harris on the job and he could liaise with Cambridge.

Half an hour later, Sergeant Harris was in the office receiving instructions to seek out the girl. 'It may be a dead end, but it's only right that we explore every avenue,' the inspector said sternly.

Harris nodded vigorously. 'Couldn't agree more, sir. We don't want to be caught napping, do we.'

Jennings winced. 'It has nothing to do with being caught napping, it is a matter of principle and sound police work.'

While rereading Dewthorp's words Jennings had left the copy of *Men Only* on his desktop and open at the opulent photo of 'Miss Maisie' (as the model was dubbed). Harris glanced down, and then gave a sharp whistle. 'Cor, she's a bit of all right, that one. Very easy on the eye, I must say. In fact I wouldn't mind—'

'Be quiet,' Jennings snapped. 'We don't wish to hear your observations.'

'But you were enjoying it,' the other replied a trifle truculently.

'I was not. I was giving it my consideration, that's all,' Jennings said stiffly. 'I've already told you that it's in there the Dewthorp note was found, the two need to be filed together.

'Hmm,' Harris remarked, 'it's a pretty vintage issue, I should say. Not that she looks vintage, except for that silly little beret and those old-fashioned earrings. My mum had a pair like them before the war.'

Together they studied the silly beret and earrings. And then Harris began to chuckle and looked closer. 'You know, sir, you may think me daft, but she almost seems familiar. I can't help feeling I've seen her somewhere.'

Jennings gazed at the bosomy blonde, and shrugged. 'Familiar or not, I doubt if she appears quite like that these days.'

There was a sharp intake of breath from Harris, and the sergeant's jocular tone suddenly darkened as he said slowly: 'No, you're right. She wouldn't, sir. She wouldn't look like that at all . . . She's dead.'

It was the mole under the left eye that had caught Harris's attention, and convinced him that the busty Miss Maisie was in fact the younger Mary Peebles. There had been other features, of course – the wide mouth, high forehead, the slight cleft in the chin – but it was the mole that clinched it. He had noticed it when he had gone to deal with her complaint about boys scrumping her apples. He had seen it along with the haughty stare she had given him when he had advised her to invite them in to tea. That same stare was in the photograph, but on the younger face not quite so unnerving – a bit sexy, in fact.

'You are absolutely sure?' Jennings had demanded.

'Yes,' he had replied stoutly. 'I go to art lessons in the church hall. Mr Furblow gives them once a week after evensong and he teaches us to notice details.'

'Of sheep?' Jennings asked absently, still trying to digest the thought of Mary Peebles as a pin-up girl.

Harris shook his head and looked puzzled, as well he might.

After the sergeant had left, Jennings continued to gaze at the photograph before him, scrutinising the face Harris had been so certain was the victim's. He saw what he meant about the haughty stare: defiant, vaguely challenging. A come-on, perhaps, at that age. But in middle age? Not exactly. A slow smile began to spread across Jennings' face. He had seen Mrs Peebles only once before the tragedy, and that was when she had been in the newsagent's querying her bill. The stare had been on display then, and he remembered feeling glad that he wasn't the newsagent. But could they really be one and the same?

Hastily he reminded himself that haughty expressions were ten-a-penny – and yet there was something about the quizzical lift of the eyebrow and the curl of the mouth that brought to mind that particular one. And he certainly recalled the mole, a mark under her left eye as Harris had observed. He suspected it had enlarged since the pose in the photograph.

Shoving the magazine aside, Jennings went to the back window and stared out at the marsh. It sprawled before him empty and silent. A flight of birds fluttered past, and further off a kestrel circled for its supper. Simple, predictable activities; not like those of humans, which seemed so waywardly odd and perverse! He closed the window, and returning to his desk began to review matters.

What had he learnt? That Harris thought he recognised the girl in the photograph as being the murdered woman; that Dewthorp, looking at the same photograph, had also been startled by what he evidently saw as a resemblance. Why else should he have slipped the letter to his niece between its pages? Presumably because he had the picture to hand when writing his comments. But then, of course, those comments had not been confined to Mrs Peebles. In his little scenario for Lily's novel, Dewthorp had also enigmatically referred to another who shared her practice of concealment; one who also portrayed themselves as being decorous and seemly when in fact a past life hinted at something else.

Jennings looked down at his blotter; and then taking his biro idly wrote the name of the Reverend Stephen Hapworth M.A., embellishing it with rococo whirls and twirls. He was pleased with the effect. Sergeant Harris wasn't the only bloody artist! Obviously, he thought, it must be Hapworth. Stephen Hapworth, who in London had moved in dubious circles and who in Cambridge had donned a cassock, filched church funds and fumbled choirboys. Yes, that was the chap. To link the two of them might be arbitrary were it not for Joy Goodhart's assertion that a Stephen Hepton from Cambridge had been seen in Orford with Mary Peebles . . . Two birds with one stone? Yes, but in this case the two birds were not only the victims of brutal murder, but very possibly also the hypocrites about whom Horace Dewthorp had wanted his niece to write a novel. And why should Dewthorp have picked on Hapworth for one of the two characters? Because also living in Cambridge, and attached to one of the colleges, he was likely to have been aware of the cleric's developing reputation – could even have known him, perhaps. And disliked him? Probably.

So far so good (or goodish). At least now it would seem that the haughty Mary Peebles was not all she appeared – or had not been in the past. But was posing semi-nude in a racy magazine really so dreadful? Plenty of girls did it and there were far worse things. Surely in itself the activity wasn't enough to invite murder (unless from some crazed puritan). No, the modelling was more likely to be indicative of a wider, more ambiguous hinterland. A hinterland from which sprang the cause of her death? It was certainly conceivable, particularly as there appeared to have been that association with Hapworth.

On the other hand, he reflected wryly, his original idea may have been right – she had been exterminated by some wrathful religious rival driven barmy by her assertive ego, and who had resolved to stifle it once and for all. Gaye Goodhart?

Jennings smiled wearily and sighed loudly, stretched his arms above his head and leant back in his chair. He almost felt like putting his feet up on the desk but refrained. Chief Inspector Nathan might do that, but it wouldn't be suitable for a mere inspector. Besides, his legs were shorter. And in any case, dignity must be maintained in front of Harris at all costs. Instead, he opened his desk drawer and pensively consumed a Penguin biscuit. The cascade of crumbs put him in mind of the victim's kitchen and the missing dog. Where was it? Who had it? He sighed again. Life was full of such teasing perplexities.

CHAPTER TWENTY-ONE

As instructed, D.S. Harris contacted the Cambridge police and was put in touch with D.S. Hopkins. Hopkins and Harris had never met, but instantly struck a mutual chord, which set them chatting about their respective soccer teams and the fragility of their superiors' nerves.

When conversation lapsed, Harris raised the question of Lily, explaining why they hoped to find her. 'It may all be a wild goose chase,' he said encouragingly, 'but I'd be grateful if you would give it a go.'

Hopkins, still chuffed with his investigation of Hapworth's background, replied that he was an old hand at tracing people and that if the girl was anywhere in the area, he would be the one to find her. 'Leave it with me,' he said confidently.

The confidence was justified, for the next day he rang to

report that Lily had indeed been found and was working for a Cambridgeshire weekly newspaper. 'Her name is Dewthorp,' he explained, 'but these days she calls herself Lily Lopez as she thinks it will help her image as a budding crime writer.' Harris replied that whatever she chose to call herself, what mattered was whether she had received her uncle's letter suggesting a theme for her next plot.

The short answer was no. The girl had received no such letter and only wished she had. Although not knowing him well, she had been fond of her uncle and on returning to England had been very sorry to learn of his sudden death. She had asked Hopkins if she could read what Dewthorp had started to write as it might indeed spark an idea for a new novel. But he had explained that such material couldn't be released until a case was closed – which could of course take years. 'I told her she was bright enough to invent her own plots and not rely on other people's ideas,' he said to Harris, 'but she looked a bit miffed and gave me a funny look. It's these youngsters, they get hoity-toity.' The other had agreed, adding that in that respect they were a bit like senior officers.

Before the other rang off, Harris asked how they were getting on with the vicar murder. 'Slowly,' Hopkins had replied, but added that the form of despatch – the blow on the head followed by the public hanging – at least made a change from more commonplace attacks.

'Bound to be significant,' Harris had asserted.

'You think so? I don't. Entertainment most likely. I mean to say, if I was a professional hitman, I'd get pretty bored with all those slick back-alley knifings and quick headbashings. Routine can get you down. I think I might be looking for something more dramatic, more inventive. Not just your everyday killing, but something more elaborate – more artistic, you might say.'

Harris considered the observation, and then asked if the other felt that by being a policeman he had mistaken his métier. Would Hopkins be more comfortable as a Mafia boss, perhaps? 'I believe they do some pretty spectacular take-outs down in Calabria. That might be just up your street.'

Hopkins replied that he wouldn't have been suitable. 'That sort of thing runs in families, it's bred into you from childhood. I grew up in Surbiton, the Mafia would never have looked at me.' He sounded regretful.

Harris was just preparing to break the negative news about Lily to his boss, when he was grabbed by Bert Hill at the desk. 'Constable Bowden is off sick,' he said, 'and there's no one else available, so you'll have to go.'

'Go where?'

'To see about Miss Phipps's gun licence. It's run out, or she's lost it or something and she thinks she isn't legal. She's a bit het up. You know where she lives, don't you – that old white house on South Green not far from the cannons on Gun Hill.'

Detective Sergeant Harris was indignant. 'I do know where she lives but it is hardly my duty to be running after lapsed gun licences. Send someone else, I am far too busy to be dealing with that sort of stuff!'

'I am sure you are, sir,' Bert replied woodenly, 'but like

I said, there's nobody else just now. And Inspector Jennings thought you might like to stretch your legs after all that telephoning you've just been doing. A nice day for it too – all bright and breezy. You'll enjoy taking a little stroll up to the South Cliff.'

Harris glared at Bert and silently cursed Jennings. It would serve his boss right when he told him about the abortive Lily hunt!

At that moment, the inspector himself appeared and asked Harris what he had learnt from Cambridge. The latter took mild relish in telling him that he had learnt very little. 'They traced the girl, and she says she never got any letter.'

Jennings grunted. Well, it had been worth a try; and even if a fuller version had never existed, at least they still had the opening draft. Quite possibly the writer had intended to continue it but then fate intervened, as it frequently did . . . Not for the first time he lamented Dewthorp's fall and the perversity of circumstance.

These musings were broken by Harris who somewhat querulously asked about his instruction to deal with the gun licence.

'What? Oh no, you are needed elsewhere. One of the Goodhart twins has just rung to say that her bicycle was nicked when she was communing with nature on the common. She's convinced that it was one of the boys from the Eversley prep school there. The headmaster has also rung, furious at the accusation and wants to know what we propose to do about it. Unless we want blood on our hands you had better go and sort it out. I need to see Chief

Inspector Nathan, and if there's time I'll drop in on Miss Phipps before I go.'

Harris thought that dealing with a bloodletting spat between an enraged headmaster and a Goodhart twin was marginally more exciting (and within his dignity) than checking expired gun licences. Besides, if the twin in question happened to be the one called Joy, he could take the opportunity to ask her where she got the pink galoshes. He left hastily before the inspector could change his mind.

Picking up a new gun certificate from Bert, Jennings went back to his office to collect his briefcase. There was still an hour to go before his appointment with Nathan, and so there would be just enough time to fit in a visit to Miss Phipps. From what little he knew of the woman, she seemed the dependable type and not one to be remiss in renewing her licence (what did she shoot – marauding seagulls?). He was surprised by her oversight but since he had always found her agreeable, a quick visit was no penance. He visualised Sergeant Harris engaged on his current task and grinned.

Isabel was slightly taken aback to find the inspector at her front door. Goodness, was the matter so serious to need a visit from the hierarchy? Noting her surprise, Jennings explained that they were short-staffed. 'And I have drawn the short straw,' he joked.

She started to apologise for her carelessness, saying she was afraid the thing was a good month out of date, but she had had a lot on her mind recently and it wasn't the only piece of paperwork that had been overlooked. She lowered her voice: 'I have two guests to look after, one being my brother from Cambridge. He's an elderly professor and very exacting. It rather flusters me sometimes!'

Jennings smiled sympathetically and followed her into a little study partly curtained from the main room, and where the matter was quickly completed. She had brought the gun downstairs for him to check, and he enquired where she kept the cartridges. 'Not with it, I trust?'

'Oh no,' had been the blithe reply, 'in my knicker drawer.'

Having given such assurance, she asked if he would like a coffee. Slightly pink in the face he was about to politely decline when a voice from a few yards away said, 'Aha, did someone mention coffee? That would be most acceptable, don't you agree, Dillworthy? Most acceptable – especially when taken with one of Southwold's senior law officers!' Isabel shot the senior law officer a helpless look and ushered him into the larger room to meet the two guests.

After brief introductions, Aldous Phipps remarked with only mild sarcasm: 'A fortunate amendment. Now we can sleep peacefully, safe in the knowledge that should we be so unlucky as to be shot, at least the weapon will be legal.' He beamed at his sister who, po-faced, went off to deal with the coffee.

Cedric frowned. Considering that the inspector was handling the dreadful Peebles killing, the professor's 'joke' seemed somewhat ill-timed. He studied the officer, feeling awkward. Should he mention that he was a close friend of Felix Smythe – the 'lodger in the case' and a key witness? Such gratuitous information might look pushy and out of place. And yet if Jennings should later learn of their link, to withhold the fact might make him appear unduly evasive.

Such deliberation was cut short by Jennings himself, who, turning to Cedric, said, 'Ah, yes of course, Professor, it's with you and Dr Loader that Mr Smythe is staying in Blythburgh. We saw him there a couple of days ago. I believe he is currently in London supervising his flower business. A tricky time for him – and I imagine for you. A nasty business altogether, I'm afraid. Very nasty.'

That would have been the end of the subject had it not been for the intervention of Aldous Phipps. With a brisk clearing of throat he said, 'I gather from the local paper that the police are requesting anyone who may have observed something unusual on the night in question to come forward. Well, I might just—'

'So that lets you out, Aldous, doesn't it,' Isabel interrupted briskly as she returned with the coffee, 'you weren't even here when it happened.'

Phipps gave her a cold stare before resuming his point. 'I was going to say, Inspector, that although – as my sister so thoughtfully points out – I was naturally in no position to see anything, I do have certain general observations, which may or may not be relevant to your enquiry.'

There was a polite silence as the old man savoured his coffee.

Oh God, thought Isabel, *I suppose he's going to hold forth.*

Anyone would think he was conducting a seminar, thought Cedric.

How am I going to cut him off while still sounding polite? thought Jennings.

Assured of the inspector's attention, Phipps set down his cup and said: 'First of all, I must declare my interests in this little affair. In Cambridge I happen to have been acquainted with the unfortunate Mrs Peebles' erstwhile guest Horace Dewthorp, who, alas, recently died here. I also knew, albeit slightly, the cleric Hapworth, whose grisly fate is naturally the talk of town and gown. The one gentleman I considered questionable, the other unremarkable but sound. The cleric's death, and especially its manner shocks me; Dewthorp's saddens and – I have to say – perplexes me.'

Isabel sighed. 'Why are you perplexed, Aldous? We all know he fell off the cliff chasing that wretched dog of hers.'

'All know, my dear? Who knows?'

His sister shrugged impatiently, 'Well, the police and everyone. And it was in the local paper.' She looked at Jennings for confirmation. Jennings said nothing, apparently transfixed by his coffee.

At the time, the cause of Dewthorp's death had seemed obvious – he had slipped when running after the dog and fell headlong over the cliff. Lead and dog whistle were found near the body. He had hit his head and died from heart failure. On the face of it, the thing had seemed one of those unfortunate but not uncommon accidents. Death by misadventure, the coroner had recorded. There had been nothing to suggest otherwise . . . Such were the thoughts that crowded Jennings' mind as he carefully stirred his coffee, avoiding Isabel's eye. Inexplicably, the old man's beady look and the trenchant tone of his question had bothered him, had wakened a nascent doubt, which he now realised had been nagging him for some while, though he couldn't say why. Perhaps this professor could. He stopped stirring and looked up at Phipps.

'You see,' the latter continued, 'from what I have observed of our canine friends, unlike the Gadarene swine they have an innate instinct to veer away from the rim of steep cliffs and not throw themselves off in an access of zeal – though their owners sometimes fear they might. No, I doubt if the little thing was in danger of falling. And even if Dewthorp had thought so, the creature is likely to have swerved and held back.' Phipps emitted a wry laugh. 'My little Popsie most certainly would! And so even if Dewthorp had tripped, he would simply have landed flat on the turf, not on the rocks below.'

'But supposing the pursuer were running so fast that even if the dog stopped, he couldn't?' Isabel asked.

Her brother raised a quizzical eyebrow. 'Rather improbable, I should have thought. A man of sixty with a dicky heart is unlikely to be sprinting for England.'

Switching his brief attention, Phipps turned back to Jennings. 'The other thing that strikes me as a trifle odd about the incident is that Dewthorp should have been carrying a dog whistle – I gather one was found near the body. Anyone would think that his charge was a fox terrier or rampant springer likely to career over hill and dale, not some piffling miniature Yorkie with a red bow and short legs. A sharp command would normally be enough. As far as one is aware, Dewthorp didn't have a dog of his own, so presumably the whistle belonged to Mrs Peebles, though why she bothered to give it to him, I can't imagine – unless somebody else did, of course. Either way, an extraneous item, I should have thought.'

Phipps bent down to pat Popsie. 'You don't need a whistle do you, little girl? And you're much bigger than a titchy Yorkshire!' The slightly larger Norfolk looked up and then, perhaps assured of her superiority, promptly went to sleep again.

Jennings had listened to Phipps's commentary without expression but was inwardly disturbed. So what was the old boy saying? That given a dog's alleged aversion to heights, Dewthorp's fall was due to some other cause, e.g. he may have stood too near the edge and suffered an attack of vertigo; he had been trying to reach a wildflower and slipped; or it had been a suicide jump, after all. But why all this stuff about the dog whistle? Because it didn't fit the scene, it was out of place. That's what Phipps had seemed to be saying: that the man's fall had been engineered, stage-managed; and the whistle had been simply an intrusive prop placed by someone who wished him dead . . . Hmm. Interesting. But was it plausible? A fanciful conjecture, surely.

'Well,' Isabel said briskly, 'that's fascinating, Aldous, and I'm sure the inspector is always grateful for the views of the laity' – the term was lightly stressed – 'but we mustn't detain him, must we. He's bound to have pressing things to do. Though I like to think it won't be anything so trivial as chasing up recalcitrant licence holders!' She laughed and stood up, and glancing at his watch, Jennings said he must fly.

After he had left, Isabel retreated to the kitchen to

prepare lunch and to indulge in a stiff gin. Really, who did Aldous think he was – Sherlock Holmes? It was all those crime dramas he had taken to watching. She wished she had never shown him the television!

Like the other two listeners, Cedric was also sceptical of Phipps's hypothesis. It was all pretty speculative and seemed to hinge largely on the psychology of dogs and the usefulness of dog whistles! Still, however tenuous, speculation could often be a signpost to truth. It was just possible that Aldous was on to something, though he rather doubted it.

What was it the old boy had said to him the other day? Something about engaging in a spectator sport. Was that what it was all about? Stirred by the Cambridge and Southwold scandals, was he now seeking further 'sport' to feed that agile mind? Cedric recalled how at Isabel's dinner party he had talked of the 'Company of Coincidence', that in the case of the three recent deaths, not only had he been acquainted with two of the victims, Hapworth and Dewthorp, but it was ironic that they too had apparently known each other. Yes, the links had amused him. So, was he now trying to embellish the triangle by implying that Dewthorp's death had also been sinister? Quite possibly. The old could be fanciful. It was something he must guard against in his own twilight years.

But once upstairs in his room Cedric felt a twinge of guilt at being so dismissive of the old man's theory. Phipps might have a mischievous mind but he was no fool. His analysis of the Peebles letter had been interesting and certainly supported his own view that there had been something vaguely artificial about it. So, who knew, perhaps that argument about the dog wasn't so crazy. His thoughts returned to the letter: was it really relevant? Well, that was anyone's guess – and the people to make that guess were the police, not a pair of obtrusive outsiders. It was Jennings & Co. who should make the assessment. Perhaps he ought to produce it for them even without Felix's permission . . . Or should he? It seemed a bit unfair and the dear boy might be furious.

Angry at such dithering, Cedric stared gloomily at his reflection in the mirror. The face confronting him was no longer that of a young man, far from it. Perhaps after all he and Aldous were just a couple of elderly dons playing at detectives and seeing innuendo and coded references where none existed. Besides, even if they were right about the letter, did it matter? Perhaps Mrs Peebles and her brother had been in the habit of exchanging enigmatic notes, it was part of some elaborate word game they played. A game in which Felix had fouled up the final clues.

Such vexations were interrupted by the loud crashing of a gong – clearly his harassed hostess summoning him to lunch. Hastily adjusting his tie and adopting a jovial face, Cedric descended to join his companions.

CHAPTER TWENTY-TWO

That evening, as soon as supper was over, Isabel went to bed with a sleeping draught. It wasn't something she normally took, but for some reason in the last two nights she had slept badly. 'I deserve the sleep of the just,' she told them, 'and I'm damn well going to have it.' Pausing at the door, she suggested that they might like to get on with the jigsaw puzzle. They nodded politely and wished her goodnight.

When she was safely gone, Aldous looked at Cedric. 'Get out the playing cards, Dillworthy, I think a little cribbage is in order, don't you? Unless of course you would prefer snap.' Cedric hastily opted for cribbage and the two colleagues rapidly became engrossed.

A little later, just as they broke off to enjoy a glass of whisky, there was a rap on the front door. Phipps pulled a face. 'Now who can that be at this time of night – Jehovah's

Witnesses? Or perhaps one of those tiresome political canvassers. We are besieged with them in Cambridge, they're even worse than the Witnesses.' He asked Cedric if he wouldn't mind seeing who it was.

Cedric went to the porch, and on opening the door was confronted by a tall, burly figure. He had heard enough from Felix about Harold Dagwood to guess immediately who the man was. Dagwood removed his hat and smilingly enquired if Miss Phipps was at home. Cedric told him that she was, but unfortunately had retired early. He asked if he could take a message to give to her in the morning. Still smiling, Dagwood replied that that wouldn't be necessary and that he would come in anyway. Before Cedric had a chance to say or do anything, the man was inside and standing with his back to the now closed door.

'Look here,' Cedric protested, 'I don't think—'

'That's all right, Mr Dillworthy. This won't take long, but I'd like to have a word with you and the other professor, if you don't mind.' In themselves the words were perfectly civil but it was their tone that was offensive – curt and offhand.

'That would not be convenient,' Cedric replied stiffly.

'Tough,' Dagwood suddenly snapped. 'Now lead the way, I haven't got all night.'

It was pointless to resist and Cedric did as he was bid. Being in front of the other he was able to give Phipps a frowning wink as they entered the sitting room, a warning the old man was quick to grasp. 'So,' the latter enquired drily, 'to what do we owe this pleasure?'

'The pleasure of returning my letter, the one that my sister wrote and which that fool Smythe never posted,' Dagwood suddenly snarled, all pretence of affability gone. 'The letter that you two seemed so fascinated by. Whatever's in it, I can bet that in the wrong hands it won't be to my profit. And it certainly isn't to yours. Those who snoop and talk about snitching to the police must take the consequences.' His lip curled.

Aldous Phipps blinked. 'Er, well we do have such a letter, and of course you are welcome to take it, if it means so much to you. But may I ask how you know of it and indeed of Mr Smythe's mistake?'

'I know about a lot of things, Professor, you have to in my line of business.' Dagwood gave a jeering laugh. 'Walls have ears, as we used to say in the war, and it's amazing what can be overheard by those sharp enough to listen.'

Grimly recalling their conversation in the crowded café, Cedric opened his briefcase. 'Here, take the stupid thing and get out. We've had enough of this!'

Dagwood snatched the letter. 'Get out? Hmm, that's a bit premature. There's something else I need to attend to, but first I'll have a glass of your nice whisky. It's been a hard day.' He strode to the decanter on the sideboard. Cedric was incensed and protested, but slightly to his surprise Phipps said quickly, 'Oh no, I think we can spare a little of that. Mr Dagwood looks as if he could do with a tot, though I fear it's only a blend.' He smiled graciously at the intruder.

The brute looked slightly taken aback by such compliance, but poured himself a generous glass and started to read the letter. When he had finished, he thrust it into his wallet and muttered something. It could have been 'ow' but sounded more like 'cow'.

'I am calling the police,' Cedric declared, 'this is disgraceful.'

'You'll be lucky, old boy, I cut the wire before I came in.' Their guest drew a penknife from his pocket and waved it mockingly. But the smile vanished as he withdrew something else; something he did not wave but levelled menacingly: a small, neat pistol. 'Amazing how handy these things are,' he said coldly.

There was silence as the two captives – for that was clearly what they were – gave it their sober regard. 'People who try to mess with my plans live to regret it. Regret, at any rate,' Dagwood added ominously. 'I've got too much at stake and can't afford to take risks, even with old fools like you.'

Stifling his fury and with supreme self-control, Cedric asked him what he proposed to do.

'I am about to go to London, and you are coming with me. We'll drop you off along the way.' He spoke with steely menace.

Hearing those last words, Cedric's anger changed to a rising fear as their implications sunk in. Until that moment, and despite the pistol, he had persuaded himself that for some reason the intruder was mounting a gross charade, a crude attempt to inspire terror. But now he knew otherwise. He meant every word, and he evidently wasn't alone. The man was clearly barking, horribly unhinged; but somewhere there lurked accomplices. Two against how many? They didn't stand a chance. Cedric swallowed, and retaining his calm, he enquired who the 'we' were. 'Your pals, presumably?'

'Pals? No, they're not pals – more like adjutants, they do what I tell them.'

'And so where are these gallant helpers now?' Phipps enquired quietly.

Dagwood nodded towards the conservatory. 'Tim's in there, Tom's out front in the car. They are waiting for my signal.'

'The signal to go off to London and take us with you?'

'That's it, squire. Go to the top of the class.' For some reason, the man seemed to think the riposte rather funny, and with a chuckle poured himself another large whisky. He sat down on the sofa and lit a cigar, the pistol, however, stayed close to hand. Nevertheless, he was visibly more relaxed and seemed in no hurry to make a move or give a signal to his waiting 'adjutants'.

Seeing the tension subside, Cedric wondered how long that ease could be sustained. In the films, captives played for time, knowing that rescue was at hand – was that what Phipps was doing? The prisoners would spin things out, getting the aggressor to talk until, lo and behold, the cavalry or Gary Cooper arrived over the hill and all was safe. *Well*, he thought grimly, *that wasn't going to happen here . . . unless of course Isabel rose from her drugged sleep and tottered downstairs for a glass of water. Not that that would help anything.*

Yet despite such gloom, he was curious about the letter. Although they had been puzzled by it, clearly it held a significance deeper than either he or Aldous had grasped. If the man was prepared to kill to get possession of it, what revelations had he feared it might hold? What was it that was making him so rash . . . and so dangerous?

As it happened, whether the result of the whisky or the effects of his 'hard day', Harold Dagwood suddenly seemed in the mood to chat, unprompted by anyone. He took the

Peebles letter from his wallet, glanced again at it briefly, grimaced and then folded it into his inside pocket.

'Yes,' he mused, 'a strange girl my sister – complex, you might say. Still, that's all over now and I suppose she's at peace. Funny the way things go . . .' The rough voice took on a puzzled, pensive note. Despite his revulsion, for an absurd second Cedric almost felt sorry for him. 'Still,' he continued briskly, 'I dealt with Hapworth all right, taught that bugger a lesson. A nice little drama it was. Oh yes, very nice!'

Hapworth? What's he got to do with things? Cedric thought. And then he gasped. 'You are not saying it was you who killed him are you! But why, for God's sake – and why in that frightful way?'

For a few moments Dagwood chewed thoughtfully on his cigar. And then he said, 'Oh no, I didn't go near the chap. You don't think I'd be mug enough to play silly beggars like that, do you? But yes, I did issue orders – though I agree, the manner was a trifle unsubtle, but that was the London boys. They had a grudge, he had shopped one of their mates, and I think they relished the drama. Very slick operators they are – learnt it all in the Scrubs – and told me the job couldn't have been easier. "Well," I said to them, "if you say so."' Dagwood flicked his cigar ash and gave a snort of laughter.

'I see,' Cedric said bleakly. 'But, ah, these orders which you issued – may I ask what was their purpose?'

'Purpose? To get rid of the bastard, of course. I should have thought that would be obvious, Professor.' Dagwood turned to the other professor and gave a broad wink. Wisely,

Phipps merely gave a frigid smile and remained silent.

Ignoring the sarcasm, Cedric persisted. 'Oh indeed, obvious. But why was his disposal so imperative? From what one has heard, although clearly distasteful, he was hardly a major threat to anybody – in fact rather third-class, I should say.'

'You would say that, would you? Well I can tell you, my friend, that this third-class little shit was getting on my nerves. He actually—'

'Oh yes,' Aldous Phipps broke in earnestly, 'these lesser types are good at that. I remember once having a student who drove me absolutely insane. Kept interrupting my tutorial with damn-fool questions. He thought he was the cat's whiskers. But I did for him in the end.'

'What? Strung him up, do you mean?' Cedric asked drily.

'No, but I got him sent down. Quite a neat little manoeuvre, I recall.' Phipps nodded with evident satisfaction.

Somewhat dazed, Dagwood stared at the old man. But before he could say anything, the professor continued: 'Now, Mr Dagwood, do tell us more about this rotter Hapworth. Apparently more dangerous than one would think.' He raised an enquiring eyebrow.

Harold Dagwood was unused to being examined by elderly academics. But he was now on to his third whisky, and given the chance to destroy his victim for a second time and to assert his own ego, he said: 'As you would evidently agree, idiots can overestimate their value. Stephen Hapworth was a paltry piece of work but he possessed certain talents and was therefore useful to my enterprises. Unfortunately for him, he overestimated both his talents and his usefulness. He got above himself.' Dagwood paused to relight his cigar and sprawled back in his chair.

Cedric questioned gently how far above himself, and was told impatiently in every bloody way that he cared to think of. 'The fool had the brass neck to think he could put the frighteners on me – to blackmail me in the same way he had the other sods. The effing cheek of it!' For a moment Dagwood's swagger was replaced by cold fury; his eyes narrowed and jaw tightened. It wasn't an attractive sight.

'Absurd,' Aldous Phipps murmured.

If the remark contained irony, Dagwood did not hear it, for he continued angrily. 'Exactly. Absurd. But unfortunately he was just sharp enough to be dangerous, and I wasn't having that. Oh no. You don't mess with H.R. Dagwood.'

Despite being only too alert to their own danger, Cedric couldn't help being intrigued by the link between the vicar and Dagwood. It seemed an unlikely combination. Casually he enquired how the two had met, and in what way he had found the vicar useful.

The question seemed to have a calming effect, for a slow smile crept across Dagwood's face; and in a quieter tone he explained that they had come across each other just before the war in a dive off Compton Street. 'The Pink Partridge, it was – all the best boys went there. And the worst. I expect you and your florist friend knew it,' he added casually.

The remark stung Cedric and he was about to snap a cold negative when he was forestalled by Phipps. 'Oh, but everyone went there,' he exclaimed, 'boys, girls, dowagers, chimney sweeps, the military. My younger sister was a member for a time, but she became convinced they had started to water the cocktails. Perhaps she was right; I believe it was closed down not long after – or did a bomb get it?' He beamed at Dagwood. 'Anyway, happy days, eh? Happy days!' And as if to resurrect the happiness, he withdrew a slim cigarette case from an inside pocket, and lighting an Abdulla proceeded to puff discreetly.

For a few moments both Cedric and Dagwood regarded their white-haired companion in startled silence. And then in a tone of rare civility, the latter agreed that those days could certainly have been a lot worse. 'Mind you, they did get worse, didn't they? But not for yours truly – or at least, not after the Yanks came over. Huh! You could sell 'em anything. And then afterwards there was all the black market stuff and, er, other lucrative lines. Then things really took off and got me where I am today: what some would term a successful entrepreneur of "unorthodox" methods.' He leered. 'And, I might remind you, a top-ranking member of the local Rotary!' He gave a shout of laughter and waved his cigar.

'And a crook and a murderer?' Cedric asked quietly.

Given the situation, it was a stupid thing to say, and Cedric was annoyed at his own thoughtlessness. Instantly the mirth vanished and was replaced by an icy stare. But again it was Phipps who intervened: 'Circumstances alter cases,' he told Cedric sternly, 'and there are times when pragmatism is all. Isn't that so, Mr Dagwood?' The latter looked blank but nodded vaguely. 'So, tell us about

Hapworth, and how you handled him.' The reedy voice assumed an ingratiating note. It was a handy cue, one that elicited a vigorous and expansive response. Cedric sensed that the man was enjoying himself. The swaggering self-regard was appalling. Had the situation been less fraught it might have seemed pathetic.

As he had earlier mentioned, Dagwood had met Hapworth in the Soho nightclub. He had pursued him there to pick a quarrel over a girl he was dating. But it seemed the girl had been of little account and not really worth the kerfuffle. In fact, to his surprise, he had found the young Hapworth considerably more engaging. He had enjoyed the youthful wit, the carefully cultivated manners, his readiness to buy the drinks – and above all, his apparent lack of any moral persuasion or backbone. Such a type might be useful to Dagwood's burgeoning business interests. As he indeed proved to be. At the time of their meeting, though well educated, the young man had been a social drifter with no secure job or goal: able but unfocused. His main talent – and, it seemed, pleasure – lay in minor embezzlement and petty blackmail; a bent which Dagwood had been quick to exploit for his own purposes. In this respect, and in other ways, Hapworth had become a useful lackey in ensuring the smooth running of the other's London enterprises (exploitative rackets would be the cruder term).

At this point Dagwood paused in his narrative and frowned. 'You would have thought that should have been enough, the chap had found a role and was being decently paid for it. He was one of my watchdogs – Steve the Sniffer,

I used to call him. But then do you know what the bugger went and did? He got ordained – yes, became a vicar! Well, I can tell you, that took the wind out of my sails all right. Tickled my arse with a feather, it did!' He gave a wry chuckle, and grinding out his cigar asked Phipps for an Abdulla. 'I fancy one of those – haven't had that sort since I was a boy. Used to smoke them with my sister in the attic – though she preferred the gyppos. Said they were more refined. Typical.'

With a silken smile Phipps obliged. 'And then what?' he enquired benignly, 'a trifle tricky, I imagine. I mean if he had a call from God, didn't that rather interfere with your business arrangements?'

'No, surprisingly not. That vocation, or whatever it's called, was just a cover, a convenient means of securing respectability and status; a way of worming himself into "polite" society. By being a clergyman, he felt safe and could enjoy a deference – something he never got from me. Nobody gets that from me, least of all a creepy little toad like that.' Dagwood gave an indignant snort.

Aldous Phipps nodded with apparent approval. 'And so what happened?' he asked.

'What happened was that he left London for Cambridge, got installed in a parish there, sucked up to the bigwigs of town and gown, and to augment his stipend practised a bit of blackmail on the side. Probably gave him a buzz, a change from all that holy church stuff. He kept a few sprats for himself but the big fish he would pass on to me for a commission, a bit like in London.' He paused, and with a laugh said: 'You know, he had grown quite fly by then and

247

had actually started to hear confessions like the RCs do. I gather there was quite a regular clientele. He told me that most of the stuff was dull as hell. Still, now and again there would be something juicy and with good mileage. He would supply the names and I would investigate, and if I thought it was worth my while I'd take the appropriate action . . . Yes, it was a nice little setup and worked well for a time.

'He would come up occasionally to discuss the names, review matters and collect his cut. We would meet in Orford and do business over lunch at The Crown – which suited me better than him turning up at my place in Aldeburgh. It suited him too, because he had got wind of that religious bunch that Mary was attached to and felt if he could insert himself among them he might find some rich pickings – like one of the devout ladies peddling dope or the chairman with his pants down. You know the kind of thing, the louder the virtue the cruder the vice.' Dagwood gave a loud guffaw and dropped his cigarette butt on the Chinese rug, where it lay smouldering before being extinguished by his heel. Cedric winced, imagining Isabel's fury.

'Well,' he continued, 'I doubted if there would be much chance of that, they always sounded a dreary lot to me. But he seemed keen, so I suggested that Mary could introduce him. They had known each other in London – not that she had ever liked him, and at first wouldn't play ball. But then she changed tack. She had become envious of some woman who was tipped to take the current leader's place when it should rightfully be hers, or so she believed. God almighty, they get paranoid, don't they! Anyway, she seemed to think that Hapworth might be able to dig up some dirt and put the frighteners on her. So he started to attend their meetings.

'But then the fool went and blew it all: wanted more money "commensurate with my worth and status".' Dagwood had assumed a mincing voice. 'Huh! And not just for that particular line, but – can you believe it? – a fifty per cent cut in all my operations. Well naturally, I told him precisely where he could shove that idea. And was that the end of it? No, it was not. He was stupid enough to start making threats, said if I didn't agree he knew what to do and that I'd better watch out as things could get embarrassing.'

Dagwood broke off, and turning to Cedric, expostulated, 'So would you have stood for that?'

Cedric shook his head dumbly.

'Well neither did I; risks like that are a mug's game. Besides, I wasn't going to have my life turned over by that grasping little toerag, so I brought in the heavies. And Bob's your uncle, he was gone. Like I said, nobody messes with H.R. Dagwood Esq!'

The esquire leant back in his chair, flushed and somewhat breathless. Then, with a curt nod at Phipps, said, 'I'll have another of those Turks if you've got any.' With the merest hesitation Phipps produced his case. It contained a solitary cigarette, which Dagwood took. Watching the operation, Cedric thought it was the first time the old man's face had registered any concern.

Listening to these revelations, Cedric had been sickened. What a pair! One was an arrogant thug who thought he was Hercules or Al Capone, the other had been a sleazy hypocrite feeding off the fallible. Both were repellent. Still, he reminded himself, moral distaste wasn't going to solve the practical problem of what the hell to do next. The man's insouciant despatch of Hapworth hardly boded well for their own fate, especially since the man had taken such obvious pride in divulging his crimes. You don't admit to murder and then let your audience go free. Especially if you have henchmen in the offing.

He glanced at Phipps, who, evidently resigned to the loss of his last cigarette, was now gazing into space apparently lost in a world of his own. Cedric found himself admiring the old man's sangfroid in the face of such danger, and his sly efforts to engage politely with the Dagwood maniac. All the same, he thought, he must be feeling pretty tense, and given his age and frailty was bound to crack at some point.

It was just then that Phipps spoke. 'I visited a brothel once' he announced conversationally. 'It was just after the Great War when I was in Cairo; one of their better ones – or so they told me. But, of course, in those days one was too callow to note the niceties . . . though I do remember the management were charming – yes, most obliging. Tell me, was the bordello trade also one of your London operations, Mr Dagwood? I imagine competition in the metropolis must have been quite fierce. Still is, presumably.' He cocked his head slightly, looking not unlike a wizened and inquisitive fox terrier.

Rather like a bemused bulldog, Dagwood gazed back nonplussed, eyes bulging. 'Er, yes . . .' he said slowly, 'now you mention it, one did dabble a bit – in fact quite a lot, early on. But as you say, things got congested and it didn't seem worth the trouble. The protection game was a surer bet.' He paused, and added, 'Besides, Mary was being difficult and said she'd had enough. According to her, the wrong class of tart was applying, and she had no intention of managing an inferior setup. I tried to persuade her to keep at it, but she said she was bored with London and wanted a change and some sea air. Naturally, I suggested Brighton – she'd have made a nice little packet there. But no, she was set on Southwold – said it had a refinement I wouldn't grasp.'

Even Aldous Phipps looked astonished. He blinked, and then said 'Are you saying that Mrs Peebles had been a madam? You do surprise me. I think Professor Dillworthy's friend found her a trifle starchy.' He turned to Cedric, 'Wasn't that so?'

Before Cedric could reply, there was an outburst from Dagwood. 'Starchy? You can say that again. There was enough starch in her to fill a laundry!' For a moment his face flushed angrily, then in a milder tone he said, 'Funny, really, because as a girl she'd been good fun, full of dash and vim. Tough as old boots, mind, but fun all the same. She was helpful, too, with my other enterprises; had some shrewd ideas. We made a good team in those days. But then, after she'd sent that fool of a husband packing, she seemed to change – became sort of colder and more critical. Less easy-going, more . . .' he hesitated, 'more dictatorial. And then she got entangled with that religious group over in Orford, God knows why. But she took it seriously enough, or seemed to.' He shook his head and frowned, and then murmured, 'Yes, that was the problem – too damn seriously. If it hadn't been for that caper, things might have . . .' He stopped and shrugged.

'Might have what?' Cedric ventured.

'Been different,' Dagwood replied sardonically. 'As it was, she had to get rid of the Dewthorp cove.'

Cedric nodded. 'Ah yes, didn't he move out to some place near the pier?'

This was met with a snort of laughter. 'Yes, you're right, but he still had to be got rid of.'

For a couple of seconds Cedric was unclear what he meant. But then meaning dawned and he stared aghast. 'You're not saying she killed him, are you!'

'That's about it, old son. Needs must, as they say; especially if you have become a pillar of the establishment.' Having taken the last Abdulla, Dagwood selected another of his own cigars and proceeded to clip the end.

CHAPTER TWENTY-THREE

In the ensuing silence the first thought that tumbled into Cedric's mind was to do with Felix.

Naturally his friend had been horrified to discover he had been so close to the murderous intruder, but to learn that he had been under the roof of not just one killer but two, would shatter him! Yet despite his present alarm, Cedric's mouth twitched ever so slightly, knowing full well that after the shock Felix would dine out on the tale for months – years, no doubt.

But instantly such levity vanished. Dine out? Would he and Felix ever meet again to enjoy the tale? If this moronic thug had his way, never. He closed his eyes and felt sick.

'So, if you don't mind my asking, what exactly were those needs?' Aldous Phipps asked softly.

'She was fearful he would dig up her old brothel

activities. He was a nosy little bastard and he had somehow got wind of her earlier life in London. I gather from what Mary said that she had found a half-finished letter in his bedroom together with a photo of herself posing for *Lilliput* or one of those mags years ago. It was written to his niece, some girl with ambitions to becoming a journalist and crime writer. Apparently, he thought the discrepancy between Mary's past and current image highly diverting, and had suggested the niece explore the idea with the aim of making it the basis of a novel – or, Mary feared, even a newspaper article. I don't think there was any malice or hint of blackmail, he just sounded intrigued and amused. But Mary was furious, and more to the point, she was worried. If it became public, either deliberately or otherwise, then her precious reputation in Southwold, let alone among the Orford crew, would be scuppered. Personally, it wouldn't have mattered much to me. But what did matter was that if this young reporter started to investigate, then other things might emerge to do with me and my "pristine" activities in the smoke. It's amazing how one thing can lead to another – like fun and childbirth, you might say.' He glanced at the po-faced Cedric and winked.

It was not an observation Cedric would have made, but he took the point about the domino effect and the precariousness of secrecy. 'But did she push him over?' he asked, unable to visualise the scene.

'No, but she engineered it. Asked me to recommend someone for the job. As it happened, I had just the man.' Dagwood grinned. 'One of the chaps that had dealt with Hapworth. The two of them came up here for a powwow and reconnaissance. We discussed logistics but weren't getting very far; and then Mary caught chickenpox and took to her bed. And that was when she had the idea about the perishing dog and getting Dewthorp to exercise it. Yes, she could be bright like that, you know. Wasted talents. She should have stayed in London . . .' Dagwood cast a rueful glance at the ceiling, as if recalling the deceased's lost potential.

'Anyway,' he went on, 'I was pretty dubious about the whole thing. But she directed the operation from her sickbed and the thing worked just as arranged. Tim stopped Dewthorp to ask the time and engage him in conversation; then at the right moment gave him a rabbit punch and tipped him over. And that was that.'

Despite his revulsion, Cedric's literal mind demanded details. 'How could he be sure he was dead?' he asked sternly.

'Tim's nobody's fool and he had brought a revolver just in case the chap was still kicking. If so, he would have slipped on his glove and plugged him and thrown the gun over to look like a cack-handed suicide. Not that it would have fooled the police for long as they wouldn't find the victim's dabs, but at least he wouldn't be alive to talk. Anyway, it didn't matter because when Tim peered over the edge, he could see that the blighter was definitely dead. Head smashed and neck broken. He then hopped into Tom's waiting car and they took off pronto back to London.'

'But wasn't it rather risky in broad daylight?' Phipps enquired.

'Only up to a point. That bit of the coast doesn't attract

many people, and it was a weekday with the kids in school and residents at work or doing the shopping. Tom was the lookout and would have hit the horn if he had seen anyone.' Dagwood paused, and then added, 'Besides, the boys have always enjoyed a bit of risk. It's the drama, gets them excited. Something to do with adrenaline or whatever it's called. Like with the Hapworth job, it amused them no end.'

There was a further silence while he smoked and regarded them speculatively.

Aldous Phipps cleared his throat. 'Talking of risks,' he said, 'might I risk asking if I could pour myself a glass of my sister's sherry? At this point in the evening I always find a dry manzanilla most refreshing.' He looked hopefully towards the drinks cabinet.

'Help yourself, cock,' was Dagwood's lavish response, 'It'll probably be your last.'

Despite the impassive face, Cedric saw Phipps stiffen as he walked slowly towards the cabinet, and with a slightly shaky hand pour himself a sherry. He took a sip.

He then suddenly swung round and said: 'And if I am not mistaken, I suppose you did your sister in as well.' The suave politesse had gone, and in its wake was a challenging voice of cold, withering scorn. Thin, not loud, but acid in its effect.

Cedric was shocked, not so much by the allegation than at the change in Phipps. Time had done a nosedive and he saw Aldous Phipps not as a fey doddering don of ancient years, but one who in his youth must have been the scourge of Trinity – or certainly its debating society – even perhaps among the English hierarchy in Cairo.

Dagwood too seemed shocked, and for a moment the airy nonchalance wavered. But then, collecting himself, he said casually: 'Got it in one, old man; she had become a bore. I couldn't stand the bitch.'

'Ah, bores and bitches – we are beset by many such irritants, Mr Dagwood. But extermination seems a trifle extreme; tiring too, I imagine. Tell me, did your sister belong to a special category of bore?' Phipps's tone had resumed its usual polite urbanity as if he were conducting a viva.

'If you mean why did I have her killed, the answer is I had to. Couldn't afford not to. Hapworth was a danger but he was small in comparison to her. Like I said, the girl had changed. We had used to work well together but she was becoming increasingly difficult and demanding. Ruthless, you might say. She wanted to control and dictate everything, every single thing – as you will have doubtless gathered from this patronising note that your friend kindly screwed up.' He patted his inside pocket. 'Ticks here, bossy orders there. Just like some bloody schoolmistress! And all that fake bilge about her roses. So clever, I don't think! Who did she think we were – MI5?' Dagwood's face had flushed with fury.

'Naturally,' he continued more quietly, 'I could and did resist such interference. We had some hellish rows. But it was after I had helped her with the Dewthorp business that I suddenly realised that things were out of hand and that with one word from that caustic little mouth she could blow me to buggery. She had to be stopped. It was as simple as that.'

If Dagwood's garrulous discourse had relaxed him, it certainly hadn't altered his hold on the pistol, which was now firmly in his hand again. He looked at his watch and stood up. Evidently it was time to alert the waiting adjutants of their departure.

However, Aldous Phipps had both an observation and a question: 'Well, Mr Dagwood, you've certainly had quite a tough time dealing with all these malcontents, it's a wonder you've managed to keep sane. But tell me, who did you get to . . . er . . . dispose of your sister? Quite a tricky job, I imagine.'

'Ah, that was my best man: Ezra. Not his usual line but the other two were on holiday and I hadn't got time to mess about.'

'Ah, no, of course not. On holiday, you say?' Phipps looked mildly surprised. 'Yes, yes, I can see that would present a problem. But tell me, is he reliable? One has to be so careful in these matters; people are not always what they seem.'

'Ezra? Oh straight as a die, is Ezra, I'd trust him with my life.' Dagwood smiled indulgently.

Considering Ezra had apparently put paid to the man's sister, Cedric couldn't help feeling that such trust was ill-judged, but tactfully kept silent.

'Yes,' the other continued, 'an admirable chap; no side there like with the Hapworth sod. As long as he can do his gardening and tootle his flute, he's as happy as Larry. Mind you, we did have a few grumbles over that last instruction, but I gave him a damn good bonus and told him he could keep the blithering dog. That did it, worked like a charm.

He made a good job of it too, very swift and neat.'

He gave a nod of approval, and then added, 'But his real flair is accounting, of course, which is why I put him on the payroll. As you can guess, my business activities are what you might call complex, but he's a brilliant bookkeeper and keeps everything shipshape . . . above and below board.' He leered. 'Yes, he's a man of talents, Ezra is. Started life as a cat burglar with his brother Tom – one of the pair I mentioned who settled Hapworth's hash – but he feels the cold and said he couldn't stand icy drainpipes in winter. Said they gave him chilblains. I ask you!'

Cedric closed his eyes, his mind in rare turmoil. How to get away? It was a nightmare, a sheer nightmare! The man was patently off his head and they were going to die. He started to sweat. He never sweated, but he was certainly doing that now. His shirt felt clammy, his collar hot. Even his socks felt damp. Was he about to expire and pre-empt Dagwood? He had a fleeting image of his funeral – hymns, flowers, choirboys and dear Felix, brave but tearful. He stared fixedly at Phipps's barely touched sherry. Really, some people could be so picky.

Cedric's whirling thoughts were pulled up sharp by their captor's next utterance: 'That's it then boys, the party's over. It's time, gentlemen, please!' he announced loudly. 'Your carriage awaits!' Taking a final gulp of his whisky, Dagwood waved a mocking hand in the direction of the door.

CHAPTER TWENTY-FOUR

When Felix learnt that Miles Loader's wife was returning from her profitable jaunt to Las Vegas, he was slightly relieved. He had been grateful to his host, but the attic, though acceptable, was not the most spacious of bedrooms. With that in mind, for his return to Southwold prior to the Norfolk tour he had managed to book a couple of nights at The Swan.

Having dealt with matters at Bountiful Blooms he had meant to leave early to avoid the rush hour. However, the intention was cancelled owing to a call from the *Tatler* requesting a brief interview plus photographs for an item they were featuring on London florists. 'Naturally, Mr Smythe, you were one of the first we thought of,' the ingratiating voice had said.

Few things stand in the way of commerce and vanity,

and an early trip up the A12 was not one of them. Thus, having sensibly waited for the evening rush hour to abate, Felix set out briskly – only to be faced with an interminable tailback of cars behind an accident in the Ipswich area. All traffic was at a resolute standstill and remained like that for well over an hour. It was exceedingly vexing and would clearly frustrate any plans for the evening.

As a consequence, it was quite late when Felix finally arrived at The Swan hotel. In fact, it was possibly a bit too late to drop in on the Phipps house, and he decided to leave it till the following day. Still, he could certainly telephone to have a quick word with Cedric and to apologise for the delay. He dialled the number but nothing happened; no buzzing, not a sound. He tried several times and then gave up. Perhaps the bedroom phone was kaput; he would go down to ask at the desk. But when he got there the receptionist assured him that all the hotel sets were working and the fault must be at the other end.

Felix was put out. Perhaps after all he would stroll over to Isabel's, it was unlikely they would have gone to bed just yet. Besides, it would be pleasant to sniff the night air and stretch his legs after the tedious journey.

He crossed the now deserted Market Place (only half past nine but what a contrast to the noise and bustle of Sloane Square!) and turned up Pinkney's Lane. Passing Reggie Higgs's shop on the corner of the little alleyway, he took a quick look in its window and was about to go on, when he heard a groan and a rasping cough. A few yards from Reggie's doorway lay the figure of a man slumped on the pavement.

Oh really, he thought in some distaste, doubtless it was a drunk or vagrant being sick. His instinct was to scuttle past looking the other way. He remembered his mother's words: *'What yer don't see, Feelo, yer can't know about!'* But just as he was on the point of following such sage advice, he was pulled up sharp.

'Help me,' a croaking voice implored, 'I'm dying.'

Felix froze. Nervously he cast a sideways glance at the person on the pavement. He emitted a gasp of incredulity as he recognised the man's anguished face . . . and then stared fixedly at the pool of blood seeping from beneath Ezra Simmond's jacket.

He stooped down. 'Yes, yes,' he muttered in a voice almost as hoarse as the injured man's, 'I'll help you. What's happened, for God's sake?'

For a few seconds there was silence. And then Ezra whispered. 'It's Tom. He was always jealous and hated me since I pinched his boyfriend. He said he would get even, but I didn't think it would be like this, not like this . . .' The words were lost in a spate of coughing.

Even amidst his shock and consternation, Felix made a mental note to watch his own step in future. He stood up and looked wildly for a phone box. Thank God, there was one on the corner. 'I'll get an ambulance!' he exclaimed.

He was about to rush off, when Ezra muttered, 'Fetch the police too.'

'Police? No, you need an ambulance first.'

'Get the bloody police, Felix,' the other gasped. 'Tom's at the Phipps's house with Dagwood. They mean business. He's got a gun.'

Felix gazed down at the white face, not comprehending. And then he did. He pelted wildly to the phone box and was about to yank the handle when he saw the dreaded sign: OUT OF ORDER. He stood stock-still, panic mounting. He started to run back to the hotel and then faltered, as he imagined his way blocked by chattering guests or a bemused receptionist slow to act. Polite questions might be asked, and he would have to explain. It would all take too much time! But suddenly he recalled the phone box on Queen's Road, and without further thought turned and ran on towards it. Surely to God that would be working!

Breathless from his exertions and mind in turmoil, he could barely focus on its display of emergency numbers. They seemed to swim and dance before his eyes. But miraculously he managed to cope, and in a voice high with fear delivered his message.

When Bert Hill received the garbled call, he thought it was some inebriated prankster. But as he patiently listened, he realised it was from Felix Smythe, the little cove who his boss had interviewed on the Peebles case. Peculiar, really, all about somebody on the verge of expiring in Pinkney's Lane and the people in Miss Phipps's house being in violent danger. He would have liked to ask a few questions, but the caller's insistence suggested a brisker response. He telephoned for an ambulance and alerted Inspector Jennings, still doing late work in the office.

Leaving Ezra to the ambulance and his fate, Felix hared on in the direction of South Green. As he got close to Isabel's house, he expected to see its lights shining, but it was shrouded in peaceful darkness. Panting, he stopped and took stock. Scanning its rear side, he could just make out the drawing room. Its curtains were drawn but there was the faintest chink of light. Whatever was going on, must be happening in there.

Cautiously he sidled round to the front. There was a large car parked under some trees a few yards away – the Rover he had seen at Aldeburgh? Its headlamps were off and at first he assumed it to be empty, until he glimpsed the fitful glow of a cigarette. Oh Christ, was that Dagwood, or the Tom person who had knifed Ezra – or some other bugger waiting and watching? Felix stood irresolute. What could he do, burst into the house like a *deus ex machina* and be shot in the process? Or wait meekly for the police to turn up? The latter was certainly easier, but they might be too late. Too late for what? Felix closed his eyes and thought of Cedric.

For one glorious moment it flashed through his mind that the dying Ezra had been delusional. Clearly there had been an attempt on his life, though in that condition anyone might get wild ideas. But it was a straw that quickly slipped from his clutch. No, the chap had known what he was saying, all right.

Holding his breath and keeping close to the hedge, Felix stealthily approached the front door. Gingerly he turned the handle and it opened. He slipped into the hall, still unsure of his purpose – at worst simply to be with Cedric. But at best maybe he could create some sort of diversion: announce he had come to read the gas meter or was collecting for the church bazaar . . . But even Felix's colourful mind rejected that idea. From the drawing room there emanated the faintest whiff of cigar smoke and he could just hear the rumbling tone of Dagwood's boorish voice. Swine. He had never liked the man!

He was on the point of tiptoeing out again in the hope that at any minute the police would arrive, when he suddenly saw what looked remarkably like a twelve-bore shotgun tucked under the hall table. It was dark in the hall and he thought he must be mistaken but as he peered more closely, saw that he wasn't. How curious. He certainly didn't remember any such weapon being there when they had come for dinner. Apart from being an expert on lilies, was Isabel Phipps a gun-runner in her spare time? Hardly! A gunsmith, perhaps. It was amazing the hobbies some ladies took up.

Felix knew nothing about guns, and whether it was loaded or not, he hadn't a clue. But in an unthinking instant, he had grabbed it, walked boldly towards the drawing room and flung open the door.

Looking back on that evening, the thing that Cedric most vividly remembered was the image of Felix framed in the doorway, white-faced, bow tie unfurled, hair wildly on end and brandishing a twelve-bore . . . Given their dire situation he thought at first that he might have been gripped by some absurd fantasy. However, the fantasy had spoken and the voice was distinctly real.

At the sound of the intrusion Dagwood had leapt up, knocking aside both whisky and pistol. 'Sit down,' Felix snapped, sounding perhaps like the Queen Mother addressing a recalcitrant corgi, 'or I'll blow your head off. You haven't a chance, the cops are coming.'

Though shocked, Dagwood quickly recovered and instinctively stooped to retrieve the fallen weapon. His broad hand stretched out to grab it. In vain – a thin, scrawny one had got there first. Pointing its barrel at the man's head, Professor Aldous Phipps looked smug as he said: 'My trick, I fancy.'

Stupefied, Dagwood gaped at the two 'marksmen' and sensibly sat down. Barely moving his head, he glanced sideways at the French window as if expecting some intervention. But all that was heard was the distant wail of a police siren, and then much closer, the sound of an engine revving and a car taking off into the night. He shut his eyes.

The fading engine was replaced by the sound of others approaching, and then a screeching of tyres followed by heavy pounding feet. As Felix had warned, the cops had arrived. With a clatter he dropped the twelve-bore and crumpled to the floor in a blissful faint.

The following day, greatly refreshed by the effect of a sleeping pill and extolling its efficacy to Aldous and Cedric, Isabel was surprised to learn what had occurred the night before . . . in fact so surprised, that she told them they were lying in their teeth. Her guests were mildly pained, and it took them some time to persuade her otherwise.

CHAPTER TWENTY-FIVE

It had to be said that Detective Inspector Wilfrid Jennings had done a grand job in rounding up and arresting Dagwood and his henchmen, Tim and Tom. As their boss had feared, at the sound of the siren the two adjutants had moved with maximum alacrity to what they hoped would be the safety of the A12 to London. But Jennings had also been quick and ordered an instant alert. As a consequence, their flight had been briskly interrupted by flashlights and barricades in the Woodbridge area, and it was unlikely that they would drive or walk on any cliffs again.

Jennings' efficiency in the arrest had been much applauded. His skills of detection had perhaps been less obvious, but as Nathan had said, they were "coming along" and he had the makings of an excellent and reliable senior officer. The superintendent, too, was complimentary and offered him a glass of whisky – not quite up to the standard of his old gran's, but nearly.

As for H.R. Dagwood Esq., he had been hauled off cursing and dribbling to a place of temporary incarceration before facing trial in the High Court – and whatever the judge deemed appropriate for his particular mode of entrepreneurship. In 1961 the death penalty was still operating.

Contrary to his own expectation, Ezra Simmonds did not die. Initially he was nursed in Lowestoft Hospital where, over time, his punctured lung recovered moderately well and he was able to stand trial. In the course of that trial and in a moment of curiosity, the judge had asked why, after disposing of the deceased and quitting her establishment, the accused had bothered to relock the kitchen door. Ezra had replied primly that he had always been brought up to leave things exactly as he had found them. The judge had given a nod of approval and passed on to other matters. The upshot was that, owing to mitigating circumstances (ill-health, a plea of guilty and having committed only one assassination as opposed to several), the accused was sentenced not to the scaffold but to life imprinsonment.

On the prisoner's way to the relevant institution, a friendly guard enquired if he was minded to take his flute with him. Ezra was heard to mutter that he was tired of the effing flute and was in no condition to blow it anyway, but that he wouldn't mind trying the guitar as he believed that instrument was becoming very fashionable. He subsequently became a model prisoner, and over the years would give the most enlivening recitals to staff and inmates alike. As for Freddie, being a man of great Christian charity, the Reverend Furblow offered to adopt the little fellow. It is reported that under the pastor's benign influence he became almost likeable.

Reggie Higgs and Miles Loader remained good chums and continued to enjoy gossipy drinks in The Crown and the Lord Nelson where, on the first day of every April, they would solemnly raise a glass to Horace Dewthorp, their erstwhile friend. Reggie's antique business thrived, but as a lucrative sideline he also started to do a brisk trade in vintage magazines of a certain style; items which became surprisingly popular during the scandal of the Peebles affair. He would occasionally remark that he owed the lady a great deal.

Miles Loader also thrived. Despite a tense period when the national press was full of unseemly stories about the murdered Hapworth and his dubious doings, to his lasting relief his kinship with that cleric remained unknown to all but himself and Isabel Phipps. His precious reputation was safe.

Thinking about the case sometime afterwards, Jennings pondered about the central characters – Dagwood, Hapworth and Peebles – and asked himself what it was that they had had in common.

Of course, they were all disagreeable and intent on dominating others, but there was more to it than that. They seemed to have shared one overriding feature: an inordinate amount of self-regard and the desire to see that regard reflected in the eyes of society. Hypocrisy could be a means of concealment for bad behaviour, but it was also a potent force in preserving public acclaim and personal dignity, or what one took to be dignity. Dagwood had relished being applauded and kowtowed to, and his sister had been increasingly scrupulous in her external deportment. Hapworth too (though somewhat less adept at its maintenance) had clearly enjoyed the role of righteous pastor and the respect it commanded.

Jennings didn't know much Shakespeare but he recalled the Iago chap and his enigmatic malevolence. 'Honest Iago' they had said of him. The cover of honesty had been of practical use in promoting his villainous schemes; however as a schoolboy Jennings had always suspected that, at bottom, such face-saving was simply the need to be esteemed . . . And wasn't there a bloke in the same play who kept banging on about reputation? He had been quite decent, he remembered, but public respect had clearly meant a lot to him as well, and he had been desperate to regain it. Yes, he told himself sagely, deep down that was what everyone craved, both the good and the bad: to be well thought of by their peers. Although Jennings could not have known it, this was a conclusion that Miles Loader would have doubtless endorsed.

Such philosophical musings were curtailed by a sudden knock on the door. The inspector hastily shoved his cache of Penguin biscuits into a desk drawer, and sat up straight and orderly to receive the cheerful face of Sergeant Harris.

Given the peculiarities of the circumstances and the wear and tear on their nerves, Cedric and Felix decided to cancel their Norfolk trip and return instead to London, where without any further distractions, they could rest in comfort. After all, it was essential that they be in fine fettle for their sojourn chez Mr S.M. in September. This was a prospect both soothing and uplifting and did much to restore their exhausted spirits.

Wisely, Felix had decided not to confide in his royal patron about his recent exploits. After all, one did not wish to spread alarm and despondency among the denizens of Clarence House. (And if truth be told, he feared she might be sceptical and think him a fool.) No, such tales were best kept for the eminent gentleman on St-Jean-Cap-Ferrat and other amusing literati. Indeed, the former might be sufficiently impressed to adapt the material for a novel. Already Felix was busily honing the finer details of their exploits: details to be recounted over cocktails and leisurely luncheons on their host's vine-clad veranda.

Cedric meanwhile had a slightly more arduous task, albeit nothing compared to his recent challenge. He had been invited by Rosy Gilchrist to deliver the principal address at her forthcoming wedding to her boss at the British Museum, Dr Stanley. It was an honour, of course, and he had few problems in finding gallant things to say about Rosy (whom he and Felix had known for some years). The difficulty was Stanley. What could he say about that barbarian? It needed supreme tact. Still, compared with a barbarian of his more recent acquaintance, Dr Stanley was quite couth – almost civilised, in fact. No doubt some suitable rabbit could be pulled from the hat.

Yes, charming though Southwold most certainly was,

it was good to be back in London, and eminently safer! And thus, clasping bone-dry Martinis the two friends toasted each other and their lucky escape. Copiously and frequently.

A CAMBRIDGE EPILOGUE

On the morning of his return to Cambridge, Aldous Phipps sat on the promenade and again stared at the sea. He was no more enamoured of it now than when he had first arrived. Apart from that stretch of water so shockingly sullied by the hanging corpse, he much preferred the languid beauty of the meandering Cam.

But other than the sea, it had to be said that his visit to Southwold had been a most interesting little interlude – most invigorating, in fact. He patted the little Norfolk. 'You've enjoyed yourself, haven't you, Popsie. Full of fun and frolic! Although you were a very sensible girl to stay tucked up in bed when the nasty man was with us, very sensible.' He gazed fondly at his companion. Given the curious events, dog and master looked remarkably spry.

Phipps gave thought to his Cambridge home. Apparently,

the frightful building works were finished, the workmen gone and peace restored. All was as it should be again. He smiled, envisaging his return to St Cecil's Senior Common Room and the tale he would regale them with. Inevitably, the obnoxious Smithers would try to interrupt but he would settle his hash all right. He must devise a tactic. After all, if he had kept his nerve with that Dagwood bounder, he could certainly parry John Smithers! The light of battle gleamed in the old man's eye.

'I see that Aldous is back,' the bursar announced.

'Hmm. How delightful,' said the Master of St Cecil's. The observation was made without much verve and he suddenly looked rather tired.

'I expect the sea air will have done him good,' someone remarked. 'Very nice to be in that cheering presence again and listen to those incisive words of wisdom.' The speaker giggled.

'Exactly. And that being the case, we must give him a warm welcome this evening,' Dr Maycock, the senior tutor, said benignly. He turned to Mostyn Williams: 'Perhaps, Bursar, you would allow us some extra bottles of that alarming sherry he is so fond of.'

'You can count me out,' John Smithers said.

'Well, John, you don't have to drink the stuff. You can always stick to port or that questionable vodka you seem so attached to. Perhaps you could bring a hip flask,' Maycock replied lightly.

Smithers sighed. 'I don't mean the sherry. I mean I shan't be here at all. There are more pressing matters to attend to than listening to Professor Phipps discoursing upon his happy hols and surfing exploits.'

'Oh, come now, Smithers,' Dr Maycock said smoothly, 'where's the Dunkirk spirit? I am sure Aldous will be most disappointed not to see your smiling face.' He took the younger fellow aside and murmured: 'I have advised you before to observe these social conventions. They matter and their breach will be remarked. And as I have also told you, it would be unhelpful to your career. Take my tip, be here. In fact, if you have any sense, you will be the first to shake his hand.' Giving a firm but kindly smile, Dr Maycock drifted away to administer comfort to the master. He was an old campaigner and knew what he was talking about.

Thus, Professor Aldous Phipps was welcomed back by a full complement of his scholarly colleagues. They in turn were treated to an account so outlandish that even the cynical Smithers was silenced. Naturally one or two little sorties were tried, but these were briskly dealt with. And for the time being, at any rate, callow Youth had to bow to the superior canniness of Age.

SUZETTE A. HILL was born in East Sussex, and spent much of her childhood playing spies and smugglers on Beachy Head and picnicking at the foot of the Long Man of Wilmington. Hill worked as a teacher in both public school and adult education before retiring in 1999. She now lives in Ledbury, Herefordshire. At the age of sixty-four and on a whim, she took up a pen and began writing. Hill has since published ten novels, including the Reverend Oughterard series.

suzetteahill.co.uk

Rosy Gilchrist and her sidekicks, Felix Smythe and Professor Cedric Dillworthy, are visiting Cambridge to attend the unveiling of a statue. But plans for the statue are far from set in stone, and the meddling Gloria Biggs-Boothby is determined to see it created by another artist. It's inconvenient, then, when the artist turns up dead ...

As Rosy and her associates become increasingly embroiled in events, they face a number of teasing questions: is the deaf and frail Emeritus Prof. Aldous Phipps quite as benign as he seems? Is the Bursar a secret misogynist? And who is the unwitting husband that Dr John Smithers is so busy cuckolding?

'CHARMING, ASTRINGENT AND WITTY'
THE GUARDIAN

Shot in Southwold

SUZETTE A. HILL

Lady Fawcett is eager to vet her daughter Amy's current beau, film director Bartholomew Hackle, who is shooting his first major project in Southwold. Amy is unable to accompany her mother, and so Rosy Gilchrist is convinced to tag along.

On the set of the production, nobody really knows what is going on – least of all Felix Smythe, whose part is constantly changing, thanks to Hackle. But the very real death of a female cast member brings a drama to proceedings that the film itself lacks, and Lady Fawcett, Rosy and Felix are at the centre of a murder mystery in which further victims may face the cut . . .

'A PERFECT MIXTURE OF FUNNY AND ACERBIC WHOLLY DELIGHTFUL'
LAURA WILSON
AUTHOR OF STRATTON'S WAR

A Southwold Mystery

SUZETTE A. HILL

Suffolk, 1955. Rosy Gilchrist is asked by her friend Lady Fawcett to join her on a trip to Southwold to visit Delia Dovedale, an old school chum she hasn't seen in years. Rosy reluctantly agrees to be her companion on the jaunt, but on arrival they discover that their hostess is dead; recently murdered at the local flower festival.

Rosy's old friends Cedric and Felix saw Delia cry out her final words on stage before meeting her untimely end. The friends then decide to take on the near-impossible task of tracking down the killer in a town of suspicious characters, before the body count rises.

If you enjoyed *Shadow Over Southwold*, look out for
more books by Suzette A. Hill . . .

To discover more great fiction and to place an order visit
our website
www.allisonandbusby.com
or call us on
020 3950 7834